THE TORTURER RAISED HIS CLUB . . .

He grimaced at the awful mess he'd already made, and lowered it. He nodded at the ones near the girl and said, "All right. They want to be stubborn. Let's work her over, eh?"

The one holding her asked, "Can I rape her first, Boss? It's not much fun when they're all bruised and bloody."

The boss shrugged and said, "Sure, why not? We can *all* rape her. We've got plenty of time."

Then Captain Gringo stepped over to the window, nodded pleasantly, and said, "You're wrong. I'd say your time just ran out."

As long as there was a free field of fire, Captain Gringo started using it!

Novels by Ramsay Thorne

Renegade #1
Renegade #2: Blood Runner
Renegade #3: Fear Merchant
Renegade #4: The Death Hunter
Renegade #5: Macumba Killer
Renegade #6: Panama Gunner
Renegade #7: Death In High Places
Renegade #8: Over The Andes To Hell
Renegade #9: Hell Raider
Renegade #10: The Great Game
Renegade #11: Citadel of Death

Published by
WARNER BOOKS

Renegade #11

CITADEL OF DEATH

by

Ramsay Thorne

WARNER BOOKS

A Warner Communications Company

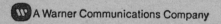

As the sun was setting in sultry Cayenne, a body lay staring up from the street below as Captain Gringo came out on the balcony again. The tall blond American soldier of fortune grimaced as he saw the corpse was still there. It explained the silence of the street outside the hotel. In the tropics people were usually out on the streets at sunset, cooling off in the sea-scented trade winds as they sized up each other for later, when it would be even cooler and comfortable enough to screw.

Captain Gringo found it amusing to watch the paseo in a new town. So he'd brought his smoke and bottle out on the wrought iron balcony to check at a safe distance on the local talent. But until somebody hauled away that white clad stiff down there, few femmes in fresh flouncy skirts were likely to be strolling by.

But what the hell—it was cooler out here, so he pulled out a spidery chair from the painted metal table on the balcony and sat down with his drink and smoke. His more-or-less trustworthy sidekick, Gaston Verrier, was off trying to collect for some smuggled arms they hadn't been paid for and, if Gaston met anything in a skirt, he'd probably be late getting back to this hotel. It was shaping up to be a dull evening.

As a conspicuous Anglo Saxon with a price on his head, Captain Gringo felt a certain hesitancy in exploring a strange town, and Cayenne was shaping up to be strange indeed. As the capitol of French Guiana Cayenne was busting a gut trying to be Paris. The populace seemed divided on the subject. The British, French, and Dutch had played musical colonies along this stretch of the South American coast until nobody knew what lingo they were supposed to speak and the

5

resultant creole dialect was a weird mixture of bad French, bad Spanish, with some pidgin English and a Dutch accent thrown in. The customs seemed different, too. He'd been in some rough towns since escaping from the U.S. Army stockade in the States, but up to now, they'd generally done something reasonably sanitary about corpses in the streets.

The sunset was at his back as he sat there, morosely smoking and sipping. The eastern sky was purple and Venus, the evening star, winked at him. He knew that Devil's Island was out there somewhere just over the horizon and he assumed that was why the body spread eagle on the cobble stones below had a red target painted on it's white cotton shirt front. The one on the back of the shirt was probably the one someone had put a bullet through, since he couldn't see any blood from the balcony. The poor slob had been one of the French prisoners from Devil's Island and it seemed only reasonable that someone had shot him for the standing reward he'd heard about. But, for Chrissake, were they going to just *leave* him there? He'd be stinking by morning in this heat and Gaston had assured Captain Gringo that this was supposed to be a decent hotel.

Of course, Gaston could get sort of weird, too, now that he thought about it. The little legion deserter had been on the run so long he probably thought the Algerian Cashbah was a fancy neighborhood. Like most men on the dodge, the Frenchman preferred to hole up in places neither too fancy nor too disreputable. Local police always seemed to keep an eye on the fancy hotels to make sure no tourists were robbed, and of course they expected to find the people who robbed them on the darkest street in town.

This waterfront hotel had seemed a safe bet to Captain Gringo, too, up until now. But sooner or later, someone had to report that stiff to the authorities. So why in the hell was he just sitting here? Why wasn't he running, like any sensible knock-around guy?

"Easy does it," he warned his itchy feet as he forced himself to take another casual sip of whatever the hell they called this green stuff he'd ordered from room service. The stiff was obviously an escapee. The police should see no need to question anyone in the hotel, and if they did, he'd look more innocent cooling off out here than he would if they found him holed up in a stuffy room at this hour, right?

Captain Gringo glanced along the row of balconies adjoining his. He saw no other guests enjoying the view with him.

Was it the slack season, or did they know something he didn't?

Captain Gringo decided to go for a stroll—whatever the local form. But as he started to rise, the French doors of his hotel room opened and a woman came out on the balcony to join him. He frowned and removed the cigar from his lips, musing, "M'selle?" For, unless he was losing his touch, the door inside had been locked.

The woman was young and pretty with long black hair, and was dressed like a lady in a white lace bodice nobody but a European was foolish enough to wear in the tropics. She sat down, uninvited, and said, "You have to help me, Captain Gringo."

So he sat back down, too, but said, "I'm afraid you have me mixed up with someone else, M'selle."

She sighed and replied, "I know what you wrote on the hotel register, M'sieur Walker. I, too, found it prudent to use an alias. I am Claudette Pardeau. I knocked on your door and when I heard no answer I took the liberty of trying the latch. As you can see, it was not locked."

Captain Gringo saw no such thing. But why argue with the lady? He shrugged and said, "Howdy, Pard. Have you any ideas about that dead man down there?"

Claudette gasped as she glanced where he was pointing. Then she made the sign of the cross and said, "Oh, thank God it's not him! When I saw the prison uniform I thought for a moment . . . . But let us get back to my reasons for approaching you, hein? I knew the moment I learned you and Gaston Verrier were in town that you were just the men I was looking for. You are my last hope, M'sieur."

Captain Gringo didn't answer as he studied her. She obviously knew who he was. He could rule out a police informant, since all one had to do to collect the rewards was inform the police. Ergo she had something else in mind, and he didn't think it could be three in a bed with him and Gaston. He took a drag on his Havana Claro and waited.

Claudette saw it was her move, so she sighed and said, "I represent a clandestine organization interested in a prisoner out there on Devil's Island. You, of course, are interested in money, no?"

He blew a smoke ring and raised an eyebrow.

She said, "A hundred thousand in U.S. currency." So he said, "Keep talking, Pard. You have my undivided attention."

7

She leaned forward earnestly and said, "You have heard, of course, of the *Dreyfus Affair?*"

"I've seen something about it in the papers. Some French officer got nailed on a spy charge, right?"

"Wrong!" Captain Dreyfus is innocent! The French high command accused him simply because they are anti-Semitic."

"Oh, is Dreyfus Jewish?"

"*Oui,* an assimilated French Jew like myself. There was a scandal in high places. Some French battle plans were smuggled to the German High Command by someone at French headquarters who had access to them. Most naturally, it was assumed the Jew must have been the one. After all, all the others were Christian gentlemen, hein?"

Captain Gringo shrugged and said, "I used to be a Christian gentleman and my army framed me anyway. How do you know Dreyfus is innocent, and what's the fuss about in the first place? Last I heard, Germany and France weren't at war."

"Not at the moment," Claudette said. "The Germans won in '70 and France means to win the next time. The stolen plans were for the defense of France in case of another German invasion. Naturally, the French high command must now start from scratch on new ones. As to how we know Alfred Dreyfus was innocent of the charges, there are two reasons. Captain Dreyfus is a most dedicated and patriotic French officer. No other man of Jewish birth could have risen so high in our very discriminating army. Captain Dreyfus made it to the general staff on merit alone, since he had no friends in high places."

"I'll buy that." Captain Gringo nodded. "What's the second reason?"

"His so-called trial was a farce," Claudette replied, adding, "the evidence presented against him was irrelevent and the only thing the prosecution seemed able to prove was that Captain Dreyfus was a Jew."

The tall American noticed a wagon coming down the street. As he watched it, he mused aloud, "Prejudice works both ways, you know. What was this evidence you seem to find so flimsy, Pard?"

"Are you mocking my Jewish name?"

"No, I thought it was French. But I stand corrected if it bothers you."

She sniffed and said, "My name does not bother me—I'm

proud of it. My family *had* a Sephardic surname when few of your kind were called anything but Tom The Miller or John The Weaver!"

"I think I must be related to some peon who walked a lot. But let's get back to the evidence against Dreyfus."

She looked mollified as she sniffed again and said, "There was no real evidence. A French agent stole an unsigned letter from the German files. It appeared to be an offer from some French officer to betray his own command. It was never proven the Germans had even received the plans, but of course one must assume they may have. Someone at French Headquarters decided the handwriting was similar to that of Captain Dreyfus. Impartial handwriting experts declared in court this was not so, but the judges decided otherwise, and now poor Captain Dreyfus is out there on Devil's Island, dishonorably discharged and serving a life sentence at hard labor!"

Captain Gringo didn't answer. He was watching them load the body down there on the wagon. There were two cops or soldiers in tropic whites and a couple of guys wearing the same shabby prison uniform as the dead man. But he noticed neither had a target stenciled on his shirt. He asked the girl if she knew why and Claudette said, "They are, how you say, trustees? Prisoners from the island and transferred here to the mainland after a few years good behavior on the island. They serve out the remainder of their sentences here, as laborers. Naturally, only those serving less than a life sentence are so fortunate, if one calls being an unpaid slave good fortune."

He watched the casual work detail and when he saw they didn't seem at all interested in him, he turned back to Claudette and said, "Somebody must have shot that guy on sight and gone for help with the body. I was afraid they were just going to leave him there for the pigs and vultures. Let's get back to your Captain Dreyfus. Assuming, for the hell of it, that he's innocent as you say, what am *I* supposed to do about it? I'm no lawyer even if my French was worth a damn."

Claudette said, "You and Gaston are soldiers of fortune. You have a boat and a machine gun, no?"

"No. The launch we coasted down here aboard is on the mud flats with a leaky bottom and a rusted out boiler. Gaston sold the heavy weapons we had on board to some local thugs who shall be nameless. Right now he's looking for another

9

slob who owes us money and as soon as he gets back we'll be long gone. This town makes me nervous and Gaston's wanted by the French, too."

She looked discouraged. He discouraged her some more by adding, "Even if we had that little launch in running condition, it's too big a boo to consider. Devil's Island is way off shore, in green water that goes splash splash. I've never been there and never intend to be there if I can help it; but an island prison intended for desperate lifers strikes me as a place that one would expect to find some guards. A lot of guards."

"But if you had one of those machine guns you use so well, Captain Gringo . . ."

"Hey, come on," he cut in. "A landing under fire on an island fortress, with one lousy machine gun? A battle cruiser, maybe. I guess a few salvos of eight-inch shells would reduce the place pretty good. But I don't have a battle cruiser and, even if I did, would you be doing your Captain Dreyfus a favor by pounding the rock he's on to dust?"

"We have to help him escape. He's innocent," she insisted, stubbornly.

They were hauling the dead escapee away now, so it was safe to risk a scene as he said, "Why don't you take a hike, Sis? I don't know what your game is, but I won't call the cops if you don't."

The brunette gasped and said, "I don't understand, M'sieur!"

So he said, "I do. They call it the Spanish Prisoner Con back in the States. It's usually a rich political prisoner being held in one of those new Cuban concentration camps, but the rest of the story goes the same. A pretty lady comes to the mark with a wild scheme to get the Spanish prisoner out and everybody's supposed to make a lot of money, right? The man the *Dons* are holding has a treasure map or funds tied up in the Morgan Trust in New York until he can get to them."

Claudette laughed incredulously and asked, "Are you suggesting I'm party to a confidence scheme involving the notorious Captain Gringo?"

He nodded and said, "Yeah, and I'm pretty insulted, too. I know I'm a Yanqui in banana land, but for Pete's sake do I look *that* green?"

"You don't understand!" she said. "I know the trick you're talking about. It's been in more than one newspaper as a

10

cautionary tale, but this is different. I haven't come to you asking you to finance a rescue attempt. I've come to offer *you* the money! A great deal of money. Cash up front!"

He took another sip of his greenish drink, swallowed, and said, "You mean we don't get the money after Dreyfus is free to tell us where it is?"

"Of course not. Alfred Dreyfus has no money. The people I work for have the money. They want to *hire* you, you idiot!"

He cocked an eyebrow again and asked, "Who are these mysterious people and while we're on the subject, what happened to that slight French accent you started out with?"

"If you must know," Claudette said, "I am working for the freedom of Captain Dreyfus with a . . . well . . . international Jewish group. I didn't know I had any accent, speaking English. I was educated in New England, but of course, since I've been speaking French the past few months . . ."

"Aw, come on, why play chess when the name of the game is checkers, Doll? You lied about the way you got through the door inside. You made the sign of the cross, like a Catholic, when you spotted that dead body over there. Now we're talking about a mysterious organization of international Jews. But you just told me this Dreyfus is an assimilated Jew who considers himself a Frenchman."

"If only you will let me explain . . ." she began, but he was on his feet and lifting her to hers as he cut in, "I'll show you the way out. I'd let you find your own way, but I'm afraid you'd steal the hat I left hanging in there."

"Please," she pleaded, as he firmly led her inside. She twisted free and plunked herself down on his brass bed to add, stubbornly, "I'm not leaving until you hear me out."

"I don't want to hear you out," he said. "You lie too much. So upsy daisy, Doll. Your charade's over, whatever it was."

"Listen, I'm offering you a lot of money, damn it!"

"I don't want your money. I just want you out of here."

"Don't you trust me, Dick?"

So she knew his first name, too? That was sort of interesting and he'd have been tempted to question her further about it, if he'd thought she knew how to level with a guy. He noticed she was fumbling with the buttons of her bodice in the semi-gloom, so he said, "I don't want your fair white body, either, if it means exposing mine to the bullets I smell in your hair. What the hell do you think you're doing, Claudette?"

She opened her dress, exposing a pair of small but perfectly formed breasts as she sobbed, "I have to show you I can be trusted, and you men are all alike!"

He knew she had a point, as he felt a tingle in his groin, but he made his voice deliberately gruff as he said, "Hey, you're pretty, but a man who can turn down a hundred thousand dollars can turn down almost anything!"

Claudette moved back on the bed and began to wriggle out of her dress like a pretty snake shedding it's skin as she asked, "Are you sure, Dick?"

He went to the door, checked the lock, and started unbuttoning his own shirt as he replied, "Well, I wouldn't want you to leave calling me a sissy. But don't get the idea I'm agreeing to anything else. I still don't trust you farther than I could throw you and that bed put together. But if you just want to have some innocent fun . . ."

She kicked free of her skirts to recline invitingly in nothing but her gartered stockings and high button shoes. Her curves were carved in old ivory by the soft light and she was breathing rapidly as he joined her on the mattress to shuck his boots and pants. As he turned to take her in his arms she panted, "Do you trust me, now, Darling?"

He chuckled and said, "At least I don't have to worry about concealed weapons." As he moved to mount her, he wedged one knee between her soft pale thighs, but she held them close together, insisting, "Wait, I have to know if we have a bargain!"

"Sure, Doll," he said, "anything you say." As she opened her body in welcome he almost meant it. He hadn't had sex since he'd been in Cayenne and as he entered her it seemed to be true what they said about Cayenne pepper no matter where it came from!

She gasped, "Oh, my God, it's so big!" And he said, "You can call me Dick, under the circumstances."

She got it, and laughed, "That's funny. The joke, I mean. I'm not sure about that rather alarming thing you're trying to shove in me."

She did seem sort of tight for such an adventurous lady. So he moved gently at first, letting her get used to his thrusts until she suddenly laughed, wildly, and purred, "Faster! I didn't think I could take anything that deep, but I see I can, and I want it all!"

So he hooked his toes under the brass rails at the foot of

the bed for purchase and proceeded to do it right as Claudette wrapped her legs around him and proceeded to ruin his back and behind with her nails and high heels. She was a biter, too, and it was a good thing he wasn't a poor married john who'd have to explain those bruises on his collar bone to anyone important. He came fast, surprised at how much he'd needed it. Then he withdrew, rolled her over, and draped her over a pillow to pound her into the mattress some more, face down. She was rolling her head from side-to-side as she clawed at the sheets, arching her spine to rub her firm buttocks against his belly as he bounced his gonads against her aroused clit with every long stroke of his shaft. She clamped down hard and sent a muffled scream into the bedding she seemed to be chewing to death. As he felt her go limp, totally dominated, he joined her in a long, lingering orgasm. He threw his head back, looked up at the dark ceiling, and muttered, "Thank you, Lord. You've been swell today."

Face down, Claudette giggled and said, in a rather surprised tone, considering, "I really came. You're as amazing as they say you are. But why did you throw me on my face like this, you brute?"

He thrust teasingly and said, "I don't want to be clawed to death. If I turn you over and do it right, can you go easy with those teeth and nails?"

"My God, are you still able to?"

"You said I wouldn't be able to resist you, didn't you?"

They were both grinning roguishly as he rolled her on her back, hooked one of her knees over one of his elbows, and re-entered her in a semi-reclining position with his weight on the other arm. Claudette sighed and said, "Oh, it feels even wilder this way. But I don't remember getting to say much of anything just now. You were on me and in me before I could settle anything with you, you naughty boy."

He kept on screwing her, conversationally, as he said, "Honey, all we've settled is that I'm a human male who leaps on a naked woman when he's invited to. Don't spoil a budding friendship by more garbage about being some sort of Jewish secret agent."

"Damn it, I told you I was assimilated. I don't know why I make the sign of the cross when I'm upset. I just do. What do you want from a nice Jewish girl raised in a Catholic country?"

13

He noticed she wasn't trying to remove any more of his hide, now that she'd settled down, so he rolled more atop her, got the other leg up, and said, "Look, I don't care if you're an Eskimo nun, right now."

She laughed and asked, "What's wrong with Eskimo nuns? Have you ever done this to an Eskimo nun?"

He didn't answer as he started to pound her, tonguing her right ear. She hissed in pleasure and sighed, "Oh, I'll bet you have had an Eskimo nun, if there's any such thing. Where did you learn to do this so well, Dick?"

He still didn't answer. He could tell from the way she was moving that *she'd* learned a lot somewhere. And there went those damned *nails* again! He couldn't fault Claudette on technique and he knew some men liked to think they were in bed with a tigress, but despite her remarks about him being a brute, Captain Gringo considered himself a gentle lover. The difference between their styles was that he genuinely liked women and got almost as much out of giving sexual pleasure as receiving it. Claudette was the brute if anyone here was. He knew she'd started this to twist him around her finger. But she'd lost sight of this in enjoying her own sensuous little body's needs. He knew she wasn't a whore. No whore with any brains ever sent a customer home covered with marks. So what the hell was she, aside from a hell of a lay?

It didn't seem too important until he'd come again, stayed in politely long enough to rouse her to another earthy orgasm, and rolled off for a breather with her head on his shoulder as he groped for a smoke in the shirt he'd dropped by the bed. He couldn't reach it without shoving her away, so he gave up on the idea. They said it was dangerous to smoke in bed, anyway.

Claudette began to purr and run her nails over his sweat soaked chest until he said, "Hey, sheathe your claws, Kitten." Then she laughed and ran her free hand down to fondle his sated shaft, fortunately not with her nails. She began to stroke it gently and teasingly as she asked, "My, did I do that to the poor thing? It feels like I broke it."

He patted her and said, "What you're doing down there sure beats pissing, but it's an exercise in futility until I get my second wind. Should I still call you Claudette, or do you want to tell me who you really are, now?"

She hesitated, began to stoke some more, and said, "I thought we had all that settled, Dick."

14

"No," he said, "We've settled that *you're* a woman and *I'm* a poor weak-willed man. But I had that part figured out pretty early. All bullshit aside, why did you really come here this evening, aside from wanting to come, I mean."

"My," she laughed. "I did come a lot, didn't I? Would you be angry if I confessed I didn't expect to enjoy it?"

"No, I'd be flattered. I enjoyed it, too. But I warned you up front that this was only for fun. What the hell do you really want with me, Claudette?"

She moved his foreskin experimentally and mused, "Right now I just want to get this damned thing up again. You're a devastating lover, as you must have been informed by that Eskimo nun in the past. But, screw me all night and I won't change my story. I can't. It's the truth."

"Well," he chuckled, "I like the part about all night. But, I'm not sure about that, either. I promised Gaston I'd meet him later and if he's got our money . . . well, it's been swell."

"Don't you want to see poor Captain Dreyfus free, Dick?"

"Hell, if it were up to me, everybody would be free. But you said yourself he's on Devil's Island. That's a rock in the ocean, Kiddo. You'd need a battle wagon to take out the garrison and even then they'd probably kill the important prisoners before they surrendered. If the people you work for are as powerful as you say, they should be hiring newspaper men, not soldiers of fortune. His only chance would be a new trial with the press covering it in open court."

She was still jerking him off, as he added, "Let's not worry about the impossible. Let's see if it's possible to get it in again at half mast."

She giggled and rolled on her back to go along with his suggestion. But as he started to remount her they both stiffened to the sound of discreet tapping on the door.

Captain Gringo rolled off Claudette and snagged his .38 on the fly as he moved barefoot to the door to growl, "Is that you, Gaston?"

"*Mais non*, a voice on the other side of the panel replied. "It is your *très fatigue* Santa Claus from the North Pole. Open this species of door, you shrinking violet! I may have someone on my derrier!"

Captain Gringo threw the bolt as his smaller and older sidekick slipped into the dark room. Gringo muttered, "Careful, I have company."

15

Gaston sniffed and said, "Congratulations. Your quarters reek of amour and *très* expensive perfume. One assumes this is a private affair, or can any number play?"

"Don't talk dirty. The lady speaks English, you old goat. Claudette, may I present Gaston Verrier, late of the French Foreign Legion and not as uncouth as he might seem?"

The girl in the bed gave a strangled gasp of embarrassment. Gaston said, "Enchanted, M'selle" and then shot a burst of rapid fire French at her that Captain Gringo couldn't follow. Claudette replied in return, sounding a lot more refined, and then said, "I think we should speak English, M'sieur Verrier."

"*Oui*," Gaston said. "My friend, Dick, speaks at best the grotesque French of the Yankee high school and M'selle no doubt finds my Left Bank argot distressing to her ears."

"Never mind all that, Gaston. Did you get our money from the Dutchman?" Captain Gringo asked.

Gaston groped for a chair in the gloom and as he sat down he replied, "No. It was *très* distressing to be treated that way by an old legion comrade, too."

Captain Gringo took a deep breath, let it out slowly, and said, "Damn it, Gaston. I told you I didn't trust the son-of-a-bitch. What happened?"

Gaston shurgged and said, "The details are a bit blurred. As we were discussing the bill for our arms delivery the conversation became heated and when I slapped the Dutchman gently to remind him of the small print, the insect pulled a knife on me. Naturally I kicked him in the head and so the two thugs with him became *très* unpleasant, too; so by the time I had them all calmed down the three of them were unconscious and . . ."

"I've seen you fighting *à la savate*, you crazy bastard," Captain Gringo interrupted. "Where's the Dutchman right now, in case he recovers?"

"I left them in an alley behind a waterfront bistro. As I made a rather hasty departure the rest of the gang was pouring into the alley, shouting abuse at my poor mother, so I did not have time to inquire as to the health of the gentleman I kicked and perhaps, how you say, stomped a few times. I, ah, got the distinct impression I may have overdone it with the Dutchman, alas. How was I to know his skull wasn't as thick as it looked, hein?"

Captain Gringo muttered, "Oboy. That's swell. I send you

out to collect a debt and you knock the guy off! Damn it, Gaston, we *needed* that money!"

During the conversation Claudette had slipped her clothing on with smooth motions that hinted at practice in this sort of situation. As she swung her feet to the floor she said, "Dick, if you need money, that's what I came here to discuss with you, remember?"

Captain Gringo didn't answer as he went to put his pants on, now that the party seemed to be getting formal. Gaston chuckled and asked, "M'selle wishes to pay my athletic young friend for his, ah, services?"

"Knock it off, Gaston," Captain Gringo growled. "Claudette's in some wild bunch that wants us to rescue Captain Dreyfus from Devil's Island. I was just telling her what a lousy idea it was."

"Ah," Gaston said, "that accounts for the heat of your discussion. I agree the idea seems wild. On the other hand, sometimes you seem rather wild to me, too, Dick. How much money was M'selle talking about?"

Claudette answered, "A hundred thousand, U.S. I brought one thousand with me as earnest money. I've been trying to convince Dick, here, to take it."

Gaston whistled softly and said, "Perhaps I spoke in haste about poor Captain Dreyfus, hein? After all, Devil's Island is only an island, for all it's dramatic reputation. How about it, Dick?"

Captain Gringo had moved automatically to the window in his pants and mosquito boots despite Gaston's casual attitude on alley homicide. He raised a slat to peer out as he growled, "You're right about it being a lot of money and I'm right about it being too risky for a hundred. Come over here and tell me who that guy down there might be."

Gaston and Claudette joined him at the shuttered window. A man in a white panama hat was lounging against a lamp post, like he was waiting for someone. Gaston asked, "Ever see him before, M'selle?"

Claudette shook her head and replied, "I have no idea who he might be. Couldn't he just be waiting for a friend?"

Captain Gringo frowned and said, thoughtfully, "He smells like a cop. Are you sure you weren't tailed here, Gaston?"

Gaston snorted in disgust and replied, "It has been a long time since anyone has been able to follow me through dark side streets without my being aware of it, my old and rare. If

17

the local authorities were after us we would have heard them knocking by this time, hein?"

"Maybe. He still smells cop and he's covering the front entrance."

"Oui, but alone. If he's at all aware of our existance he knows a full platoon would be indicated if he wishes to take the two of us! I think M'selle is right. I think he is waiting for someone down there. You're just becoming suspicious in your old age, Dick."

"Yeah, I got this old by being suspicious a lot, too. We've got to get out of here, Gaston. If that guy in the white hat's not interested in us, the Dutchman's friends are, and how many hotels are there to check out in a town this size?"

"Oui," signed Gaston, adding, "We shall of course use the other way out when we evacuate these premises, *non?"*

"Right. So where do we go from here?"

Gaston didn't answer. Claudette said, "Dick, you'll be safe with the people I work for. Our headquarters are in a private home not far from here. I'll just duck out the back way and let them know you're coming, all right?"

Captain Gringo didn't answer. He didn't like her suggestion. But he didn't like the idea of staying here, either. Gaston said, "Leave us the advance payment as well as the address and we shall join you in half an hour, hein?"

Claudette asked, "Dick?" and Gaston said, "He's thinking. A *très fatigue* habit he has. Do as I say, M'selle. Sooner or later even he will see he has no choice in the matter."

So Claudette switched on the overhead light to write the address of her outfit as Captain Gringo flinched away from the window and snapped, "For God's sake, you just outlined me against the window for that guy in the white hat!"

Gaston asked, "Did he look up?" and the tall American replied, "How the hell should I know? He's wearing a broad-brimmed hat that shades his damn face!"

Claudette had taken a pencil and note pad from her purse to scribble the address she said was safe. She handed it to Gaston. The dapper little Frenchman nodded but said, "The, ah, vile details, M'selle?" and she took an envelope from her purse to hand over as well. Gaston unbolted the door for her and said, "Expect us within the hour, M'selle."

She looked uncertainly at Captain Gringo. The tall American nodded, grudgingly, and said, "We'll talk to your people about it, since we sure as hell can't stay here tonight. But I'm

18

not promising anything until we see what we have to work with."

"Dick, I just gave you the earnest money."

"Yeah, I'll give it back if I decide it's too big a boo. You can take it back now and just forget the deal if you don't trust us."

"I trust you, Darling," she said, and ducked out into the dark hallway. As he closed the door after her, Gaston took out the envelope to count the down payment while Captain Gringo muttered, "She can trust us. But can we trust her?"

Gaston looked up and said, "It's all here. What are you stewing about now? A thousand dollars is *très* expensive bait for a trap, *non?*"

Captain Gringo shrugged and said, "Oh, I don't know. When you consider the rewards out on the two of us, a thousand is just pin money. But we know we're in the frying pan, so we'll just have to take a chance on the fire."

It was a little after sunset when the two soldiers of fortune slipped out of the hotel, hopefully unobserved. The light was tricky as they threaded dark narrow streets under a lavender sky. They knew better than to make for the address Claudette had given them until they were sure they weren't being followed. They circled a while and let it get a bit darker before they approached their goal. It turned out to be a big oak gate set in an otherwise blank stucco wall on a side street in a residential neighborhood. You could never tell how fancy homes were in this part of the world. For despite being a French colony, Cayenne was built Spanish. Each family lived in it's own private world, wrapped around a private patio. There were both advantages and disadvantages to this old Iberian custom. You didn't have to worry about what the neighbors might think if you didn't wash the windows or mow the lawn. You didn't know what your neighbors were up to, either.

Gaston squinted at the number chalked on the door and said, "This is it." But as he started to knock, Captain Gringo grabbed his arm and said, "Hold it. Since when has anyone posted their house number in *chalk?*"

Gaston said, "Hmm. That does seem odd. But perhaps Claudette did it to make sure we'd see it, *non?* Many of these

19

old houses have no permanent numbers facing the street. One is supposed to know one's way to grandmother's house in close knit communities."

Captain Gringo put an eye to the crack between the gate and jam. He saw and heard nothing from the other side. Gaston kept his voice low but impatient as he asked, *"Merde alors,* are we going in or do you intend to stay out here on the street all night?"

It was a good question. Captain Gringo pointed out a drain pipe running down the wall a few yards from the doorway. "Come on," he said, "I'll boost you up for a peek over the top before we knock, okay?"

"Merde alors! Not in these pants! You climb like a monkey if you wish. The number matches and the street sign back there said . . ."

"I know we're on the right street," Captain Gringo cut in, reaching for the drain pipe as he added, "Stay out of line with the doorway. I haven't been able to make out any numbers on any other houses we've passed and anybody can use a chunk of chalk."

The tall American hauled himself hand over hand up the pipe as Gaston snorted in disgust and lit a smoke. Captain Gringo disappeared from view against the sky and a million years went by as Gaston puffed impatiently at street level. Then Gaston stiffened as he heard a scrape of metal and the big oaken portal slowly began to swing inward with a low groan of it's massive hinges!

Gaston peered into the darkness and could just make out a tinkling fountain in the dark patio as he realized the flare of his match had betrayed the fact he was standing outside. He dropped his cigar and stepped on it as he put a thoughtful hand inside his jacket and called out, quietly, "Claudette?"

A voice whispered to him from the gloom, hissing, "Yes, inside, quickly. You may have been followed!"

Gaston hesitated, then shrugged and moved inside the archway leading to the patio, eyes narrowed and one hand gripping his pistol in it's holster as he asked, "Where are you, M'selle?"

The heavy slab of oak slammed shut behind Gaston as the patio lit up like a Christmas tree and a fusilade of hot lead slammed into the oak backstop and through the space Gaston had just been standing!

But the wirey little soldier of fortune hadn't reached his advanced years by moving slowly and at the first suspicious creak of hinges he'd thrown himself headlong to the patio flags and was rolling sideways for the cover of some potted hibiscus bushes. He made it, barely, for the ambusher, manning what had to be a machine gun, traversed his weapon to tap dance slugs off the flagstones after Gaston and blew the pottery to shards, covering him with leaves and hibiscus blooms as Gaston threw a desperate round at the muzzle flash across the patio before rolling on and wedging himself between a stouter fig tree bole and the wall it was almost growing against. Shooting up the hibiscus had filled the air with dust as well as greenery and as the machine gun fell silent, Gaston lay doggo while a voice asked, "Did you get him?"

Someone else said, "I think so. He's down behind those pots. Wait 'til the smoke clears. He's not going anywhere, either way. Where the hell's the other one?"

Gaston sincerely wished he knew, too, as he tried to make himself even smaller behind the fig tree's butress roots. The smoke and dust were starting to clear, now, and he could see all too clearly what a fool he'd been. The bastards had strung electric light bulbs all along the eaves around the patio and they were set up across the way on the veranda in front of the main entrance to the house. They'd opened and shut the doorway with ropes he could now see crossing the patio, and anyone whispering could sound like a woman, and where in the devil was Captain Gringo?

Gaston couldn't make out the ambushers in the shadows over there, but he knew they'd spot him any moment. One of them said, "I don't think he could be behind those pots, Mike. You shot away most of the cover and . . ."

And then all hell broke loose!

Somebody staggered out of the shadows as a pistol went off from the doorway behind him. So Gaston happily shot the son-of-a-bitch again as he heard Captain Gringo yell, "Gaston, stay down!" A half dozen men popped out into the light, running for the way out as if the devil incarnate was after them, and they were right!

Captain Gringo had sized up things and slipped down in the dark to get inside the house behind the ambushers on the veranda via a pantry window. He'd shot the machine-gunner and his belt man right off, of course, and as the others panicked and ran across the lighted patio, the tall American simply dropped behind the machine gun, sitting on the dead gunner, and proceeded to mow them down with their own weapon while Gaston held his face flat against the earth behind the fig tree until it was all over.

It didn't take long. Captain Gringo cut their legs out from under them with his first traverse and then swung the hot muzzle back to finish off the couple who tried to rise with short savage bursts. The blood and brains spattered on the flag stones looked more like tomato sauce in the garish electric light. As he rose, pistol in hand, and stepped out to have a closer look at the results, he said, "You can come out now, you dope. What in the hell made you come inside like a big ass bird? I thought I'd shit when they opened up on you like that!"

Gaston got to his feet, feeling his crotch gingerly, and said, "I am proud to say I only pissed a few drops. They tricked me with a whisper I took for M'selle Claudette. I assume we shall not find her here after all?"

Captain Gringo rolled one of the cadavers over with his foot and answered, "She's not in the house and these guys were jabbering in English."

"Ahah! So this was not the right address, as you suspected!"

Captain Gringo shrugged and said, "Her outfit's supposed to be French and these guys are wearing American shoes. That guy across the street in the white hat looked like a Yank, too. There's a couple of ways to read this. The guy in the white hat, or somebody with him, could have followed Claudette, saw where she was going, and doubled back to write a fake number on this place's entrance. But that would call for them being mighty lucky about being on the same street. So it's more likely this outfit has been watching Claudette's outfit and, seeing a chance to lure us into this ambush . . ."

"Try it my way," Gaston cut in. "Maybe Claudette intended us to do just what we did just now, save for surviving, of course. They chalked the number to make sure we would see it. She simply gave us the address and went home to some destination I see no need to search further for, hein?"

Somewhere in the night a police whistle was blowing. Captain Gringo said, "We'd better talk about it on the fly. The neighbors seem to have been complaining about the noise we've been making!"

Gaston nodded and headed for the street entrance. But Captain Gringo snapped, "Not that way, you jerk-off! The streets will be crawling with cops in a minute! Follow me!"

They went inside and found a switch to plunge the patio and it's grim contents in darkness. Then they returned to the flat roof and moved silently across other roof tops to the end of the block before the tall American risked a peek over the edge and said, "Okay. Let's hit the pavement and try to look casual as we stroll on, right?"

Gaston waited until they were doing just that and seemed alone on a dark narrow lane before he sighed and said, "Eh bien, we would seem to be well clear. Now, are you going to listen to some fatherly advice, or do you have some insane idea about finding that damned Claudette?"

"Well, we did take her money and we don't know she set us up. I'd like to see what she has to say, at any rate."

"*Merde alors,* I know what she would say. She would say she had nothing to do with that ambush, whether she did or not. You have enjoyed her body and you have her money. When are you going to learn to quit while you are ahead?"

Captain Gringo chuckled and said, "Right about now. Even if she's on the square, her idea's pretty suicidal even without another outfit reading over her shoulder, and we just found out they were, unless she was in on it and . . . shit, it's just too damned complicated to mess with, either way! This is one time I'm going to be smart enough to just take the money and run!"

Gaston said, "That's my boy! For once you are making the sense, Dick. From what I know of the *Dreyfus Affair,* her tale is sheer madness. Captain Dreyfus is only Jewish by birth and an agnostic by conviction. I don't think Claudette is a Jewess either. Certainly not a *French* Jewess."

"Ahah! I noticed the way you practiced some quick French on her back there. She didn't have a Jewish accent, right?"

Gaston shook his head and said, "Very few French Jews speak French with a noticable accent. Dick. There are very few of them in the first place, and those that are have been more assimilated than the Eastern European Jews you may remember from the States. Poor Dreyfus is typical of the French variety. He should have known better, but he would seem to be one of those unfortunates who, how you say, bust the gut trying to pass for the French officer and gentleman. Alas, my country is *très* anti-Semitic, whether one uses the correct silverware or not."

Captain Gringo was more interested in the mysterious girl at the hotel than any officer in jail at the moment, but he'd never gotten Gaston's views on the subject. So before asking his further opinion on Claudette, he decided he'd like a quick rundown on how Gaston felt about her religion, if it were her religion. He said, "I heard you Frogs were sort of nasty to Jews. How about you, Gaston?"

Gaston shrugged and said, "We were too poor in the part of Paris I grew up to have long tedious philosophical discussions. There was a Jewish boy in the street gang I used to run with. He used to help us steal when we invaded Les Halles. We had no feelings one way or the other about his religion, since none of us prayed too often in any case. Eh bien, any sensible person knows it is better to have an honest Jew for a neighbor than a Christian chicken thief. But the French high command is not run by sensible people."

"Okay, so we can both take Jews or leave 'em. Tell me why you didn't think Claudette was Jewish if she had no accent."

Gaston shook his head again and said, "You were not paying attention. I never said she had *no* accent. She speaks French, a very, how you say *snooty* French, in a manner that hints at formative years in a *très* aristocratic *convent!*"

"She talks like a *nun?* No wonder she thought that crack about Eskimo nuns was such a belly buster! But a runaway nun makes even less sense than a Jewish girl trying to get Dreyfus out of that lockup on Devil's Island. Could it be some sort of *Catholic* conspiracy?"

"One tends to doubt this," Gaston said, adding, "considering the background of Captain Dreyfus. I did not say she had to be a nun. Many of the less aristocratic but upward climbing French families send their daughters to convent schools to give them the supposed advantages of that funny French they teach. We know she is not a *true* aristocrat simply because you don't meet girls like that in a modest hotel in Cayenne. It's possible for a wealthy Jew to send his daughter to a convent school, but in that case she would hardly have come out a Jewess. Conversion is the price of admission and the teaching nuns make sure the conversion, how you say, sticks? To have been there long enough to talk like she does, Claudette would have to know her Latin Mass forward, backward, and sideways, hein?"

Captain Gringo started to mention the Sephardic name she'd used to sign the hotel register. But that was dumb. He'd seldom signed his right name to anything since jumping the Mexican border with an army hangman after him.

Gaston was saying, thoughtfully, "Of course, as in the case

24

of Captain Dreyfus himself, we may be talking about a most assimilated person of Jewish ancestry. But in that case this business about an international Jewish group working to free him makes little sense. The only such group I know of is the Zionist Movement and they would seem to take their religion tres serious. So why should they wish to intervene for Dreyfus, a man who turned his back on them in an attempt to be an accepted French aristocrat?"

"Forget it," Captain Gringo said. "We're not getting mixed up in the crazy scheme, whatever it is. Where do you suppose this street leads? It's dark as hell and we seem to be running out of pavement."

They stopped under the last street lamp to stare thoughtfully into the pitch blackness ahead. The blank walls of houses wrapped around inner courtyards stared dimly at them from both sides of the street. Somewhere a bush full of crickets was chirping at them with a very rural sound. Gaston said. "One would assume we are near the city limits."

"Thanks. I never would have figured that out by myself. Damn it, Gaston. You've been here before. How far west can we make it on foot?"

Gaston took out a cigar, lit it, and blew a puff into the darkness before he said, "Not far. As I recall, there is only a narrow coastal strip of cultivated plantations and small holdings. Beyond that the land rises to meet *très* formidable jungle. Despite the optimism of the colonial maps, most of the Guiana back country is unexplored. One hears it is most unhealthy for white men a few miles inland from the coast."

"Swell. What makes it so unhealthy, the usual snakes and fevers?"

"Oh, they have *them*, too. But the Bush Negroes would seem to be the real menace. Most of them seem to be Ashanti, a rather truculent tribe."

Captain Gringo lit a smoke for himself as he digested this. Then he frowned and asked, "Ashanti? In South American jungles? I must have missed something in Geography. I thought the Ashanti were a West African tribe."

"*Oui*," Gaston said, nodding. "They've been killing French and British troopers with monotonous regularity over there, too. I told you they liked to fight. You may have noticed the climate here tends to be *très fatigue,* so the early would-be planters imported many slaves, siezed on the west coast of Africa, hein? The experiment did not work as well here as it did in places where the somewhat reluctant plantation labor had no place to run to. The hills and jungles of Guiana are almost exact duplicates of the ones the Ashanti left behind in Africa. So they took to them as the duck takes to water. After all, who is going to stand there like an idiot cutting sugar cane when a green wall of familiar forestry beckons to him from a few short steps away?"

Captain Gringo agreed. "Right. So these Bush Negroes are like the Cimmarons in Jamaica, hiding out in the woods after escaping from the planters, right?"

"Wrong. We are not speaking of the usual runaway slaves. The ones out there in the jungle are pure unadulterated Ashanti, Kru, Ibo and so forth. They did not see fit to cut cane long enough to pick up any of their master's habits, good or bad. They, how you say ran off lock, stock, and barrel, taking along their women, witch doctors, and drums. At the moment they seem unaware that they are runaway slaves. They are African warriors. They seem dimly aware that sometime in the past the white people along the coast made trouble for them. So they regard all whites as enemies. They don't feel like fugitives on the land they grew up on. They think of it as their tribal kingdoms. They know it as well as anyone else knows his own tribal territory and seem determined to hold it against all intruders. So while white survey expeditions occasionally go in to chart and explore, they never seem to come out."

Gaston blew some more smoke and added, "All in all, Dick, there has to be a better way out of here."

"Come on," Captain Gringo said, "I led you through Jivaro infested Amazon jungle, didn't I?"

"*Oui,* it was very noisy as I recall. But Ashanti are not Jivaro and they make Colorados look like schoolboys. There were already tribal Indians in that jungle to the west when the Bush Negroes moved in, Dick. The black warriors chewed them up and spit them out. Or, at any rate, some of them did. The Ashanti are not cannibals, but they say some of the Bush tribes are. They would kill us if we were Indians. That blond hair and your big blue eyes is an open invitation to what they call a spear washing. Besides, even if we somehow managed to avoid the Bush Negroes, the country that way is too rugged. There are unmapped mountain ranges between here and anywhere anyone would want to go. I am discussing *steep* mountain ranges with mile high cliffs and waterfalls that drop from the constant cloud cover clinging to their tops. The rivers are all white water, and running the wrong way. The constant dampness covers every tree and rock with thick green slime and leeches are big as your cock. You go that way if you want to. I would find it less fatiguing to simply put a gun to my temple if I wanted to die that much!"

"Well, we can't stay here," Captain Gringo admitted. "The Dutchman's pals are probably searching the waterfront for us. Claudette's spooky pals are watching our hotel. And if we don't go *some* damned place the local cops are going to ask us what the hell we're doing any minute now."

He headed west, into the dark. Gaston fell in beside him, but protested, *"Merde alors,* were you listening to anything I just said, Dick?" Captain Gringo nodded and said, "Sure. The jungle's a ways off. We'll see if we can find a cow path running the same way as the coast. How far are we from Dutch Guiana?"

"Too far, and they call it Surinam. It's at least a hundred and fifty miles to the Dutch border, Dick! These countries may look small on the map, next to Brazil, but let us not be carried away with this walking business! No trail we might find will lead that far. Each coastal settlement is surrounded by distressing amounts of salad greens. There are mangrove swamps between here and the next French settlements at Sinnamary!"

"Okay, how far is Sinnamary? Maybe we can hop a coastal schooner there."

"Idiot! I just told you it's jungle swamp, and over fifty miles even if it wasn't!"

"Hell, is that all? Things are looking up. We've walked fifty miles in a night before and it's early yet."

Gaston was starting to puff as he tried to keep step with the longer legs of the younger American. "Slow down," he gasped, "you species of racing camel! Even if one is intent on wading through a mangrove swamp for some reason I see no need to *run* all the way there! What in the devil is your hurry, Dick?"

Captain Gringo replied, "Butterflies in my guts, I guess. I didn't like this place even before people started playing games with us. There's something wrong, Gaston. I noticed there was no paseo in the main part of town this evening. I've noticed we don't seem to see anybody at all on the streets after dark in any part of town and it's early yet."

Gaston sighed in relief as they slowed down a bit, and said,

"Oh, that is no mystery, my old and rare. This is a penal colony. There's a nightly police curfew. Didn't I mention it to you when we arrived?"

"No, but I know it *now!* What in the hell are you using for brains, Gaston? What the hell are we wandering around in the dark like this for in the middle of a curfew?"

Gaston chuckled, "I thought it was *your* idea. The curfew only applies to the prison population. You and I have the *très* droll passports we managed in Venezuela, *non?* The police seldom stop anyone who is not wearing those white pajamas they issue the prisoners."

"I noticed a lot of trustees in town. But where are all the rest of the people?"

"There are not many rest of the people, Dick. I told you they could not get the Blacks to work for them here, so they had the practical idea of sending the scum of French prisons to fetch and carry for the very few free Frenchmen mad enough to want to live here. I would say the population of French Guiana was eighty or ninety percent prisoner at the moment. A situation hardly calling for an active night life. The planters and officials wall themselves in as they pursue the usual social activities of wining and dining and seducing one another's wives, hein?"

"I guess so. How come they have to wall themselves in if there's a police curfew after dark?"

Gaston laughed and said, "My more uncouth countrymen are inclined to scoff at regulations, which would seem to be how most of them got here. The inmates paroled here to the mainland as day labor are not under lock and key after dark, but, of course, consider themselves imprisoned and, naturally, want *out!* The discussion about the surrounding country that we just had is the reason they can't leave; unless, of course, they somehow obtain arms, money, and hopefully a boat. The droll situation makes for a tendency to lock one's door after dark, if you have anything of value to worry about."

Gaston suddenly touched the tall American's sleeve and murmured, "Ah, see what I mean?" as Captain Gringo, too, spotted the six or eight dim figures in the gloom ahead.

They were on a mere lane running along the back wall of the housing on the edge of town. To their left, the country seemed open fields of something soggy. The guys blocking their route north-east had to be dressed in white to be as visible as they were. He could see by the way they were standing, warily, that they'd spotted him and Gaston, too.

28

He asked the Frenchman, "What's the form?" and Gaston replied, "We could go back the way we came and hope they could not run as fast."

"Don't like that, much. We've both got guns."

"Oui, but guns make noise and attract the attention of the police, who, I gather, you are not anxious to discuss our affairs with?"

Captain Gringo nodded and answered, "Yeah, we'd better just bull on through 'em and hope for the best. If they had arms enough to matter they wouldn't be prowling around out here. They'd be trying to escape the colony, right?"

"Merde alors, what do you mean arms enough to matter? If they have one gun between them we are in a sticky pickle, my old and rare. I wish I could break you of your stubborn streak. Come, let us scamper gayly back to safety, hein."

"Safety where? I'm heading for that town to the north, Gaston. Are you in or out?"

Gaston swore and kept step with him as the tall American strode thoughtfully toward the line of prison inmates. The guys in the white pajamas waited, ominously. As the two parties got within earshot, one of the prisoners growled in French, "Well, well, what have we here, two sweethearts going for an evening stroll?"

"Listen, my children," Gaston replied, "you are making a big mistake." Another inmate said, "Let's take them!"

Captain Gringo knew enough French to get the message and, even if he hadn't, it would have seemed obvious that eight guys coming at you with sticks and homemade knives weren't on your side. So he dropped into a club fighter's crouch and, as he hoped, the first untrained street brawler walked into a sucker-punch wide open. Captain Gringo caught his roundhouse right on his own left elbow and decked him with a right cross as Gaston feinted with his small boney fists, rose on one toe, and kicked another one under the ear.

But this was a French prison colony and Gaston was not the only gutter-fighter from Paris who knew La Savate. So the next guy coming at Captain Gringo tried to kick his face off.

But Captain Gringo knew from watching Gaston how La Savate worked, even though it wasn't his usual style. He grabbed the attacker's ankle in both hands, holding him in the position of a can-can dancer caught in mid-air, and brought his own mosquito boot up to kick the son-of-a-bitch in the wide open groin before dropping him like a used contraceptive, with just about that much fight left in him.

Meanwhile, Gaston had put another on the ground with a well-aimed kick and the survivors were dropping back to think things over. The one who'd started the conversation had held back to see how easy they'd be as he let his less experienced pals find out the hard way. But the leader of any gang is supposed to know his onions and anybody can suggest a hasty retreat. So the boss bully grinned piratically at Gaston as he drew something that glittered in the dim light, saying, "Well, well, well, I see we have a prima ballerina dancing for us tonight, boys. Where did you learn La Savate, my little beauty?"

Gaston said, "Somewhere between the Left Bank and Place Pigale, you cocksucker. Do you wish to continue this lesson or have you had enough?"

"I'll tell you when I've had enough. How good are you with a knife, Left Bank? Just you and me, man-to-man?"

Gaston laughed, "Oh, I have always wanted to duel like a student prince. Stay out of this, Dick. But cover me in case we are not among gentlemen, hein."

Captain Gringo reached under his jacket and drew his snub-nosed .38. A more sensible member of the gang blanched and said, "Hey, *mais amis,* this is getting serious! Why didn't you guys tell us you were able to take care of yourselves? We thought you were tourists! Drop it, Marcel! The wise fox hunts the rabbit, not another fox!"

But Marcel, if that was the leaders' name, shook his head and insisted, "Left Bank and me have a deal. Isn't that right, Left Bank?"

Gaston said, "If you say so. But I strongly suggest you listen to your friends."

Marcel's answer was to move in, crouching over the blade held between him and the dapper Gaston as he said, "You're too cute to live. Where's your blade, Left Bank?"

"God preserve me from ignorant children," Gaston snorted. "He asks to see my blade. Can you believe it?"

And then Gaston sort of toe danced into Marcel in a bewildering blur and as the bully slashed wildly in the faint tricky light, he suddenly gasped in numb surprise and muttered, "Oh, no!" as Gaston held him on his feet with one arm, holding him in a tight bear hug, while his other hand gripped the hilt of the knife he'd driven into Marcel's lower chest just under the ribs. Marcel's own blade dropped to the dirt behind

Gaston as the bully tried to say something more. But he couldn't say anything. Gaston could feel the pulse beats with his own knife handle as they faded away. So he let go, stepped back, and quietly asked, "Anyone else?" as Marcel crumpled at his feet, dead.

There were no takers. The first man Captain Gringo had clobbered sat up, holding his head as he asked, "Jesus, what happened?" One of his pals came over to help him up, muttering, "Marcel just made a mistake. We've got to get out of here before the police find his body. I'm already doing twenty-to-life and I don't need anymore."

He saw Captain Gringo looking at them thoughtfully and asked, "Is that all right with you, M'sieur? We just want out!"

Captain Gringo nodded and Gaston said. "We'll be on our way while you revive the others and get them back for bed check. If I were you boys I'd hide the late Marcel somewhere; but one sees you seldom listen to your elders, so . . ."

"M'sieur, we are listening!" another cut in, adding, "How were we to know you were an old Apache? Listen, if you guys need a gang, you just showed this one you know the way it's done!"

There was a mutter of agreement. Gaston noted, "They want to join up with us, Dick? What do you think?"

Captain Gringo said, "Fuck 'em. Who needs half a dozen guys who can't take on two? Let's get out of here. We have enough on our plate without a bunch of sissies tagging along!"

Gaston had been right about the mangrove swamps. The way north-east from Cayenne had been open field and cultivated plantation for the first few hours. But long before sunrise the trail they were following petered out against a drainage ditch and all they could see on the far side was black as pitch. The night was moonless and the trades had even blotted out the stars with cloud cover. Captain Gringo pulled a clump of dead weeds from trailside, twisted it into a improvised torch, and lit it with a match. The weeds were soggy and gave a dull flickering glow, but he could make out the stilt roots of mangroves growing out of water and wet inky goo on the far side. A couple of big red eyes were gleaming in the torchlight from the drainage ditch, not

31

moving as they stared unwinking at the light. He grimaced and said, "Cayman or crocodile over there. I can't tell which, but it's a big one."

"*Oui,*" Gaston said, "I see it. Tell me, my old and rare, is there any important difference between a cayman and a crocodile once it has you in it's jaws?"

"Only to a zoologist. I think we could jump that ditch, if there was anything on the other side to jump to."

"*Merde alors,* one does not jump into a mangrove swamp. I told you this would happen, Dick. What do we do now?"

Captain Gringo held the torch higher as he stepped away from the cayman infested water. He looked around and said, "We're miles from town and nobody seems to be chasing us. What are those little bushes doing all around us, Gaston?"

"They are growing there, of course. What else would you have pepper bushes do?"

"Yeah, I heard about Cayenne Pepper. Okay, if somebody planted them, somebody must live around here. We're out too far for prison labor, so the owners of these fields are probably simple country folk and I don't think there's an alarm out on us."

Gaston glanced up at the soggy sky and observed, "I, too, see the advantages of a roof over one's head. But we had that back in town before you proceeded to gallop off through the night."

"Shelter is the least of our worries, in this climate," Captain Gringo said. "What I want is a boat. Between all these drainage ditches and the sea just over to our north-east, some villager or small holder might have a dugout or something we can use. How much could he charge us for a lousy dugout, right?"

"Not much, and if he tries we can always shoot him. But I hope you are not planning to paddle by those mangroves in a dugout, Dick."

"Why not? It beats *walking* through that bowl of soggy spinach."

Gaston sighed, "Correct me if I am wrong, but is that not the Atlantic Ocean to our right?"

"Yeah, what of it?"

"Let me break this to you gently, my old and rare. Atlantic Oceans are not places one should paddle dugouts. The trade winds have had the width of a tropic sea to pile up breakers and one does not like to consider having to swim in warm

32

shark infested water even when it's not coming at one two stories high!"

Captain Gringo said, "Look, there's a path leading through the peppers. It has to lead somewhere, so let's give it a go."

He tossed the torch in the ditch to fizzle out as he headed through the waist-high peppers with Gaston following Indian file, bitching as usual. The tall American in the lead had to navigate as much by feel as by sight in the almost total darkness; but once he was used to the trail he was able to stay on it most of the time. They followed it nearly an hour and Gaston was starting to make unfortunate sense as he complained they were obviously lost. Then Captain Gringo spotted a glimmer on the horizon and, since there were no stars out that night, said, "Hey, I see a light. Looks like the window of a house. So keep it down and follow me."

The farmstead was further away than it looked, but as they trudged on, the light indeed resolved itself into a square window with a coal oil lamp burning inside a frame dwelling with a corrugated iron roof. Captain Gringo drew his gun and murmured, "Watch your legs. There might be a watch dog and when they don't bark they come in biting."

Gaston drew his own gun, saying, "I hear something. But not a dog barking."

Captain Gringo heard it too, and couldn't figure out what it was. It sounded like someone in the house was beating wet laundry on a rock, which seemed reasonable. But whoever was doing their primitive laundry at this hour seemed to be moaning a lot about it.

He stepped off the path into the peppers growing almost to the beaten earth of the yard, trying to get a better view through the mysterious open window. He could see movement, now. Something was casting a repeated blur of shadow on the far wall. He kept going and the moans and sounds of wet slapping grew louder as he moved in.

And when he was close enough to see inside, he stopped and muttered, "What the hell?" as Gaston joined him. They could both see a quartet of roughly dressed men in there, giving an old man and a girl a hard time. The girl was in her late teens or early twenties, with features of a pretty mestiza of White and Indian blood. One of the men was holding her from behind, twisting an arm up in back of her. One of her breasts had popped out of her thin cotton blouse above a clean but ragged peon skirt. Her long black hair swished like

33

a horse's main in the face of the grinning lout holding her as she struggled to get free.

The old man was being held face down across a simple plank table, bare to the waist. One of the slobs was beating him slowly and methodically across the back with a riding quirt. The reason it sounded sloppy was because the old man's back was already a red hash and the quirt was soaked with his blood.

Gaston nudged Captain Gringo and whispered, "Stay out of it, Dick."

"Jesus, do you know what's going on?"

"Oui, they seem to be having a dispute about his rent. Nobody but a, how you say share cropper would be dwelling in such a little shack, and it may be he's been late delivering his share to the landlord. Those thugs are the usual bully boys one encounters in backward rural communities, hein?"

Captain Gringo growled low in his throat as the man holding the girl noticed the exposed breast and began to paw it, trying to nibble her ear from behind as she struggled with him. Gaston said, "We can't change the way it's always been, Dick." The hell of it was, Captain Gringo knew Gaston was right. He'd promised himself not to get mixed up in any more crusades after learning many times, the hard way, that the little people down here could act just as dumb as the big shots. He'd told himsllf that was probably how they'd gotten to be little people in the first place. Even those Ashanti slaves had had sense enough to buck the system, damn it!

The man doing the beating stopped, maybe to catch his breath, and Captain Gringo was getting used to the local creole enough to follow the drift as the bully asked his victim, "Well, old man, have you had enough?"

The badly beaten man raised his head from the planks and croaked, "More than enough, if I had what you are looking for! But I swear to God I don't know what you're talking about!"

The torturer raised his quirt, grimaced at the awful mess he'd already made, and lowered it. He nodded at the ones near the girl and said, "All right. They want to be stubborn. Let's work her over, eh?"

The one holding her asked, "Can I fuck her first, Boss? It's not much fun when they're all bruised and bloody."

The boss shrugged and said, "Sure, why not? We can *all* fuck her! We've got plenty of time."

Then Captain Gringo stepped over to the window, nodded pleasantly, and said, "You're wrong. I'd say your time just ran out."

There was a collective gasp as all four of the ruffians went for the side arms they wore. The girl broke free and darted to the old man, throwing herself down on him. As long as there was a free field of fire, Captain Gringo started using it!

He shot the boss and sent him crashing into the far wall with a look of horror in his dying eyes. Before the boss slid all the way down the planks, Captain Gringo had dropped two more and the fourth was cringing in a far corner, hands reaching for the rafters as he gibbered in fear and pleaded, "No, not *me!* I meant no harm!"

He was the one who'd suggested raping the girl. But Captain Gringo held his fire as he cocked a leg over the sill to join the party. The girl raised her head from the old man's back. Her cheek was covered with his blood. She stared numbly at Captain Gringo, who smiled and pointed his muzzle at the last man on his feet, saying, "It's up to you, Señorita."

The girl hissed like a cat, turned and bent to pick up the bloody quirt, and advanced on the cringing bully as Captain Gringo came inside, still covering him. The girl bared her breast with her free hand, saying, "You admire this, eh? Take a good look, you bastard! It's the last thing you'll ever see!"

She meant it. The quirt lashed out and caught him across the eyes, tearing one from it's socket and not doing the other a hell of a lot of good. The would-be rapist screamed and fell sobbing to the floor on his knees with his hands to his bloody face. By this time Gaston had come in more sedately by way of the front and only door. He started to ask the girl what was going on, but the blinded man was screaming too loud for anyone to hear, so Gaston stepped over to him, placed the muzzle of his pistol against his skull, and blew his brains out. As the body thudded quietly to the dirt floor, the girl asked, "Why did you do that? I wanted him to suffer!"

"We noticed," Captain Gringo said, as he stepped over to the old man still sprawled across the table. He was in bad shape and belonged in a very well-staffed hospital. But he raised his head, groped for Captain Gringo's free hand, and pressed it to his bruised lips before saying, "If there is a just God in Heaven, he shall reward you for this, my son. You and your brave comrade arrived just in time. They were about to . . ."

35

"We know what they were about to do, old timer," Captain Gringo cut in, adding, "Can you move your legs?"

"My what? I seem to be able to move them, now that I try. I fear I am not well enough to rise without help, though."

Captain Gringo put a hand on one of the few places the quirt had missed as he soothed, "You stay just as you are until we can patch you up." Then he blinked and marvelled aloud, "Hey, we're speaking English."

The old man said, "Of course. You spoke English when you called out to them from the window. For a moment I thought you were the U.S. Marines, but, personally, I think you do a better job!"

The old man didn't make it through the night. The shock would have done in many a younger, stronger man, and he'd been seventy-eight when they started beating him to death. They knew this because he lasted long enough to tell his tale while they tried to help with rough first aid as his life ebbed out of him between their fingers.

He was a well educated Frenchman who said his name didn't matter, although the girl, Mimi, kept referring to him as grand père. He didn't want to talk about his past life, either, but he'd obviously done something in France one time that had earned him a long stretch on Devil's Island.

Like many others he'd served a stiff jolt at the maximum security facilities out on the rock and then been made a trustee, or unpaid slave, of the main colony to serve out the remainder of his sentence.

Again, like all too many others, the old man had served out his time and, broken, stayed on as a "Colonist" with no place else to go and no way of getting there. With prisoners working for next to nothing, a flat fee going to the prison authorities, there was almost no way for any free white or native to make a living in French Guiana. Those French planters who didn't want to use prisoners as servants could get a free native for room and board, period. The old man had managed to barely survive as a tenant farmer, as Gaston had surmised.

In exchange for half the crops he raised, he'd settled down to raise peppers and kids with a creole woman who hadn't had anything better to do either. Mimi was their granddaughter. All the other children and grandchildren had died or wandered off some where. The old man wasn't making much sense near the end. Gaston had already hauled the dead outside, but when Captain Gringo caught his eye after feeling the dying man's pulse again, Gaston led the girl outside with some muttered excuse in Creole.

Captain Gringo closed the dead man's eyes and looked around for something to cover him. But he could see there wasn't a scrap of textile or matting that could be spared, so he settled on dimming the oil lamp to a soft glow and composed the cadaver's limbs in a more dignified position as he waited for the others to come back in.

He lit a smoke and had a third consumed when Gaston stuck his head in and murmured, "Dick?"

"It's over," Captain Gringo said. So Gaston brought Mimi in. The little creole girl was stone-faced as she knelt beside her grandfather and made the sign of the cross. But the soft light betrayed the tear running down her cheek. She murmured, "They are dead, too, but it does not help one bit."

Captain Gringo nodded and said, "I know. Who were they, Mimi? What were they after, the rent?"

The girl shook her head and said, "We never saw them before. They were not from our landlord. This season's crops are not ready for to harvest yet, and, in justice, the planter who owns us has always been willing to wait."

"They were after something. I heard your grandfather tell them he didn't have it."

Mimi said, "I think they just wanted an excuse for to abuse us. They said my grandfather was a smuggler. They said he had money and guns hidden somewhere. At first my grandfather laughed, and then they started hitting him."

"That's where we came in, Mimi. I have a reason for asking, so are you sure they had the wrong people? Sometimes men making a little money on the side don't see fit to tell the women in the family about it."

Mimi smiled bitterly and replied, "Look around you! Is this the tenant shack of a rich man? Look at all the peppers my poor old grandfather planted and tended with no sons to help him. Then tell me when he'd have had the time to smuggle guns or anything else!"

Captain Gringo nodded and said, "We just came through a lot of pepper fields, Mimi. Your grandfather didn't grow it all, right?"

"Of course not. We only till five *hectares* and he was hard pressed to manage that as he got older. When it is light you will see there are other shacks such as this one all about. There are perhaps forty families working for the same planter as tenants on shares."

Captain Gringo glanced at Gaston who shrugged and said, "*Mais oui,* it seems obvious they came to the wrong place if, indeed, any of these poor people have been dabbling in gun running. Some sewer rats assume anyone who bathes regularly is rich and the old man was once a cultivated Frenchman. Frankly, I don't see how anyone near here could be smuggling anything. We are far down the coast from the border, hein?"

Captain Gringo said, "Somebody could be landing stuff in a cove of that mangrove swamp from the sea, but you may be right. They could have just been roving thugs who thought anybody can come up with something if you hit him long enough."

He saw the girl was taking it well, considering. She'd probably had some practice, living on the edge of famine all her life, and the old man had mentioned burying a lot of her relatives over the years. That reminded him to ask Gaston about the disposal of the bodies and the Frenchman said, "There is another drainage ditch a short distance from here. I kept their guns and the contents of their pockets. They are piled outside."

Captain Gringo nodded and turned back to Mimi, saying, "We have to be on our way, Honey. But we'll help you get your grandfather's body to the church or whatever before we leave."

She looked blank and replied, "Church? We have no church. We have nothing but the rags on our backs. We don't even own this shack or the fields around it. If you will help me, I will bury my grandfather in the yard. There is no other ground to be spared, for the price of pepper is low and every bush must stand. May I ask where you gentlemen are bound?"

"Hard to say," he said. "If we can get through those mangroves, we had the next settlement up the coast in mind."

Mimi brightened and said, "Oh, I have relations in Sinnamary! Will you take me with you?"

"What about your pepper farm here, Mimi?"

"Pooh, it's not my pepper farm. It was not my poor grand père's pepper farm. The only thing I own is my body, and if

38

those bad men had friends I may not be able to keep that for myself. Won't you take me with you, please?"

Gaston murmured, "Dick?" but Captain Gringo said, "We'll think about it. Is there a shovel anywhere around here, Mimi?"

She said her late grandfather's tools were leaning against the wall outside. So he rose and said, "Stay here while we dig the grave, Mimi. Come on, Gaston."

Outside in the dark, Gaston protested, "I admire the body she owns, too, but do we really need more complications, my old and randy?"

Captain Gringo found two spades, handed one to Gaston, and pick up the other as he said, "Keep it down—she speaks English. It might be more complicated for us if we leave her here. She's right about another visit, you know. Somebody must have told those guys you chucked in the canal that there are buried treasure here. Even if she's not in danger, do you really want her gossiping about tonight with the neighbors?"

Gaston grimaced and said, "Oui, I vaguely remember hearing it was against the law to shoot people in French Guiana without discussing it with the authorities. But do you think that barefoot little thing is up to a fifty-mile romp?"

Captain Gringo sunk his spade into the red soil near the edge of the yard. "Nobody is up to a fifty-mile romp on foot," he said, "if he or she can get their hands on a boat. That's another reason we should take her under our wings. She knows the country and might be able to put us on to some second cousin with a dugout for sale. Are you just going to stand there? Help me dig, you lazy old bastard!"

Gaston started at the other end of the planned six-foot slit, muttering to himself. The soil was soft under it's hard surface crust and cut like cheese. So they were soon knee-deep in the grave. Gaston threw another blade full of dirt on his spoil pile, leaned on his handle, and suggested, "Eh, bien, this is deep enough, if we are all leaving, hein?"

Captain Gringo hesitated, then nodded with approval. "You're right. It's not as early as it used to be and the worms will get him no matter how far down we go."

He went inside, moved Mimi gently out of the way, and proceeded to wrap the old man in a straw mat as he said, "Gather your things, Mimi. I'll take care of your grandfather."

"Oh, am I coming with you?"

"I wouldn't be using half your furniture if you weren't. You'd better stay in here, Honey. We'll call you when we're ready to say a few words over his grave, okay?"

He picked up his surprisingly light bundle and lugged it outside. As he dropped it in the shallow grave he told Gaston, "It's no wonder he died. The pool old bastard was nothing but skin and bones before he started bleeding. Your countrymen have a lot to answer for down here, Gaston. This prison colony is pretty shitty!"

Gaston shrugged and said, "One must admit my people can be a bit more *practique* than Christian. That was my main reason for deserting La Legion. But let us not be unfair to France, Dick. A lot of these prisoners would have hanged in your country."

"Oh, shit, even if a guy deserves a hanging there should be limits. They give a guy no way out down here. They work his ass off until he serves his time and then they work his ass off afterward."

"Tragique, perhaps, but, to repeat, most of the men sent to Devil's Island would have been executed by any other government. One does not come here for stealing a chicken, you know. France has quite ordinary jails for petty criminals. I feel sorry for this poor old failure, but he might not have lived to be so old had he spent the time on one of your lovely American chain gangs. Are you suggesting no American serving hard labor has ever been exploited and abused?"

"Okay, you got a point. But remind me never to go to a French jail."

"Mais oui, all jails are *très fatigue,* and if we don't plant this wilted cabbage and get out of here the discussion may not be as academic, hein?"

They smoothed the loose soil over the wrapped corpse with their blades and Captain Gringo said, "I'll get Mimi. Where are those guns and things the gang dropped on their way to hell?"

"By the door, as I said. On that bench there."

Captain Gringo moved to the open doorway and nodded to Mimi, who was tying up a small bundle in a red calico bandana. As she carried it out to the grave with her, Captain Gringo pulled the bench into the light for a better look at the spoils of war. There was a nice brace of single action .45 peacemakers, with the bullet loops filled. So he strapped it around his hips, adjusting the double action .38 under his jacket as he did so. He'd been wondering when and where he could pick up extra rounds for his sidearm. There were some small money bags, none holding more than a few coins. But that could be ammo, too, so he emptied them into his own pocket. He picked up a gunbelt for Gaston and another with a single holster for Mimi. Then he strolled over to join them as they mumbled over the grave. He handed Gaston his extra arms. Mimi was fingering her rosary, eyes closed, so he stepped behind her and buckled the belt around her hips, noticing they were tighter and firmer than the peon skirt suggested. She flinched, then nodded as she got the picture and said, "Yes, I shall never let a man near me again, now that I have a weapon!"

Gaston grinned and muttered, "Stupid move, my old and rare."

The tall American smiled wearily and said, "I hate to rush you, Mimi, but it's time to go. Do you have any idea where we can pick up a boat?"

"A boat? No. Why do you need a boat, ah, Deek?"

"I don't know if you've ever noticed, but there's a mangrove swamp between here and Sinnamary."

"Oh, that is no problem, Deek. I know several trails through the mangroves. I used to play in the swamp as a child. My poor grand père and I often hunted in the mangroves until his shotgun rusted away a year or so ago."

Captain Gringo cocked an eyebrow at Gaston and asked, "Still think I'm crazy?"

Gaston laughed and replied, "But of course. And most favored by Dame Fortune, too. Never have I seen such a fool for luck. Any other man would have drowned us in the swamp, or at best made it around in a boat. But *regardez,* you have to find a beautiful woman who can lead you through it dry shod!"

Captain Gringo glanced up at the sky and said, "Moon's rising at last. You'd better take the lead, Mimi." So the creole girl did, setting a good pace through the peppers. The light was improving rapidly and as he followed close behind he noticed she had a very nice walk indeed. She didn't wiggle it like a cantina gal showing off at the paseo to get whistled at. But a man could tell it was all there. She walked with the graceful strides of a barefoot woman used to carrying parcels on her head. A lot of high-toned society girls back home tried hard for such a dignified, albeit, seductive walk. She came to a cross path and moved west, looking back over her shoulder as she asked, "Are you still coming with me, Deek?" and he

41

said, "I sure hope so." But of course she didn't get it. He hadn't intended her to. He knew the smart thing would be to drop her off with her relations as soon as they could, and he knew how relations down here could cloud up and rain all over a stranger who'd messed with one of their womenfolks, too. But damn, if only he'd met her some other time and place!

They were about a mile from the old shack when they heard hoof beats and Gaston snapped, "Down!" before Captain Gringo could. He saw Mimi didn't know the form, so he lunged forward, grabbed her, and dove into the peppers with her, clapping a hand over her mouth as she started to scream.

For a moment Mimi struggled, confused, as he lay half atop her amid the crushed peppers, saying, "Quiet, someone's coming!"

She nodded, eyes wide in the moonlight through the overcast and he let go of her face as she huddled closer, stiff with fear. He could smell her musky unwashed flesh, spiced with the tang of hot pepper, and he knew she was aware he was a man, too. So as he slid his hand down between them he whispered, "Don't take this the wrong way, Doll. I'm after my *gun!*"

He got to the .38 between them, but it was a tight fit and the nipple he'd brushed with the back of his hand was aroused. Probably just nerves, he told himself. The hoof beats came closer, then stopped. Mimi buried her face against his chest and fought not to sob aloud as he held her tighter to comfort her. He had no idea where Gaston was. He wasn't about to ask. A distant voice called out, "See anything?" and another replied, "No. But the little cunt couldn't have gotten far!"

Captain Gringo was aware that somebody was pissing in his lap, and he didn't think it was him. Mimi sobbed, "Please, Deek, save me!" and he whispered, "Easy, Honey. The man just said he didn't know where we were!"

They heard the hoof beats fading and he called out, softly, "Gaston?" "I am here, smeared with crushed peppers, *merde alors!* Someone seems to be wondering why their wandering boys failed to come home to supper, hein?"

"Yeah. Let's get out of here some more."

He sat up, looked around, and seeing nothing but the tops of more peppers, started to help Mimi to her feet. She was bawling like a baby. He patted her on the shoulder and said,

"It's okay. They're gone and the mangroves can't be far, right?"

"Oh, Deek, what must you think of me?"

"I think you were scared. Welcome to the club."

"But . . . I went pee pee on you! I am so ashamed! How can I ever face you in the light again?"

He laughed, gently, and said, "I won't tell if you won't. I didn't think you did it to be mean, Honey. These pants need pressing anyway. Let's just forget it, okay?"

"How can either of us ever forget such a disaster? Nice girls are not supposed to go pee pee!"

"Oh, hell, Queen Victoria must have, at least once. We can worry about it later, Mimi. Right now I'm more worried about your path through the mangroves."

She turned away and started trotting, holding her skirt away from her legs with her hands. As they staggered after her, yelling for her to slow down, she started bawling again. After she'd run a quarter mile she stopped, dropped to her knees and covered her face with her hands to cry in earnest.

Gaston sidled up to Captain Gringo and whispered, "What's wrong with her, Dick?"

"She pissed her pants back there and she seems upset about it."

Gaston chuckled, "I doubt if she's ever worn pants. But that's the trouble with growing up in poverty. When dignity is all one has, one tends to overdo it, hein?"

It sounded reasonable. But Captain Gringo wasn't sure. He'd learned on the run to frisk the Bluebird of Happiness for concealed weapons and Mimi was a mélange of presumably peasant Indian, Spanish, and French. He'd always thought the lower class French took pissing more casual than Hispanic peones, and Hispanic peones didn't get this excited about having to take a leak. He bent and hauled Mimi to her feet as he said, "Come on, Doll. This is getting silly. Don't you want to get away from those horsemen after all?"

That seemed to straighten her out. She gasped, "Oh, they called me a bad thing!" and headed out again through the moonlight. Captain Gringo let her take a longer lead, now, since he could see her better and wanted a word with Gaston. Gaston was starting to frisk bluebirds, too. He said, Dick. I think those others came to the right place, don't you?"

The American answered, in a low voice. "Yeah. I'm not sure she knew the old boy was guiding smugglers through the swamps, though. He told her his gun was rusted out and stopped taking her with him into the mangroves a while back. That was probably shortly after someone contracted with him to lead more important woodland romps."

Gaston nodded. "She'd have told them if she'd known where the old man hid his gold. But he must have been a determined miser indeed to hold out as he did."

The tall American shook his head and said, "I don't think he had anything worth the beating he took. Nobody's that tough. He couldn't have been more than a local guide, paid off in peanuts. The oil lamp and one of the shovels back there were new. Some wise asses just used an old exile as a guide, tipped him a few francs, and moved on with whatever those other guys were after. The thugs were from a rival gang, or maybe neighborhood bullies who'd just noticed the old man's modest prosperity and decided to shake him down."

Gaston patted the gunbelt he was wearing and opined, "I like a rival gang better, Dick. These are new well-kept weapons—not the sort of thing one usually sees in the company of the bush league bandito. Their friends had horses, too. From the hoofbeats I heard I would say they were well shod and spirited saddle mounts, too."

Captain Gringo saw the black wall of mangroves beyond Mimi as he said, "Let's drop it for now. We have to close up." He walked faster to catch up with the girl who acted as if she knew what she was doing, considering how dark it was. There was no beaten path he could see in the moonlight but Mimi went directly to some weeds growing on the banks of the drainage ditch separating the swamp from cultivated land. She hunkered down and said, "Ah, here is the log poor *grandpère* used to bridge the ditch."

Captain Gringo hunkered down to help her and together they lifted the hidden rough plametto log. They got it upright on one end and he heaved to drop the other end on the far bank. It landed with a dull damp thud. He asked the girl, "Are you sure it's not rotten, Mimi? Palmetto doesn't last long on the ground in this climate and you said it's been a year or more since you were out here, right?"

Mimi didn't answer as she scampered gracefully across to the other side and called back, "See?"

He saw. The log had bent under her ominously and she couldn't weigh more than a hundred and ten. He said, "Gaston, you'd better go next."

44

Gaston had been watching. He said, *"Oui,* I think it will hold me, but what about you?"

"If I have to swim I have to swim. Here, take my gunbelt."

Gaston did so and gingerly crossed the log to join Mimi. Captain Gringo noticed it bent even more under Gaston's weight and he had a good fifty pounds on Gaston. He didn't see any caymans or salt water crocs, but the ones who got you were seldom the ones you saw. He took a deep breath and started running, or, rather, splashing, for the log bent under the surface as he crossed it, but it held—just. So when he joined the others on the far side he lifted the end and swung it around to send the improvised bridge floating off in the gentle current. Then he said, "Damn, we should have brought that lamp from the shack. It's black as a bitch in here."

Mimi said, "I can feel the path with my bare feet, Deek. Everything else under the mangroves is wet."

So he told her to lead on and followed, strapping on his gun rig again as Gaston brought up the rear. He wasn't barefoot, although his mosquito boots had taken some water over their tops and his toes were squishing, but he could feel the so-called path under them. It felt as if they were walking across a big spring mattress. There was no dry earth in a mangrove swamp, but floating weeds and rotten vegetation tended to raft thickly between the stilted trunks of the close-packed trees. Mimi and Gaston were shorter, so Captain Gringo caught most of the low branches with his face in the dark. He held a hand up. It helped. But not much. Aside from mangrove twigs the air seemed filled with hanging Spanish moss and spider webbing. He sincerely hoped any spider who took umbrage wasn't one of those big bastards that ate birds. Spiders down here had something wrong with their glands and could grow as big as a man's hand. The natives said the ones with fatal stings were smaller. He hoped they knew what they were talking about, and that he didn't wind up kissing any of them in the dark. He called ahead, "Mimi, you're walking too silently. Scuff your barefeet to let the snakes know you're coming."

Behind him, Gaston muttered, "Leave her to her own devices, Dick. It's true the ground snakes tend to slither off a trail when they hear the footsteps of creatures too big to swallow. But the tree boas can swallow anything and tend to, how you say, home in on the sounds of movement in the dark."

Captain Gringo grimaced and said, "Jesus, you just cheered me up a lot! Do you know where you're going, Mimi? There are no stars to navigate by even if we could see the damned sky."

"I told you," Mimi said, "I grew up playing in these mangroves, Deek." So he felt a little better for a while. Then they were out in the open on a sandy hammock and Mimi stopped. The light was better in the clearing, so he could see the puzzled expression on her face. He asked, "What's wrong?" and Mimi said, "I do not understand. This island was never here before."

"Merde alors," Gaston said. "We're lost!" So Mimi started to cry again. Captain Gringo said, "Hey, everybody calm down. We're ahead of the game since nobody could possibly find us, wherever we might be. We'll build a fire in the sand and dry out. As the sun comes up we'll be able to tell east from west, so what the hell."

Mimi pointed uncertainly and added, "I think Sinnamary must be that way." But Captain Gringo insisted, "It'll still be there in the morning. The first thing you do when you're turned around in the woods is stop and think it over. Plunging on wildly is the way you really get lost."

"But, Deek, I am sure I am only a little turned around. I could not have taken more than one or two wrong turns back there."

He started kicking fallen branches into a pile and replied, "Yeah. One wrong turn would have done it. We're on dry land and all three of us are soaking wet. We'll dry out, catch forty winks, and back track when we have more light on the subject. Didn't I hear someplace that you can eat mangrove fruit?"

"Oui," Gaston affirmed, "but mangrove wine makes more sense. The fruit is *très* insipid, since it is little but sweet pulp."

"Okay, you two gather some anyway. It's been a while since our last square meal and the sugar and water will at least keep us going. This sand will be dry enough to sleep in our clothes, once it bakes near the fire a while. You and I will take turns on guard, Gaston."

"Merde alors, what are we to guard against?"

"I don't know. That's why one of us has to stay alert at all times. Are there any natives in this swamp, Mimi?"

The creole girl shook her head. "Nobody lives in here, but of course people hunt and gather the mangrove fruit and Spanish moss from time to time."

"There you go, Gaston. Want to flip a coin for first watch?"

"No, I want a steamboat ticket back to Costa Rica. Come, Mimi, let's gather our mundane midnight snack, hein?"

They left Captain Gringo to build the camp fire and once he got the damp punk tinder going it was no big deal. He'd learned in Apache country long ago to make his camp fires small, like an Indian. Aside from casting no sky glow, a small fire was easier to keep going and, since a flame was a flame, gave off more sensible heat than a white camper's roaring blaze. You could sit close to an Indian fire and get warm all over instead of baking on one side and freezing in the other. As he hunkered over the smudgey fire he realized for the first time how much he needed to dry out. A little known danger of the tropics was pneumonia. Many a so-called "jungle fever" was the common cold. It never got really frigid in the tropic zone, but the contrast between the baking days and cool clammy nights could lead to nasty chills. He took off his boots and wet socks and put them on sticks driven into the sand to dry. He sat with his clammy barefeet near the coals and let the heat soak into his moist crotch as he luxuriated. As his pants began to dry he could smell Mimi's urine mixed with his own groin sweat. He saw no need for this rather distasteful blend of body odors to give him a dawning erection, but that was the trouble with sexual instincts—they never acted sensible. The whale shit and musk they put in expensive French perfumes were more subtle, but had the same sneaky effects. He wasn't sure if he bought that Darwin theory, but there sure were times when he suspected some of his ancestors had been stinky little critters sniffing at one another a lot.

Mimi and Gaston rejoined him, carrying some fruit that looked like plums. As the three of them sat by the fire chewing and spitting the pulp in the flames he said, "You're right, Gaston, there's not much to them. But what the hell, maybe we'll meet a deer or something someday."

"Someday ought to be soon," said Gaston. "for all this is doing is giving me an appetite for solid food. I did not get as wet as you, since I had sense enough not to grow up so alarmingly. I think I shall take the first watch. I had better patrol a bit, too. To mount the proper guard, one should

47

know how many directions the foe can approach one's camp, *non?*"

Captain Gringo nodded and Gaston rose, leaving most of his share of mangrove fruit unconsumed. The little Frenchman was tenser than he let on and the walk would probably do him good. Captain Gringo reached for another faggot for the fire. Then he hesitated and said, "These hardwood branches seem to make nice coals and I don't want to bounce any light off that low overcast above us, Mimi. Are you warm enough?"

She said, "Yes. I did not get very wet, except when I . . . oh, God, don't look at me. I am so ashamed."

He sniffed and said, "Hey, it's all dried up, so forget it. This sand is pretty dry, too. You'd better get some sleep."

Mimi said, "I have no place to lay my head." So he took off his linen jacket and spread it on the sand between them, saying, "Here, put your face on this and you won't wake up spitting sand."

"What about you, Deek?"

"I'll lay my head beside yours, of course," he replied, removing his guns and setting them aside not out of reach. He saw she was reluctant, so he swung his legs away from the fire and drew her down beside him, saying, "See? There's room for both of us. I hope you don't snore."

They lay side-by-side, their breaths mingled as he patted her and added, "You really need the rest, Honey. I know you've been through a lot and you don't feel sleepy yet, but it's a good idea to catch up on one's beauty sleep whenever there's a chance. God knows when we'll have another chance."

She lay quietly, almost against him, and said, "I feel so ashamed. I feel like I am in bed with you."

"That's nothing to be ashamed of," he added, telling his erection to knock if off for God's sake. Mimi giggled shyly and said, "This is silly. I feel very wicked, even though I know you don't want me."

"Hey, let's not get sickening about this, Honey. I never said I didn't want you. I'm just well bred."

"Pooh, you're being gallant because I shamed myself back there on the trail. You must be very disgusted with me. I can still smell what I did to your pants and my skirt."

"You want to take them off?"

"Oh, Deek, don't be naughty."

"I'm trying not to be. It would be a lot easier if you'd stop talking about your body functions. I told you everybody does

48

it, Mimi. They do other things with the same parts, so let's drop the subject or get to the nice parts."

She gasped and asked, "Oh, are you talking about the wicked things men and women do together down there, Deek?"

He said, "I wouldn't say it was wicked. Maybe a little, uh, informal."

"Oh, I think you are just trying to make me feel better about soiling myself. I know you must be disgusted with me."

He snuggled closer, held her against him with one arm, and ran his free hand down her flank as he kissed her and reached under her skirt to pet her where she seemed to feel so ashamed. She responded to his kiss but tried to cross her legs as he cupped her firm warm mons. Her pubic hair was perfectly dry, now, although one finger seemed to be getting very wet at the moment. She rolled her lips to one side and gasped, "You mustn't! I have not had a chance to bathe since I went pee pee!"

He said, "I don't mind. If we have to keep harping on your sweet little pisser, we may as well get to know it better." Then he kissed her again before she could start the usual guff about being a nice girl. He knew she was experienced as soon as she began to move her hips in response to his clitoral stimulation. He didn't want to hear who'd broken her in, but it had obviously been an expert. He was wondering how he was going to unbutton himself without losing a tactical advantage when Mimi reached down between them to unfasten his fly, protesting all the while that he was being most wicked. He rolled into the saddle as she hauled his organ grinder out and spread her thighs in welcome as she guided it into position. But as she felt it entering her she gasped, "Oh, whatever must you think of me!" So he said, "I think you're wonderful" and drove it into her to the hilt.

She wrapped her arms around him, raising her knees and spreading them wider as she complained, "Your belt buckle is scratching me and you are going too deep!" So, knowing he was home safe, he stopped and got his pants down around his thighs without removing himself from the scene of action. As they started again he knew she was fibbing about it being too deep because she was trying to inhale him, balls and all, as she bounced her firm little rump on the hard packed sand under it.

His scrotum had to stay out in the cold between her hot

49

buttocks no matter how she tried, because she really was built nice and tight, but he had no complaints. Mimi was a great little lay. So he pounded them both to mutual orgasm and when she screamed aloud he warned, "Take it easy. Gaston will come running to see who's getting killed. And, speaking of Gaston, let's move back from the fire so we can strip and do this right!"

She lowered her feet to the sand on either side of his legs and said, "Oh, I had forgotten Gaston. He'll be shocked to discover I am not a good girl!"

Captain Gringo said, "Disappointed, maybe. I don't think you can shock Gaston. But let's not frustrate him by making him watch. Come on, let's get back in the dark a ways."

So they did so, Mimi protesting all the time he was undressing her that she felt terribly ashamed. But as he spread her skirt on the sand for a new beginning the little creole girl got on top, stark naked, and proceeded to bounce like a child on a merry-go-round as he kissed her teasing nipples and helped her with a palm cupped under each thigh. The way she could spread her legs was incredible and though they were well back from the dull red glow of the camp fire, he could see her tawny body as she loomed lovingly over him. He was fixing to come again when they heard Gaston calling out, *"Alors,* where is everybody?" and Mimi dropped close against him, face flushed and vagina twitching in mingled desire and embarrassment. Captain Gringo called out, "We're all right. Uh, it's a sort of private party, Gaston."

The old Frenchman laughed, "Ah, you have my blessings, my children. If you're at all interested in anything else, I just heard a distant steamboat whistle. We seem to be closer to the shoreline than I assumed. Now that I have reported this perhaps unimportant news, I shall resume my appointed rounds. But one assumes I am to be relieved some time in the future, hein?"

Captain Gringo laughed and as he saw Mimi wasn't ready to take charge, again, he rolled her over and got on top as she protested, "We must stop, now that he suspects us, Deek!"

He said, "He doesn't *suspect,* Honey. Now that we don't have to worry about him, let's do it right!"

He commenced to suit action to his words but though Mimi was responding nicely indeed from the waist down she went on bitching about Gaston thinking she was a bad girl and how she'd never be able to face him again in the daylight. Captain Gringo said, "You can face me, now, can't you?"

"That's different. A woman is not ashamed of her body after she's shared it with a man. Now that I know you so well I can confess I have done more than pee pee with what you are abusing so marvelously. But I am afraid to face anyone else who knows I am not a virgin."

He didn't reply until he'd had a long shuddering orgasm. Then, as he kept moving politely to help her out, he said, "Don't worry. I think Gaston has that part figured out. I don't think he'll make obscene gestures and stick his tongue out at you, Mimi."

There was a lull in the conversation as the creole girl went wild in his arms again. But after she'd subsided from her own orgasm she started muttering dumb things about Gaston again and it was getting tedious. He could understand her feelings. He'd once shared a small room with a sister he was screwing and another he wasn't.

At first, at least.

It had been a lot more comfortable after they'd all gotten better adapted to the cozy situation. So he rolled off, sat up, and said, "Wait here."

"But, Deek, I'm still hot."

"I noticed." He grinned, getting to his feet. He walked to the fire, picked up his gun rig, and strapped it around his naked hips as he called out, "Hey, Gaston?"

The wirey little Frenchman materialized on the far side of the dull red glow to say, "You must know you are nude, so let's not discuss the matter. What else is going on?"

"I'll take your watch. You'd better take Mimi. It seems we have a shy nymphomaniac on our hands and the sooner she's screwed everybody the sooner she'll shut up about concentrate on guiding us through this fucking swamp."

Gaston's teeth gleamed red in the firelight as he said, "A fucking swamp indeed, but are you sure you do not mind sharing, Dick?"

"I don't generally make a habit of it, but this may be a medical emergency. Go tell her you're not disgusted with her for Pete's sake!"

So Gaston went, as Captain Gringo moved toward the tree line, slapping at a mosquito that seemed to want to suck him off. There weren't as many mosquitoes deep in a swamp as there were around the edges as a rule. So that was something to think about. He needed to think about something as he heard Mimi's distant voice call out, "Oh, no, Gaston, I couldn't!"

51

He started to explore the limits of the sandy hammock as it seemed she could, judging from the occasional distant giggles. The hammock was surrounded on all sides by the same mangroves growing in water and muck. So they weren't on the far side as he'd thought. He cocked his ear as he heard something louder than Mimi albeit further away in the darkness. Gaston had been right: it did sound like the siren of a coastal steamer. But it was something else. He'd heard that sound before, if only he could remember where and when.

His perambulations had taken him around to where Gaston and Mimi were between him and the fire. So he stopped, bemused, as he saw them outlined by the ruddy glow of the fire. Gaston had her on her knees and elbows and was giving it to her dog style as she kept asking him what "Deek" would think if he knew they were being so wicked. "Deek" grimaced and moved on. He knew it wouldn't hurt so much when it was time to ditch the little creole, now that she'd dropped her shy act. He told himself he was finished with her, too.

He'd probably mean it until he got another hard on. Sharing, even with a friend, was pushing things to the limit for a properly raised West Point graduate; but he and Gaston had before and would probably do it again. His civilized veneer had been worn pretty thin since meeting Gaston in front of that Mexican firing squad a while back. Fortunately, both he and the sometimes-shocking Gaston were sure enough of each other's invincible male natures not to be nervous sharing the same bed and broad. He'd never met a man who attracted him sexually and Gaston had reported his few *practique* experiments in the legion and prison as totally silly and unsatisfactory disasters. It was nice to know an old goat who kept threatening to cornhole you didn't really want to.

Captain Gringo heard the distant horn again as he moved on. He looked up at the overcast, snapped his fingers, and muttered, "Of course!"

It was a conch shell fog horn. Some native fisherman was blowing the thing, the way they did off other parts of the Latin American coast in murky weather. Some native sailing vessel was sheltering somewhere in a cove. The sounds were all coming from the same direction. Okay, so why sound a conch horn when you were standing still? Easy: it was a signal for someone they expected to meet. It was dark and misty, but not really foggy enough to call for a fog horn under usual circumstances.

He moved back to the fire and put on his boots to kick it out by scattering and sanding the coals. Gaston joined him, naked in the moonlight, and said, "She's asking for you again. Why are you putting out the fire?"

"You know those smugglers the old man worked for? That's who must be tooting their tooter about a mile from here."

"Ah, I, too, thought it might be a conch blown by some unwashed type. They of course have no way of knowing the old Frenchman we buried will not be here to guide them tonight, hein?"

"Right, and they might come looking for him. We'd better drag all our stuff over by Mimi and sit tight until we can see."

So the two of them picked up and walked over to Mimi, who sat naked on her skirt and asked, in an uncertain voice, "Oh, dear, both of you at once?"

Captain Gringo told her what he thought about the smugglers and added, "No shit, now. We're all friends, and it won't hurt your grandfather if you tell us what the hell's going on, Mimi."

"I swear I don't know," she said. "I told you poor grand père no longer took me with him into this swamp. I knew of course he was doing something dishonest. After all, he was a criminal when he came here to Guiana long before I was born."

"Come on, he must have had visitors. This may not seem delicate, but you, ah, screw pretty good for a girl living all alone with her grandfather."

Mimi lowered her face to her raised nude knees and murmured, "I was hoping you would not ask about that. I am so ashamed."

"He did have visitors a lot, huh?"

"No, Deek, I swear he never brought anyone to the house. He was sometimes gone a few days. He left me there alone and told me to say he was on an errand if anyone asked, but nobody ever did. Nobody but the landlord's agent ever visited our tenant plot."

"Is that who broke you in, the landlord's agent?" he asked, and when Mimi shook her head and began to cry some more, Gaston snorted and asked, "For God's sake, Dick, I know

53

you are one of those tedious New England Puritans, but have you *no* imagination?"

Captain Gringo nodded and muttered, "The old guy *was* a criminal, wasn't he?"

Gaston shrugged and said, "He was a man. Let us leave it at that."

Mimi looked up in the moonlight and asked, "Do you both think I am a whore, now?" and Gaston sat down beside her to sooth, "But of course not, my child. Whores are terrible things who charge for it. Let us say you are a . . . well, good sport, hein?"

Mimi laughed and wiped her eyes, saying, "I feel so much more comfortable, now that we're all friends. Who's turn is it, now?"

"I think we'd better decide that later," Captain Gringo said, "after we all get some sleep. It's late and we may have some running to do as soon as the sun comes up."

He spread his jacket on the sand near Mimi's skirt and Gaston did the same on the other side. The three lay naked with Mimi between them. It was warm enough to sleep without coverings, but getting to sleep was still a problem. Captain Gringo lay quietly counting sheep as Mimi snuggled against him, with Gaston snuggled against her from the other side. Captain Gringo had a hard on, damn it, but, he'd decided enough was enough and he knew he might need all his strength in the near future. So he ignored it, or tried to, and had almost drifted off when he heard Mimi whisper, "Gaston, you old naughty thing! What are you doing to me back there?"

"Hush, child. I am only doing what comes naturally to a man with an attractive woman's derrier in his reclining lap, hein?"

She giggled, her face against Captain Gringo's chest, and whispered, "Idiot, that's the wrong . . . oh, I see it *is* in the right place, now."

Captain Gringo opened his eyes with a frown and said, "For God's sake, troops!" as Mimi began to bounce against him with Gaston pounding her from the far side. She said, "Oh are we disturbing you Deek?" as she slid a questing hand down his belly, grasped his erection, and laughed, "Oh, I see we are."

He didn't think it was funny. He told himself he didn't want the little slut. He might have talked himself into it if she had not moved to her elbows and knees, presenting her rump

54

to Gaston as she proceeded to serve her other companion with her mouth. Captain Gringo hissed in mingled pleasure and disgust, for she did that great, too, and her late grandfather should have been ashamed of himself!

He knew they'd all feel sheepish about this in the morning, but meanwhile it felt wildly wonderful and so they had a totally depraved orgy until both men were exhausted and even Mimi was ready for some sleep. As he fell asleep with Mimi's head on his lap and her thigh cocked over Gaston's chest he wondered why he felt so drained and decided, all in all, it had been a long hard day, even for him.

Captain Gringo awoke with the sun in his eyes and sat up to view the damage. Mimi and Gaston were still asleep, sprawled naked beside him. She looked even better in broad daylight and her sleeping face wore the innocent look of a simple child of nature, which she was, when you came to think of it.

He didn't see much point in anyone dressing for breakfast, but there was no breakfast, so he hauled on his clothes, strapped on his guns, and went for a dawn patrol before waking his companions.

He could see much better, of course, and headed for the sounds he'd heard in the night, following a treacherous but visible trail through the soggy floating mat between the mangroves. He slowed as the muck gave way to more sand. They'd obviously wandered into some stretch where sea winds had piled sand up between the trees as they reclaimed land from the Atlantic rollers. He saw light ahead and moved cautiously, gun drawn, to where the tree wall ended, facing an indented sandy cove with bare barrier sand banks protecting it from seaward.

A small sailing ketch lay anchored in the secluded and no doubt uncharted cove. A trio of dark mestizo youths was ashore just down the sandy beach. They were digging in the sand. As he watched, one shouted and proceeded to fill the basket he had with what looked like golf balls. Captain Gringo muttered, "Turtle eggs" as he watched from the shelter of the mangroves. He doubted if they were the usual turtle egg hunters. The ketch out there looked fast and sneaky. He decided they were the guys who'd been signaling with the conch last night for the old dead guide. An egg was an egg to anybody, and they were taking advantage of their delay to gather breakfast. It made Captain Gringo hungry as hell to think about it.

One of the others yelled something and he saw they'd caught a sea turtle in some shore brush. He knew sea turtles crawled ashore at night to lay their eggs and escape back to the sea. Apparently they didn't always make it. The poor brutes were clumsy on land and if they ran into a snag they were stuck.

The three of them hauled the big turtle clear and turned it on it's back to wave it's flippers listlessly. He'd had turtle soup, so he assumed that was what they had in mind until one of them dropped his pants. Then he muttered, "Oh, shit" as the mestizo youth lowered himself on the female turtle's breast plate and proceeded to rape her, if rape was the right word. The others were laughing like hell and even Captain Gringo thought it was sort of funny, in a sick silly way. It was one of those things a guy just never thought of until he saw some nut trying it. But the guy humping the turtle looked like he was enjoying himself. They'd doubtless been at sea a while.

The others must have been hard up, too. For when the first idiot finished another mounted the turtle in turn. He was going at it hot and heavy when Gaston nudged Captain Gringo from behind and asked what was going on. The American turned to see Mimi was with him and that they were both still nude. He said, "Put some clothes on before they see you, for God's sake. A maniac who'd screw a turtle would even rape you, Gaston!"

Gaston peered around him and cackled, *"Merde alors,* I have heard of this perversion, but I did not think it possible."

Mimi peeked, too, and giggled. She asked, "I wonder what it's like."

"Sorry, Doll," Captain Gringo said, "no boy turtles. Take her back and put some clothes on her, Gaston. I'll cover you from here. But make it snappy."

They faded back into the brush, Gaston lecturing Mimi on the astounding dimensions of a sea turtle's penis as they got out of ear shot. Captain Gringo turned back to see the third guy was screwing the turtle, now. A man came out on the deck of the ketch and yelled over to them. So they stopped fooling around and one of them even had the decency to turn his sweetheart over and let her work her way back to the safety of the sea. It seemed only right.

The three of them moved down to a little cockleshell and paddled out to the ketch as it weighed anchor. Captain Gringo heaved a sigh of relief. Apparently the smugglers, or whatever, had given up on Mimi's grandfather and were putting out to sea while they were still ahead.

By the time Gaston and Mimi rejoined him, the ketch was making it out over the bar. From the time they'd taken he assumed they'd done more than dress. He didn't know why that should give him a tingle, but it did, and that annoyed him.

The problem with sharing was that everyone got to showing off and competing, even if they were all friends. That was the trouble with Queen Victoria's rules. Some of them made sense. Next time he'd let Gaston get his own girl.

As the ketch sailed away he gave them his ideas about it and added, "We may as well gather some turtle eggs ourselves before we start looking for the right path through to the north."

As he stepped out on the sand, Gaston asked, "Can't we just follow this beach, Dick?" and Captain Gringo said, "No. That's not a point of land, there to the north. It's mangroves growing in at least three feet of water. This area's like the hammock we spent the night on. A freak sand pile in a much bigger mess of glug."

Mimi said she knew how to hunt turtle eggs. So that was what they assumed she meant to do when she scampered down to the water line. But then she waded out, clothes and all, to paddle happily about in the warm water. Gaston sighed and said, "Ah, to be young and foolish once more. About last night, Dick . . .

"Hey, I told you to get some of it while it was hot. Why should you be left out when she's even gone sixty-nine with her own grandfather?"

Gaston grimaced and said, "I am usually a good sport about that, too. But all in all, I was not up to oral sex with a lady who needed a bath so badly. I think it might be a good idea if we all had a good soak, clothing and all. Between pepper juice and Mimi juice I am *très* gamey enough to be detected hiding in a wood pile, hein?"

So they went down to the water, put their guns, boots and pocket contents on the sand to stay dry, and waded in to join

57

Mimi in a cleansing dip. Captain Gringo knew the salt would make them all itchy as it dried, but a clean itch beat jungle rot. And clean clothes and bodies were harder to smell if they had to hide close to anyone.

The wet clothing was heavy, though. So once he'd rinsed as much sweat out as he could, Captain Gringo came ashore to spread his things on a fallen log to dry in the sun as he enjoyed a cooler naked swim. Mimi and Gaston thought it was a good idea and they wound up splashing, laughing, and playing grab-ass in the water until he told them to get serious and help him find some breakfast.

The three walked naked as children along the beach until Mimi spotted a place that looked pretty much like any other and began to scoop sand away, pretty as a picture, innocent as Eve before The Fall, and lusty enough for a dozen men to elbow one another out of the way to get at. She drew a turtle egg from the damp sand, brushed it off, and began to suck it, raw. Captain Gringo grimaced but Gaston said, "Let us admit she is *practique*. The whites stay runny even when they are cooked, and taste no better."

So the three of them squatted naked together, sucking eggs, and Captain Gringo could remember worse breakfasts, although he knew it was hunger more than the taste that made the glue-flavored eggs so delicious this morning.

They moved on, sated but exploring like kids left unguarded to play pirate, or in Mimi's case, maybe doctor.

It took the creole girl an hour or so to find the right path through the mangroves again. But after that the day passed almost anti-climactically. Even Mimi was too jaded to suggest sex as they took a few rest breaks and pressed ever onward to the north-west. There was no point in stopping to eat, since they had nothing to eat, and mangrove fruit picked on the fly took care of thirst as the day wore on.

The sun was low in the west again and the sky was the color of a flamingo's ass by the time she led them out into cultivated cane fields and said, "You see? I told you I knew the way."

Gaston drew a pocket knife and cut some sugar cane to chew as Captain Gringo asked Mimi how far they were from Sinnamary. She pointed with her chin and said, "A few hours walk that way, Deek. I have been thinking and I don't think it would be wise for me to go all the way into town with you. The relations I told you about live over in that direction and it may be best if I arrived alone. I would not wish for them to think I was a wicked girl and . . ."

"I understand," he cut in, realizing that people down here seemed to think any woman left alone with a man unchaperoned couldn't be trusted. It was beginning to appear there might be a point to quaint native customs. In a society where girls never got the chance to fend off men with flutters and faints, they had no practice at saying no. He wondered if Mimi knew what the word meant.

He accepted the length of cane Gaston handed him, but Mimi refused, saying only poor people ate raw sugar from the cane. She seemed to be getting more proper every step away from the deserted swamplands. It was only fair. She'd acted the other way going in.

Mimi led them to where the path they were on joined a wagon road. Then she turned shyly and said, "I must leave you now, my friends. I thank you for all you've done for me, and I direct you to go with God."

Captain Gringo nodded and started to kiss her goodbye, but Mimi blushed and turned away, saying, "Please, Deek, don't spoil it. What if someone should see us?"

He laughed and said that sounded reasonable. So they parted with no further ceremony. As he and Gaston trudged on, Gaston asked, "Was that wise, Dick? Her grandfather was part of that smuggling gang and we still don't know what they were up to."

"Forget it," Captain Gringo said. "She didn't know anything about her late grandfather, except that he liked incest a lot."

"Ah, that one can understand, perverse as it may be, given the choice of one's hand or a beautiful young girl, forbidden by the usual customs or not. But to get back to his gang . . ."

"Hey, *you* get back to his gang, Gaston. I don't give a shit what they were up to back there. I just want to get out of this crazy colony. Everybody we meet is up to something, and none of them make sense. The Dutchman screwed us out of the money for those arms. I don't know who the fuck wants us to get Captain Dreyfus out of jail. And I'd say smuggling was a cottage industry down here. You think we'll find a shady skipper with a boat out of here, once we reach Sinnamary? By the way, what the hell kind of a name is Sinnamary? It's not Spanish or French."

Gaston said, "It's Holland Dutch. I told you they used to

trade colonies down here. Another reason things are, how you say, so fucked up. The Dutch had all of Guiana or what they insist is Surinam first. The French and British decided they wanted to play, too. So every time somebody lost a war in Europe they reshuffled the deck. I think the Dutch gave up their claims on your New York in exchange for the British agreement not to take any more of Surinam from them."

"How did the French get into this neck of the woods?"

"Oh, France wins wars once in a while, rumor to the contrary notwithstanding. I am *très* vague on ancient history, but obviously Sinnamary was once a Dutch outpost. Now it is French. Cayenne and Sinnamary form the corners of a triangle with Devil's Island at the point off shore."

"Hmm, then Sinnamary imports prison labor, too?"

"But of course. Who do you think *grows* all this cane, people who don't *have* to? Aside from the few free peasants, like the amusing girl we just left, almost anyone you meet down here without a necktie is a prisoner or paroled and involuntary colonist."

Captain Gringo said, "Let's get out of here before we meet too many more of them, then. You were about to tell me about a tramp steamer back to Costa Rica."

"I was? *Merde alors,* I am homesick for the only country down here that seems undismayed by our survival, Dick. But I don't know the knockaround crowd in Sinnamary any better than yourself. I *thought* I had friends in Cayenne, but as you know, the Dutchman and his gang are not as sentimental as myself about old comrades. The trouble with looking up French criminals in this country is that there are simply too many French criminals for them to stick together."

They trudged on as it began to darken and stars winked in a purple sky. Far ahead above the surrounding crops the sky seemed a little lighter. They were either approaching a town or the moon was coming up from an unusual direction. When Captain Gringo commented on this Gaston said, *"Oui,* Mimi said it was only a few hours walk and I feel like I have walked far too far for a man of my dignified years."

The road they were on took a gentle curve around a clump of gumbo limbo and when they could see down it again someone had built a bonfire by the roadside and some white clad men were standing around it with shotguns. The two soldiers of fortune stopped and Gaston sighed and said, *"Eh bien,* I consider hasty retreat our best strategy, *non?"*

Captain Gringo shook his head and said, "No. They've

seen us and don't seem to be getting frantic about it. If we run away they might. There's not a cross trail close enough to matter. They might be just local yokels gathered after working the fields or something."

"With shotguns?"

"Okay, let's say they're duck hunters. They're watching us and the next move is ours, so let's just stroll in and say howdy."

As they moved closer, Captain Gringo saw he'd have made a mistake in backtracking, but wasn't sure he wanted to come closer. The firelight gleamed off brass buttons and hat badges, so he knew what they were even before Gaston hissed, "They are colonial gendarmes!"

Captain Gringo nodded and kept going as a man with corporal's stripes on his shabby white jacket stepped out in the road to block their way. Captain Gringo said, "Talk some French to them, Gaston." So Gaston said, *"Bon souir, M'sieur L'Agent"* and the cop asked in French if they had any identification.

They produced their forged passports and when the corporal saw Captain Gringo was supposed to be a Canadian he switched to English, asking, "What are you two doing out here, M'sieur?"

"Uh, isn't this the road to Sinnamary?"

"Of a certainty. But where in the Devil have you *come* from? There is nothing behind you but a trackless mangrove swamp!"

"We just found that out the hard way. The coach we hired couldn't get through, so we hired a native guide. A Black boy. He just headed back to Cayenne."

The corporal motioned to another gendarme who brought a bullseye lantern over to shine on the passports. The corporal asked, "Why did you not take the regular coastal steamship, M'sieur? What business do you have in Sinnamary, eh?"

"Uh, you can see by my passport I'm a reporter for a Canadian newspaper. Our readers are interested in the Dreyfus Affair. I couldn't find out much in Cayenne, so I thought I'd see what was going on in Sinnamary."

Captain Gringo thought that was a pretty good cover story, considering how much time he'd had to make it up. But the corporal growled like a watch dog who'd just sniffed strange piss on his own garden gate and said, "I think the two of you should talk to my officers at Headquarters. You will accom-

61

pany four of my men there right now. Meanwhile, we shall keep your passports and weapons, hein?"

Before Captain Gringo could answer one of the others had stepped over to unbuckle his gun rig. Since a third man had the muzzle of a shotgun against his spine he could only smile and say, "That seems reasonable."

He hoped for a moment they'd miss the .38 under his jacket. But the man who'd removed his gun rig patted him down, found the .38, and put it in his own side pocket with a grin. The corporal raised an eyebrow and observed, "M'sieur seems well armed, for a reporter." And Captain Gringo shrugged and answered, "What can I tell you? I heard there were a lot of bad guys down here."

The corporal smiled thinly and as they'd disarmed Gaston, too, by now, he barked off two more names and as a four man detail formed around the two prisoners he said, "We intend to leave the, how you say, good guys in charge, M'sieur. Go with these men. Our officers can decide whether they want to talk to you about that accursed Jew or send you out to meet Dreyfus in the flesh!"

Captain Gringo started to argue. Then somebody jabbed him with a gun muzzle again and he said, "Okay, Gaston, let's go with these gents and get it straightened out, right?"

Gaston didn't answer. Captain Gringo knew that when Gaston wasn't talking he was coiling like a cobra and he could only hope the old bastard wouldn't kick anybody in the ear until they were well out of range of the road block. He wasn't sure it would be a good idea even then, since the bastard holding a shotgun muzzle against his spine seemed nervous enough already.

The six of them headed toward the distant lights of Sinnamary as the tall American considered their options. None of them were very good. Taking on four trained gendarmes without a weapon between him and Gaston sounded like a lousy idea. On the other hand, once they were in the hands of the police in town it would be even harder to get away. The chance of bluffing themselves out of this fix were less than fifty-fifty. The Sinnamary Headquarters would have copies of the wanted fliers on Gaston and himself and word had already gotten around that the two of them were in French Guiana. Both the Dutchman's gang and those weird French Catholics claiming to be an international Jewish organization had known they were in Cayenne. The cops had to have at least a few informers scattered around.

Their fake passports were good enough to get past the average customs inspector. They wouldn't hold water if anybody checked by sending one lousy cablegram.

They left the sugar cane behind, passed through a strip of what he now knew were more peppers, and he saw they were approaching a banana plantation. The banana fronds arched out over the road, making it a dark tunnel. He knew Gaston might think it would be the place. But he was afraid the four men guarding them might have that figured out, too. So how the hell could he signal Gaston to behave himself?

He kept his voice casual as he said, "At least we'll be close to town when we get it straightened out, eh, Gaston?" And Gaston replied, "Ah, great minds run in the same channels."

One of their guards told them to shut up, in a nervous voice. So they did. They both knew, now, that the next time either of them said anything it was time to make their move. Captain Gringo knew Gaston would start by knocking the shotgun away from his back. They seemed more nervous about him than Gaston, which was reasonable even if it was dumb. He was younger, a lot bigger, and they probably thought he was more dangerous.

A lot they knew. He hit a lot harder than Gaston, but Gaston could hit three times and kick a target six feet off the ground in the time it took anybody else to throw a solid one-two combination.

They were told to put their hands up as they approached the shadows of the bananas. So they did, and the guards marched them through, separated by a good ten feet. As it turned out, that was a good thing for them, albeit not for the guards. As they passed through the tunnel and were almost out the far side, all hell broke loose.

Captain Gringo dove headfirst for the dirt even before Gaston yelled, "Down!" for he'd heard the nasty ringing of a machete cutting through flesh and bone a split second earlier! The shotgun covering him went off, blasting a flaming hole through the air his back had just occupied as another steel blade cut the guard's head open like a cantaloupe!

Captain Gringo landed on one shoulder and rolled to the roadside ditch as somewhere in the distance a police whistle trilled above the nearer sounds of meat chopping. He yelled out, "Gaston?" and heard his sidekick call back, "Here! What's going on?"

Before Captain Gringo could reply that he had no idea,

63

human hands grabbed him by the ankles and proceeded to drag him, cursing and trying to kick, into the banana stalks beside the road. Somebody sat on his chest in the gloom and held a blade against his throat to growl, "Be quiet, *ami*." So he asked, "Who's talking?" and stayed put. He could just see well enough to make out that there were a hell of a lot of guys in here with him. They were white shadows against the darker banana stalks. He figured they couldn't be cops, so what the hell.

He knew he had that part right when, a few minutes later he heard a burst of gunfire nearby and a suddenly sounding police whistle choked off in mid-trill. There were a few more shots, a long ominous silence, then someone came over to where they were holding Captain Gringo to say, "*Merde,* I tried to avoid gunplay, but now the fat is in the fire. Let's get out of here!"

"What about these men, Chef?" asked the man sitting on Captain Gringo's chest. The leader shrugged and said, "F ng them along and we'll sort it out at the plantation. Th y are obviously not gendarmes, hein?"

So Captain Gringo was hauled to his feet, and he saw others doing the same to Gaston a few yards away. The one called Chef slapped Captain Gringo's face and asked, mildly, "Do I have your attention, M'sieur?"

"Yeah. I'm on your side, I hope."

"We shall see which side you are on. You and your friend, as well as ourselves, will have a date with Madame La Guillotine if the police connect anyone who was here tonight with that rather neat ambush. So consider this before you make any rash moves, hein?"

"I already have, Chef."

"*Eh bien,* let us march. Please forgive our surly manners, but you will not get your side-arms back until Le Grande Chef decides what is to be done with you."

"I said we were on your side. Did you get all of them? The guys from the road block, too?"

"*Oui.* We had no choice, since they responded to the sound of that gun we did not wish to have going off. We only wished to see who the gendarmes were so interested in. But every dead gendarme is a net gain for our side."

"Who's side is that, Chef?"

"Keep moving. Le Grande Chef will explain to you, if he decides you can be of any use to us."

64

"And if he decides we're not?"

The Chef didn't answer.

He didn't have to.

Captain Gringo had expected to be led to some bandit camp in the bush. So he was surprised when they crossed a drainage canal and were herded up a gentle slope to an imposing mansion built in the Steamboat Gothic style he remembered from New Orleans. Out in the open he could see the men around them wore the straw hats and white pajamas of the prison colony's trustees. The French authorities had missed by a mile in trusting *these* guys, though!

They all wore gunbelts and ammo bandoleers to go with the machetes they were packing. As they neared the big house he noticed some peeled off to head for more modest outbuildings off to one side under more trees. He and Gaston were escorted to the front veranda by Chef and less than a dozen others. A portly man in a white panama suit was standing in the doorway, smoking a dollar Havana Perfecto. As they joined him on the veranda, the man smiled and said, "Ah, Captain Gringo and M'sieur Gaston. We've been expecting you. It was good of you to come."

"We had a choice?" asked Captain Gringo.

The planter laughed and told Chef to give them back their guns and papers before he said, "Come inside, my friends, we have a lot of things to talk over."

So they followed him, strapping on their gun rigs and putting away the possibly still useful forged passports. They noticed the Chef and the others didn't follow. The planter led them into a huge parlor decorated like a whore's dream with red velvet drapes and upholstery. The Louis XV furniture was gilded and if there'd been any point in having a fireplace this close to the equator, the baronial marble job dominating the room was a pisser.

The planter sat down on a throne-like chair near the fireplace and indicated where they were to sit on the far side of a low rosewood table between them. He shoved a humidor of cigars their way as he said, "I am called Le Grande Chef, but my name is Van Horn. I have sent for some refreshments, you must be famished."

Gaston reached for a cigar as Captain Gringo leaned back

to take one of his own somewhat soggy claros from his shirt pocket and light up. He hadn't thought the guy had a French accent. His English was that perfectly pronounced and hence annoyingly officious variety spoken by a very well educated European. Van Horn didn't miss the gesture with the cigar. He smiled and said, "Ah, you still have misgivings about me. I can understand. As you see, I know all about you. So let's talk about me. Officially, I am a French national, since I was born and raised on this plantation. But this land was originally Dutch, as were my ancestors. We have never been quite comfortable under French rule. Aside from religious differences, we have never liked France's colonial policy. We Dutch learned long ago that slavery is not just morally wrong, but financially stupid. How can one hope to build a viable colony when none of the colonists have any money to spend? France doesn't want Guiana to be self-sufficient. She wants us to send her cheap sugar and spices in exchange for being a dumping ground for her most desperate criminals."

Captain Gringo blew a smoke ring and said, "I notice you have a lot of prisoners working for you, Van Horn."

The planter nodded and said, "They give us no choice. How can a planter who pays his help compete with one who does not? But, as you can see, I treat my workers better than most and they are devoted to me."

"In other words you have a private army. It's pretty slick, Van Horn. The dumb prison authorities assign trustees to you, and once they've tasted a little decent treatment they're on your side. Nobody checks on what's going on out here in the woods, as long as you seem satisfied and keep them peppers coming. I get the picture, but what's the play, a revolution to make French Guiana part of Dutch Guiana?"

Van Horn looked pained and sighed, "No. The Netherlands have a treaty with France and you know what they say about stubborn Dutchmen. Since they were recognized as a free nation after breaking away from the Spanish Empire in the fifteen hundreds, the Netherlands have never broken one treaty. They seem smugly proud of this for some reason. It's probably why they have such a small country. But that is their problem. My plan is to form a free republic of Guiana, with myself as president, of course."

"President or dictator, Van Horn?"

Van Horn smiled. Captain Gringo had noticed he smiled a lot. Van Horn was one of those big pink men who look like giant infants. But there was nothing harmless about his rather feline eyes. They looked like the eyes of a tiger staring out of a chubby infant's face. Van Horn said, "My provisional government may hold elections some day, after I'm dead. Meanwhile, I see no need to act so reserved. Surely you can see that almost any government would be an improvement over the one the French have imposed here. Ninety percent of the population lives under the gun, with no rights at all."

"Right. So if you take over they'll all live like you run this plantation? As well treated servants?"

"They see it as an improvement, too. But enough about me. My cards are on the table, since I know you two are the last people on earth the French authorities would listen to if you tried to stop me. I don't have to pay my prisoner recruits anything but a little drinking money. But officers who know modern weapons are worth a thousand a month to me. I understand you were a heavy weapons expert in your own army, Captain Gringo. M'sieur Verrier, here, can be almost as valuable as an ex-legion man who knows how to whip French scum into soldiers. Are you interested?"

Captain Gringo heard Gaston whistle thoughtfully, since the offer was better than they usually got. Five hundred a month was the going rate for soldiers of fortune and that was ten times what a skilled worker got in the States these days. He said, "The money sounds fair. But let's backtrack a bit to stuff I'm really interested in. How in the hell did you know we were coming? We didn't know ourselves until we were half way here!"

Van Horn chuckled and said, "I know about the trouble you had collecting from the Dutchman. You see, some of my men hijacked the arms he was supposed to sell for you. You'll be paid, of course, if you see fit to join us. As to how I knew you were heading this way, I didn't. My men saving you was our mutual good fortune. They were covering that road for other associates of mine. I'm as puzzled as anyone as to what could be delaying them."

Captain Gringo smiled and said, "Things are beginning to fall into place. Let me see if I've got it right. A certain ketch carrying certain arms from overseas was supposed to meet up with an old ex-prisoner in the mangrove swamp, right?"

Van Horn frowned and asked, "Who told you this?" and Captain Gringo answered, "Relax, the cops don't know anything. We found the old guide dying on the far side of the

67

swamp. Some toughs who suspected he wasn't buying new lamps and so forth on pepper profits beat him to death trying to cut themselves in. He died without talking."

"Oh, damn! He had a woman living with him! If she talked to anyone . . ."

"She didn't. She can't. The old man was slick about living on one side of the swamp and guiding your landing parties out the other. The girl had no idea what was going on."

"You know her, too? They say she's a wild little slut with a big mouth."

"She didn't tell us anything and we were on better terms with her than any cops are likely to be if they ever question her. She didn't know what the ketch was doing in that cove. We spotted them, too, coming through the mangroves. They gave up and sailed away. So noboby else knows they were ever off this coast with anything."

Van Horn said, "Damn! They had machine gun ammo on board, too!"

"Oh, you have machine guns, Van Horn?"

The planter nodded and said, "Of course. Three Maxims and a Spandau that I'll expect you to train my men to handle. We've enough for training and perhaps a spot of guerrilla, but to mount a full scale independence movement we'll need more. Oh well, now that we know what went wrong with that shipment it will be easy enough to work out another way to bring it in. It just means waiting a bit longer than I'd planned, but I am used to a waiting game. Ah, here comes the refreshments, gentlemen."

The planter wasn't kidding and it was easy to see why he was so fat, now. Two black girls loaded the little rosewood table to overflowing with big silver trays of hors d'oeuvres, cold cuts, red Dutch cheeses, and a choice between coffee, tea, or Holland gin, depending on which jug you fancied. The Black girls wore the black uniforms and white caps and aprons of French parlor maids. But one of them had tribal scars on her otherwise pretty face. As they left, Van Horn said, "They're Ashanti. If you like dark meat I'll tell them to sleep with you, later. I have them nicely domesticated."

Captain Gringo helped himself to a slab of ham between slices of cheese as he said, "I thought the Bush Negroes had given up on slavery, Van Horn."

The planter nodded and said, "They have. Both those girls had been condemned to death for adultery by the tribal elders. I talked them into letting me have them. To an Ashanti, being a servant is a fate worse than death, so the elders found it amusing, too."

"You're in contact with the wild tribes in the interior? I thought they killed white men on sight."

Van Horn laughed and said, "They do, usually. I told you I was raised here and my people were Dutch. The Netherlands signed a peace treaty with the tribal elders a while back and both sides seem rather oblivious to the advantages of ignoring a promise. Suffice to say, I'll need the co-operation of the Ashanti, Kru, and Ibo tribes when it's time to take over. I've been cultivating them with occasional presents and medicine. They have brains enough to take quinine for a jungle fever and there's a lot of that going around in the hills."

Captain Gringo was about to ask a dumb question about runaway slaves in a French colony having a treaty with the authorities of another colony just to the north. He helped himself to some coffee as he considered the awesome chips Van Horn was piling up without the French government having a clue about his game plan. He'd seen a rag-tag bandito make himself the dictator of a country with less. It was small wonder Van Horn seemed so smug. He had a mess of pissed off French toughs ready to fight for him and his rear was guarded by tough African warriors as well!

He didn't see how the colonial authorities would ever stop Van Horn's power play, and what the hell did he care? The colony was already being run by a brutal system and if Van Horn and his gang didn't revolt against it, somebody else was bound to. At least Van Horn seemed to know what he was doing, so the bloodshed would probably be less than if there was just a mad uprising by the oppressed prisoner population.

Captain Gringo would have liked to keep some things to himself, but that damned Gaston started asking about the Dreyfus Affair and how the conspiracy to free him fit in with Van Horn's plans.

The planter frowned and said, "I don't care one way or the other about Captain Dreyfus. He doesn't sound like the kind of recruit I'm looking for. They say the idiot is still patriotic to France and considers himself a French officer and gentleman, despite all they've done to him. He'll be set free with the others when we take over, of course. After that, if he behaves himself, he'll be treated like anyone else. I can't see giving him a position in my new government. They say he's a bit stuffy about due process and the French constitution."

69

Since Gaston had opened the sack, Captain Gringo said, "This international whatever must be planning some sort of coup to get him off the rock. Are you saying you haven't heard about other rebel bands, Van Horn?"

The planter shrugged and said, "Oh, there are dozens of conspiracies going on all the time here on the mainland and out there on the island. Most of them are simply concerned with escape. But since nobody ever escapes, one tends to doubt they're important."

Captain Gringo took a sip of coffee and said, "I seem to have heard or read some escape stories from Devil's Island. Somebody must get out once in a while."

Van Horn shook his head and said, "Not from Devil's Island itself. It's never been done and never will be, unless and until I take over, of course. The popular tales of escape from Devil's Island are concerned with escaping from *here*, the mainland colony. That's difficult enough. The few who've made it were trustees who managed to somehow get through the surrounding swamps and jungles to the outside world. Many think of this whole colony as Devil's Island. But the true rock is an escape proof cell block complex miles off shore and surrounded by shark infested breakers. There's no way to get Dreyfus out without taking the whole island, and of course it's built like a fort to withstand such a siege."

Captain Gringo nodded and said, "That's what I keep telling people. Okay, you're not in with Claudette's gang and God knows who they are in the first place. When do I get to see my machine guns?"

Van Horn brightened and said, "Ah? You two are in?"

Captain Gringo glanced at Gaston, who reached for another sandwich and said, "Why not? We are soldiers of fortune and everyone else we meet down here seems intent on crossing us double. May one ask when we see some front money, M'sieur Van Horn?"

The planter reached in his coat and took out two envelopes. He handed them over as he explained, "I've had these ready for you gentlemen since I heard you were in the country. Had not you found me, I'd have found you, sooner or later."

Gaston opened his envelope to count the money, but Captain Gringo just put his away. He was feeling better about Van Horn, even though he still didn't like his type. The deal seemed up-and-up. What was the point of feeding and bank-rolling guys you meant to screw in the near future?

70

Of course, what happened in the *distant* future was still up for grabs, but it looked like they were okay for the moment, and a guy on the run took his moments as they came.

He yawned and Van Horn said, "Forgive me, I can see you gentlemen have had a long day. The guns and further planning can wait until morning. Why don't you two get some rest? I'll have my servants show you to the guest rooms."

The planter reached for a bell cord and pulled it. The two Black girls came in and he spouted something at them in Dutch, Ashanti, or some other odd lingo. So each took one of the guests by the hand to lead him out of the room, leaving Van Horn to eat the rest of the food, presumably.

Gaston had drawn the one with tribal scars. She giggled and said something that sounded dirty to the one leading Captain Gringo. She lowered her head and looked embarrassed.

They were taken up a flight of stairs and Miss Scar Face took Gaston into one room while the one with Captain Gringo showed him into another and switched on the lights. Van Horn lived high on the hog indeed if he had his own electricity this far from anywhere important. He wondered what the simple native girl thought of the wonders of modern science. She looked uncomfortable enough in clothes. As he inspected the luxuriously appointed room she stepped over to the four poster bed and began to undress. He asked her what she thought she was doing and she answered in the *lingua franca* of the back country, "Le Grand Chef said I was to make you comfortable. Don't you wish for to fuck me?"

He said, "Not against your will. What is your name?"

"I am called Tonda. I no longer am allowed to have a will of my own. What is the matter, sir? Am I not pleasing to look upon?"

Tonda was pleasing indeed to look upon as she peeled off her one piece uniform and sat on the bed to remove her slippers. Her body was a Greek statue carved from mahogany and polished to a smooth patina. Her face was pure African albeit fine boned and regal. As she shucked her sandals she moved up on the bed, pulled the coverlet down, and reclined on the clean linen in resigned welcome, long limbs parted to expose a smooth shaven groin. He took off his gun rig, hung it near the head of the bed, and sat down beside her to undress as he said, "I can see you're not anxious, Tonda. You can go to your own quarters, now, but thanks for the offer just the same."

71

She sat up on one elbow with a puzzled expression. She said, "I was told by Le Grande Chef to sleep here tonight. Do you think I'm ugly, or is it because I am Black? I know some of you refuse to put it in a Black woman, but . . ."

He laughed and said, "You'd be surprised where I've put it in my time, Tonda. I'm not being shy because I don't think you're pretty enough for me. I just don't like to mix pleasure with pain and you know you hate this business, don't you?"

Tonda dabbed at her eye and sobbed, "Oh, yes. But I have never met a man so understanding since they banished me from my tribe. I tried to tell the elders they were mistaken, but they said I was a woman taken in adultery and since then I *have* been, all too often!"

"It was a bum rap, eh? Well, don't worry, Honey. I'll be good. If you can't go back to your quarters without answering a lot of silly questions, we'll just pretend we're brother and sister or something."

He slid under the covers with her and as his leg brushed her warm flesh he frowned and repressed a dumb suggestion about her wearing a night gown at least. He doubted if she knew what one was. She asked, "Aren't you going to turn out the lights?" and he said, "No. I hate waking up in the dark in a strange bed. Cover your face with the sheet if the light bothers you."

He wasn't quite up to falling asleep himself just yet, so he reached out to his nearby shirt for a smoke and some matches. The door was locked from inside and Tonda sure wasn't carrying concealed weapons. But he wished she could sleep somewhere else. He wasn't feeling horny for her. Aside from the fact that she didn't want to, he'd worn himself out on the trail with Mimi.

He smoked and meditated as Tonda lay quietly beside him, gazing up at him. He ran all the tales he'd heard through his mind and decided he hadn't missed anything that mattered right now. He was still keyed up, but his muscles complained that it had been a long day and tomorrow could turn out even longer. So he snubbed out his half finished cigar and moved down into the bed, enjoying the sensuous feel of clean linen on his naked skin after the grubby sleeping arrangements he'd been having lately. He saw Tonda was still watching him and asked, "Aren't you asleep yet?"

She said, "You are very strange. I was afraid at first. But now I feel I can really trust you."

She snuggled closer and he said, "Hey, let's not be *that*
72

trusting, Tonda. I'm still a man and you're a beautiful woman. I only said I'd behave if you would. I wouldn't want you to think I was a pansy."

Tonda laughed and said, "I didn't think you were effeminate even before I saw you with your clothes off. To tell the truth, that thing of yours is frightening. Is it still soft?"

"Oh, come on, I can be as gallant as the next guy, but this is getting to be cruelty to animals! Do you want to make love or not? I told you it was up to you, Goddamn it."

Tonda sighed and said, "I know, and I think you mean it. That is what seems to be arousing me. Do you know that I have hated every man who's had me since the elders sent me here as an outcast?"

"I had that part figured, Tonda. What in the hell is your hand doing in my lap?"

She murmured, "Oh, it's even bigger, hard. If I still refused you, would you let me sleep untouched in your arms?"

"Not if you don't stop playing with me, damn it! I don't get this game, Tonda. I said I wouldn't abuse you against your will, but . . ."

"Abuse me, then. I want you to. It has been so long since I've been in bed with a man I did not hate."

He thought that sounded reasonable, so he took her in his arms and kissed her, running his free hand gently over her mahogany curves as she in turn pulled him aboard and spread her long dark thighs in welcome as she guided him in with her hand. As he entered her she gasped, "Oh, let me get used to it a little at a time. I am still very tense and confused about my feelings."

He settled cautiously atop her, noting how tight and a little dry she was as it went in a fraction of an inch at a time as she began to lubricate and pulsate around his ever growing erection. Tonda shut her eyes hard and grimaced in mingled pleasure and discomfort as he bottomed in her and lay still in her throbbing warmth. Then, as he'd hoped, the Ashanti girl began to move her shaved pelvis up to grind against his pubic hairs. He waited until she was moving well and starting to gush before he started doing it right, with long teasing strokes. Tonda kept her eyes closed and began to say nice things to him in her own African dialect. Maybe she was pretending he was somebody else. Her husband or the lover she'd been caught with?

He tried closing his own eyes and pretending she was Ellen Terry or Lillian Russell. It helped when a partner wasn't very

73

inspiring to look at. But none of his usual fantasy lays seemed more exciting than the real thing right now, so he propped himself up on his stiff arms and let himself go as he stared down at her in the Edison light. The view was wild as hell.

Tonda's dark curves were glistening with passion and her nipples stood at attention as her mahogany breasts bounced in time with their mutual attempts to get all of him up inside of her at once. She drew her long smooth legs up to lock her ankles around the nape of his neck as she cradled his balls between her love wet brown buttocks and moaned, "Deeper! Can you go any deeper?"

He tried his best and it seemed to thrill her when his shaft's head began to kiss her womb with every stroke. Despite thinking a few minutes before that he'd had all the wild sex he needed for a while, she proved him wrong. For she clamped down hard in a moaning shuddering orgasm and he joined her with a blast of lust that surprised him as much as it delighted him. She pleaded, "Don't stop!" So he didn't. He pounded on as she rolled her head wildly from side to side in multiple orgasms until he came again and had to pause, her pulsating vaginal muscles pumping their mingled juices over his scrotum as it cuddled in the cradle of her quivering ass. She opened her eyes, smiled radiantly up at him, and said, "Oh, I didn't know it could be that wonderful. I needed sex. I have not had any since my last period, even with an unwanted lover. I knew you would satisfy me. But I never thought it could be so good. Do I do it as good as a White woman?"

He grimaced and rolled over to reach for another smoke as he said, "That's a dumb question, Tonda. Some women are good in bed and others aren't. I've never noticed that their complexion had anything to do with it."

"Have you ever wanted to make love to a Black girl before?"

"Hasn't everybody? This is a pretty boring topic, Tonda. Do you want to discuss race relations or have some more?"

She laughed, "I want you to do everything to me. By the way, what is your name?"

"Call me Dick. Let me get my second wind and we'll explore the possibilities. Do you smoke?"

She said she did. So they shared a cigar as she nestled with her head on his shoulder. But she was fondling him gently as they lay together and so he didn't get to finish his cigar after all. He noticed a mirror across the room as he mounted her dog style with her knees on the edge of the mattress and his feet on the rug. The reflection looked wicked as hell and he'd have been envious of that other guy over there if he hadn't been getting the same thing. Tonda spotted it and raised her head for a better look, saying, "Oh, I can see what we're doing. It's beautiful. Turn a little so I can see it going in me, Dick."

He did and she started showing off by wagging her tail from side to side as he pounded her to another sobbing orgasm. But before he could join her she wanted to change positions. So he let her up. She took him by the shaft to lead him over to the dresser and mirror. Then she climbed up on the dresser next to the mirror with her buttocks on the edge and spread her legs suggestively. He stood at one end of the dresser to put it in again as she lay back, spine arched, admiring what looked like a twin sister getting layed at her side. It looked from where he stood that he was doing it to twins, too. The illusion inspired him to come fast and beg for time out. But as he withdrew, Tonda sat up, grabbed his sated shaft, and began to suck it from a crouched position as she shot arch glances at herself in the mirror. He decided civilized novelties were new to her. He found them sort of bawdy, but Tonda hadn't been introduced to him as a blushing virgin, so what the hell. He didn't want to waste anything on her tonsils, so they wound up on the floor, the rug under her tail bone affording a new nice angle of attack. He pounded her to glory and this time even she was ready to pack it in for a while. The rug had doubtless been a little rough on her back.

He helped her back in bed and they lay entwined, too out of breath to smoke or even talk much. He thought she was asleep, from her relaxed contented breath on his sweaty chest. But as he started to doze, Tonda asked, "Can I trust you, Dick?"

He frowned and answered, "What do you mean trust me, Honey? We've done everything I can think of that doesn't hurt."

"Not really," she said. "There are a few naughty things I only do with men I really like. But maybe later. I meant, could I trust you if I told you something?"

He patted her reassuringly and Tonda said, "I am in love. Don't be offended, I don't mean you don't fuck good or that I don't like to do it with you. But there is a boy, in my village, and . . . oh, this is ridiculous. How can a man who's just come in me be expected to understand?"

He said, "I understand, Tonda. What we have is, well, good honest lust. You mean there's a guy who means more than sex to you, right?"

"Oh, you are so understanding, Dick. I think I love you too, a little. I know M'Chuma can't make me come any better, but . . ."

"A come is a come. You're talking about a guy you want to just be with all the time, a guy you'd kill for even when you didn't feel like sex."

A tear ran down her cheek to his chest as she snuggled closer and said, "Oh, I see you have been in love, too. What *is* the magic, Dick? M'Chuma is an ordinary lover and not as handsome as many men I've slept with. But I want to be with him at sunset, just holding his hand and not saying a word as we grow old together."

He nodded and said, "Magic is the right word for it. Nothing else about love makes sense. Is this M'Chuma the guy they caught you with in your tribal village?"

"Oh, no. M'Chuma is my husband! Or he was, until the witch doctor said bad things about me. There was no other man. I swear this. But, of course, you do not believe me."

"I believe you," he lied, keeping this thought to himself as Tonda rambled on about a jungle triangle involving herself, her husband, and a horny old witch doctor who should be ashamed of himself if half she said were true. The question was how much of it was true. He knew she could trust him. But could he trust her, if this were some dumb kind of test?

His suspicions grew as she said, "If only I could get away from this plantation, Dick, I know that if I could speak to M'Chuma alone for only a moment, he'd believe me. The would not let me speak to him alone as they pelted me with dung and shaved off my hair. The elders took M'Chuma away and they were going to kill me until Le Grand Chef bought me from them as his slave. I don't want to be a slave, Dick. I am from a royal Ashanti clan. My grandfather sat on his own stool by the chief's. Will you help me get back to my village?"

It was a tough question. She was asking him to double cross the planter they both seemed to be working for. It was an even-money bet that Van Horn had put her up to it. The girl might or might not be a real wild Ashanti. She wore no tribal marks he could see and he'd seen all of her from every angle. She wore shoes like she'd grown up in them, too.

He knew she was waiting for him to say something, so he

patted her again and said, "We'll talk about it another time, Tonda."

"Does that mean you won't help me get away?"

"It means I have to think about it. I don't want to do anything Le Grande Chef would be upset about and . . ."

"Oh, I hate you!" she sobbed, pulling away and sitting up as she added, "I did everything I could to make friends with you, but you are just like all the other men! None of you want anything but pleasure from any woman!"

He watched, bemused, as she angrily pulled on her sandals and got dressed, calling him nasty names and making uncalled for remarks about his poor old pecker.

She went to the door, unlocked it, and said, "I didn't enjoy it. I *hated* it. So there!" and slammed the door behind her. He rose, smiling crookedly, and muttered, "Can't go back to your own quarters without permission, eh? Damn it, Walker, I sure admire the way your brains have started working again."

He locked the door with a grin and went back to bed. As he stretched out he sighed and closed his eyes. It felt good to be alone at last in a clean soft bed. As he pulled the sheet over him he became aware he had half an erection. He growled, "Go to sleep, you silly old bastard. I know she promised to get to the dirty stuff later, but enough is enough."

He rolled over and tried to go to sleep. He needed sleep more than he needed anything Tonda had to offer, right now.

But he couldn't help wondering, as he dozed off, what if the poor kid had been on the level? She'd sure acted sore for a gal just kidding around and if there really was anything to her story . . .

Forget it! he warned himself, It's probably bullshit in the first place and even if it isn't, you don't owe anybody a trip into the uncharted jungle to deliver a lady you just screwed hell out of to her Ashanti warrior husband!

He told Gaston Tonda's story as they had breakfast alone on a back veranda the next morning, Van Horn apparently having left earlier on some errand. Gaston agreed he'd had no other choice but to evade the issue. When he asked Gaston if the other girl had tried similar games, the little Frenchman laughed and said, "*Mais non*, she simply squeezed me dry as a lemon. One gathers she was trying to make lemonade in her

77

forbidding interior. We did not talk much. In the first place she speaks some *très* strange dialect and in the second, her mouth was full most of the evening."

"Hmm, the two of them spoke some sort of dialect that could have been African last night. Have you seen either of the girls this morning?"

"*Mais non,* as you saw when that rather ordinary mulatto served this meal just now, the valient seductresses would seem to have the morning off."

He popped some toast in his mouth as he added, "All in all, one would say they earned it. I find the story of your bedmate *très* droll. A woman trying to get back to her husband is seldom so enthusiastic with other men, *non?*"

"What can I tell you? She says it's love. The husband, I mean. She was just screwing me for laughs. It's not as crazy as it sounds, Gaston. Many a soldier away from home has pined pretty good for the girl he left behind him, even in bed with somebody closer to hand."

Gaston shrugged and said, "True, but since I will kick you in the head before I allow you to run off into the jungle with her, this discussion is pointless. If it were a test, you passed it. If it were not, you still can't help her. They have spears, Dick. Big pointed things they like to stick in white men, and you would appear to have made *la zig-zag* with an important Ashanti's woman."

"I don't think she'd tell him that."

"Believe me, Dick, women always tell. Who do you think told on Elizabeth and Essex, Essex? If they do not confess with their mouths they do it with their eyes. One men in ten may be able to keep his foolish mouth shut about such matters. Asking a woman to keep such a secret is to betray her nature. *Sacre,* what is the point of a woman having a secret lover unless her friends can envy her for it?"

Captain Gringo swallowed some coffee and said, "Let's drop it. Before we were stopped by those cops you were saying something about a boat out of Sinnamary."

"I was? I thought we just went to work for Van Horn, Dick."

"Maybe we have and maybe we haven't. Let's find out if we're prisoners here or not by trying a run into town. We're still a long ways from the Dutch border, so if there's no easy way out in Sinnamary we can always come back in time for supper."

"We took the front money, Dick."

"So what? Claudette offered more and was a good lay besides. This colony's getting on my nerves. There's too many wheels within wheels and my guts keep telling me everybody's lying to me. I'd rather hire out to a nice simple war lord having a regular old fashioned revolution, where a guy knows who he's machine-gunning, for Chrissake!"

Gaston laughed and said, "Ah, can this be the nice American boy I met in Mexico? You used to fuss at me for being *practique*, Dick. What happened to all your fine *officer-and-gentleman merde?*"

Captain Gringo smiled bitterly and answered, "I gave it up for my health. Robin Hood was a chump. He should have kept the money. I never would have gotten in trouble in the first place if I'd been thinking of my own ass instead of giving breaks to people who were going to get themselves killed anyway. You're right that I started out with some half-ass ideas about an officer's code. But it's pretty dumb to be the only guy south of the border who follows one, and I'm tired of being played for a sucker."

"*Eh bien,* I am pleased at the way you are growing up, my old and rare, but Van Horn's particular double cross eludes me. He's paying well above the going rates for what would seem a simple enough spot of gun thuggery. In what way do you think he means to double our crosses, hein?"

"I've no idea. That's his problem. Finish your breakfast and we'll see if they lend us some horses or shoot us."

Gaston put down his coffee cup and said he was set to go. But before either could rise from the table a big buxom blond in a thin cotton Mother Hubbard came out on the veranda. Her wheat straw hair hung across her awesome tits in twin peasant braids and she was barefoot, but Captain Gringo had met few women in his time who looked so snooty.

She said, "Oh, you must be the gun tramps my brother was talking about. Have either of you seen him this morning?"

Captain Gringo started to ask her who the hell she was talking about, but noticed her family resemblance to Van Horn. It was odd what an improvement her gender made. Her pink softness and sensuous mouth had looked repulsive on her big brother. On her, they looked good. She was one of those big fluffy slabs of Angel Food cake a man wanted to dive into on sight. But he said, "No, Ma'am. The servants said he'd ridden off on some errand or other."

The blond wrinkled her upper lip and sniffed, "Oh, damn,

79

he's probably off playing with his niggers again. I've told him he's going to get us all massacred in our beds by those wild Blacks, but does he listen?"

Captain Gringo frowned and said, "I didn't know the Ashanti villages he mentioned were within a morning's ride, uh, Miss . . . ?"

"Wilma. Wilma Van Horn. My brother calls me Willie and you can call me M'selle Van Horn."

"You can call me Captain, then," he laughed, "and this is M'sieur Verrier. You were about to tell us how far those Bush Negro villages were, M'selle."

"I was? Oh, very well, since you'll probably have to lead a rescue expedition in any case if Paul doesn't return by sunset. This plantation is on the landward edge of cultivation. Our back lots abut the tree line of the uncleared jungle. The Niggers are almost anywhere in there, but I don't think they have any villages this side of the foot hills of the Tumac-Humac ranges. Paul trades beads and things with them in the no-man's land between here and the treaty line. I've asked him not to do that."

Her lip curled further as she added, "Frankly, I think he mucks about with Black girls. Have you ever heard anything so disgusting?"

The two soldiers of fortune exchanged glances. Captain Gringo looked away to keep from breaking up as Gaston said, "Incredible! Surely M'selle is mistaken? I took your brother for a gentleman, and surely no gentleman would defile his flesh in such a monstrous fashion!"

The big blond shrugged and replied, "I know it's hard to believe, but you'd be surprised at how many Whites down here go in for that sort of perversion. I am driving into town, should my brother return before me. You will tell him where I am, won't you?"

Gaston started to say something, caught Captain Gringo's warning glance, and shut up as the big blond turned and went back inside. But as soon as they were alone again Gaston said, "What's wrong, Dick? That was a good chance to leave for Sinnamary, *non?*"

"No. If we offered to escort her we'd be stuck with her company. The big cheese is off the reservation and his sister's leaving. Let her get clear and nobody around here will have the authority to question our own expedition."

So they decided to have another cup of coffee after all and when they'd finished, they got up and strolled over to the compound of smaller out-buildings to the north of the main house. They heard the ringing of a blacksmith's anvil and spotted a corral of horses half hidden by the smithy, so they headed for it. As they cut across the hard packed red clay the trustee, called Chef, stepped out of the shade of an overhang to greet them. He still wore a gun belt, but he'd left his shotgun somewhere. He smiled and said, "*Ah, bon jour*. You wish to inspect the guns, hein?"

They'd had no such thing in mind, but Captain Gringo nodded and said, "Yeah, we told Le Grand Chef we'd look them over before we ran into town to see if we could scout up more ammo."

Chef didn't go for his gun, so it appeared he accepted it. He pointed at a tin roofed shed and said, "*Bien,* we have the guns in there." So they followed him.

Inside, squatting on their tripods atop supply boxes, waited three oil covered machine guns. Two were Maxims and one was a Spandau as Van Horn had said. It was nice to know somebody had told the truth for a change. Captain Gringo stepped over to the nearest Maxim and opened the breech. The action was clean and in good condition, considering the climate. But the headspacing was all wrong. He took out his pocket knife, opened the screw driver blade, and proceeded to adjust it as Chef asked, mildly, what he was doing. He said, "You have to make sure this back plate fits snugly against the bases of the ammo at all times. The last time this weapon was fired it was left to cool off without tightening the headspace. Too loose a fit means a jammed belt. Too tight means a gun blowing up in your face. It's ready to fire, now. As it warms up, you have to ease back on the headspace and give the bullets more breathing space, see?"

Chef shrugged and said, "It's not my job. You are the machine-gun expert, Captain Gringo."

The tall American didn't answer as he opened the second Maxim and saw it was okay. Van Horn had said they were to instruct his followers, not a thing was said about them doing the machine-gunning in the field. He made a mental note to ask the fat man about that the next time he saw him, if he ever saw him. Taking the money and running was making more sense by the minute.

The Spandau was a copy of the basic Maxim patent with just enough change to get around the international patent and make the fucking gun more complicated to service and fire. It looked to be in good shape and he noted all three guns were chambered for the same Belgian 9mm rounds. The Fabrique National made good ammo for anybody that could afford it. Van Horn seemed to like to travel first class in weaponry as well as furniture. Had it been up to Captain Gringo, the guns would have been chambered to take French army issue, pedestrian as it were. Once the revolution started, the French navy would be certain to blockade the coast and it made more sense to have guns that could fire captured ammo after the first few skirmishes with the colonial troops and gendarmes.

Gaston asked how many old soldiers Van Horn had in his improvised trustee army and Chef said, "None. The French army and navy have their own military prisons and the few men with military experience out on the rock are never paroled ashore."

Gaston sighed, "*Très practique* of them. A small but well trained garrison can handle ten times their number of untrained street fighters. To give the devil of Devil's Island his due, he seems to have his eye on all the chips in the game."

"*Merde alors,*" Chef said. "We can take them when Le Grand Chef gives the word. Our men are desperate and we outnumber the garrison by a hundred to one, even if we didn't have these lovely machine guns!"

Gaston raised an eyebrow at Captain Gringo, who shrugged and added, "It's a big country to cover with three heavy weapon squads. The last time I looked at the map there were five mainland towns big enough to have their own garrisons and when you throw in the island prison you get six. There's one coast road broken up in dots and dashes by swamps and lagoons. So that means some hit-and-run in small craft, and France has a big navy with guns that can fire inland all the way to where it hardly matters."

Chef pouted, "Don't you think we can win, Captain Gringo? What is your point in joining us if you don't think we can win, hein?"

The American said, "I'll tell you after we have a look around town. Our American revolution was against impossible odds, too. The first thing I need to know is how much ammo we'll have, and I want to scout the defenses of Sinnamary, too."

So the mollified Chef led them around to the corral and told a couple of trustees there to saddle two mounts for them. A few minutes later they were riding off the plantation alone and Gaston said, "I don't care for these horses, Dick. The horse is not a tropical beast and neither of these looks capable of making it to the border, even if the way were clear."

Captain Gringo said, "Yeah, they're just crow bait the Van Horns use to save on shoe leather. Van Horn and his sister probably use the only decent mounts in the corral and I told you I've been looking at the map. We could probably make it to the next town up the coast on them. But it gets pretty wild and soggy between Iracoubo and Mana, near the Surinam border. There are a couple of good-sized rivers to cross, too. So that means a ferry boat and I'd just as soon look for a tramp steamer once. Come on, let's move these nags. It's starting to warm up and I want to get there before they button up for La Siesta."

He whipped his mount with the rein ends and it managed a trot, although a more comfortable lope seemed to be asking too much of it. So neither had much to say as they concentrated on getting to town with their balls intact. Captain Gringo reined his lathered nag to a walk as they approached the outskirts of Sinnamary. There didn't seem to be a road block or guard post and the favela around the little seaport was the usual collection of shacks whipped up out of salvaged packing crates and thatch. Scrawny chickens scratched in the bare yards between the road and shacks. A lean pig dozed in the roadside ditch, a vulture brooded from a fence post as they rode by. Captain Gringo suspected the vulture knew more than the pig or chickens. They passed a shack where bare assed mulatto kids played in the dusty yard and a man in convict's whites held hands with a Black girl in a short cotton shift as they both watched the children from the shack's veranda. Captain Gringo grimaced, not at the misogynation but at the devilish ingenuity of the French prison authorities. The trustees were exploited as slave labor and fed just enough to keep them alive, but were allowed enough wine, women, and song to keep them undecided about running off into the trackless jungles all around.

It was no wonder so few escaped from Devil's Island. No matter how miserable a man is, he hates to risk the little he has if he has anything at all. It was a good way to lighten up the native population and hope for future French speaking free labor, too. He made a note that most of the prison population would probably sit out Van Horn's uprising until they knew which side was winning.

The outskirts of Sinnamary didn't amount to much, since

83

the little seaport didn't amount to much either. As they reached the plaza they could see some high bottle-front buildings leftover from the original Dutch colonists. Most of the buildings in the center of town were the Steamboat Gothic the French built in tropical climes. There was a Spanish-looking church to complete the cosmopolitan atmosphere, and as they tethered their borrowed mounts in front of a hotel, they noticed the polychrome people passing by spoke a mélange of French and Spanish Creole with what sounded like Dutch and English embedded in it like raisins of sea-man's slang. Gaston asked what the next move was and Cpatain Gringo said, "Let's split up. We'll cover more angles that way. If I'm not here when you get back, ride back to the plantation. Every time I wait for you in a strange saloon I seem to get in a fight."

Gaston laughed and said he'd see if he could bump into anyone he knew or might like to. He headed for the water-front where the funnel of an ocean-going, three-island tramp loomed above the sheds and warehouses. So Captain Gringo headed the other way, knowing Gaston was better at blending in and that if the French authorities were keeping an eye on anything it would be the waterfront. Gaston's French was letter perfect and thanks to the massacre the night before, no local gendarme should suspect his papers if he had to show them.

Captain Gringo soon saw, however, that there was little else of note in Sinnamary. It seemed all residential on the far side of the plaza. He didn't want to go to church, so he stepped into a corner tobacco shop and stocked up on fresh smokes, noting that his usual Cuban Claros were more expensive here. He bought some anyway. Gaston had warned him the French government had a monopoly on tobacco and that the results were God awful. The French had invented cigarettes, but nobody else could smoke their brands.

He noticed a rack of newspapers. If he moved his lips and took it slow, he could barely read French. So he pulled a copy from the rack. The shopkeeper came out from behind the counter protesting, *"Mais non, M'sieur!* It's I who takes the papers from the rack!"* as Captain Gringo saw him grab a couple of smaller pamphlets that had been hidden by the top paper and hold them behind his back.

Captain Gringo arched an eyebrow and asked, "What are you saving for your regular customers, dirty pictures?"

The shopkeeper looked flustered and retorted, *"Oui,* very

filthy. You have paid for your cigars, so the paper is gratis, *M'sieur*. I bid you *Au revoir*."

Captain Gringo shook his head and said, "I want the good stuff. What are you getting for those pamphlets?"

"They are not for sale, M'sieur. I can see you are a foreigner. You would not understand our humor in any case."

Captain Gringo wondered if he should let it go. It was none of his business what the bored colonials read to get a hard on. On the other hand, in a country where people pissed in the streets and sex was sold wide open, it was sort of mysterious that they'd censor "Jack and Jill Play Doctor!"

He put his smokes away and held out his free hand, saying, "I'll take one of those pamphlets the nice way or I'll come back with the police and find out why you're so unpleasant to a paying customer. What's it going to be?"

The shopkeeper blanched and quickly handed him one of the forbidden pamphlets, saying, "I assure you these mean nothing to me, M'sieur, but some of my customers will read trash."

Captain Gringo took it to study the paper cover. It read, J'ACCUSE! PAR EMILE ZOLA.

He nodded and tucked it in his side pocket as he offered to pay. But the red-faced shopkeeper said that was gratis, too, and seemed anxious for him to leave, so he left.

He walked on, chuckling. Zola was that French writer who'd written *Nana*, wasn't he? *Nana* had been a pretty dirty book, sold under the counter back in the States. If this newest effort had to be sold under the counter in a *French* shop it had to be shocking indeed. He'd read it later. He hoped he'd understand the good stuff. That scene in *Nana* where the two whores got together, after hours, for some lesbian love had been hot as hell in English translation. It was funny how the idea of two women slithering all over one another seemed so interesting to men. The idea of two men doing the same thing seemed sort of revolting. He wondered if a woman would get a charge out of watching two male homosexuals. He didn't see how he'd ever find out.

He came to the end of the street and saw nothing beyond but high weeds growing on either side of the walk. But there was a fair-sized building across the vacant lots, so he decided to check it out. He got maybe two city blocks from the building before something landed on his back like a big cat, pinning his elbows to his sides!

As he fell to his knees, cursing himself and the son-of-a-bitch holding him from behind, another man in prison whites materialized from the weeds and moved in, reaching for Captain Gringo's holstered guns as he hissed, "Hold him, Jacques!" as the mugger who'd jumped him from behind gasped, "I am trying to! Get his guns, you idiot!"

That was easier said than done. Captain Gringo had one hand down against the rear mugger's crotch, so, feeling his cock and balls through the thin cotton, he grabbed and squeezed, hard, as he lashed out with his booted right foot to break the knee cap of the one facing him!

After that, it got easier. When he had them both moaning at his feet he drew one Colt to cover them in the unlikely event they had any fight left in them. He said, "That was fun. Now who are you two working for?"

The one called Jacques hugged his shattered knee against his chest as he lay on the ground, moaning, *"Sacre!* You have crippled me!"

"You're still alive, aren't you? I asked you a question with a gun pointed at you, *ami."*

The one he'd ruined more painfully, albiet not as permanently, gasped for air and groaned, "We work for ourselves, you big moose! Damn you, Jacques, I told you he looked too big for the two of us, and now we'll have to go back to hard on the rock!"

Captain Gringo holstered his gun and looked around as he said, "We can keep this a private matter between us girls, if you're leveling with me. Are you saying you're just a couple of foot pads out to make an easy score?"

Jacques groaned, *"Oui.* Drinking money is hard to come by here. We did not know you were a fellow Apache, M'sieur. Oh, Jesus, Mary, and Joseph, I need a doctor!"

Captain Gringo could see he had a point. His chum could probably get him to some police dispensary. Then the police would ask all sorts of dumb questions about how he'd broken his knee, too. Captain Gringo looked around, saw they were screened from all sides by the weeds along the gently bending road, and sighed, "Sorry, Guys, but when it's me or you, it's going to have to be you."

He kicked Jacques flat and stomped on his wind pipe, crushing it like a beetle. As he turned the other pleaded, *"Mais non!* Have mercy!"

Captain Gringo knew what kind of mercy they'd intended to show him and it seemed no time for long conversations, so as the ball-busted man tried to roll out of his way he kicked him in the head and leaped high to come down with both boot heels in the small of his back, snapping the spine like a twig. He bounced off and landed and walked away not looking back. He knew he didn't have to. He could have hidden the bodies in the weeds, but there was nothing connecting him to either of the would-be muggers and they were going to stink like hell in no time anyway. It was more to the point to establish his presence in other parts, pronto. So he headed back the way he'd come, resisting the impulse to look behind him. He was surprised at how much open ground he had to cover before he'd reach the corner where the tobacco shop stood. Distances always seemed greater when a guy was in a hurry instead of just strolling. There were windows above, too. Could anyone have been looking out just now? If his short savage fight had been spotted and reported, he could be walking into a police patrol!

Easy does it, he warned himself, as he moved on at a desperately casual pace. This was no time to start running back and forth like a chicken with it's head cut off. He had to get out of this open space and unless he *went* somewhere he wasn't about to do so!

As he approached the corner, he saw a man coming out of the tobacco shop. The guy didn't look his way and he turned the corner toward the main part of town. But the guy had been wearing a white hat!

Captain Gringo stopped, feeling naked with no cover in any direction. He knew he was probably wrong. Lots of guys wore white hats. On the other hand the stranger was anywhere around the corner, set up to do anything he had in mind as Captain Gringo came around it blind. Could he cut through the weeds and approach the main drag from another angle? Sure he could, and anybody looking out a window up there would wonder, and remember. He turned around and headed back the way he'd just come, toward the bodies. He'd been headed that way in the first place, right? He'd find a cantina or something over in that other neighborhood and be sitting there surprised as hell when somebody came in to report the stiffs outside.

The convicts he'd had to kill hadn't gone anywhere but he had a hell of a time not looking down at them as he strode on, shoulder blades tingling as he also resisted another impulse to look back. The other buildings in the shade of the trees across the open lots looked farther than they should have, too; but in about a million years he reached them and saw the satellite suburb was simply an uninteresting cluster of nondescript buildings save for an old stucco church off the road and half-buried in greenery. He didn't see a store or cantina in the area and a man in convict whites was leading a mule loaded with firewood toward him. The guy was going to be the one who spotted the bodies out there in the open lots and Captain Gringo didn't want him to remember any faces when he reported to the police, so he cut across the churchyard and entered the open doorway as if he were on his way to confession or whatever.

He was braced for an awkward confrontation with a sexton or priest, but when he got inside he stopped in wonder and muttered, "What the hell?"

The old church was just a shell: the pews and altar had been ripped out, long ago, judging from the stains and dust on the coral rock walls, and the stained glass windows were missing, too. He nodded, remembering this had once been a Dutch colony. He'd thought the church looked a little spartan for Catholic tastes. It was an abandoned Dutch reform edifice. The stone floor was covered with pigeon droppings, broken glass, and used contraceptives. It was nice to see the local youths had found a use for the old shell. Fortunately none of them seemed to be screwing in here at the moment.

Captain Gringo wondered if he could put the old church to his own uses. He found a stairway leading up into the bell tower and followed it to the belfry. He eased over the slatted opening and saw he had a bird's eye view of the lots he'd crossed, and that he'd crossed them just in time for the convict with the mule was on the far side of the bodies, making good time for town and the police, now. Captain Gringo fished out a claro and lit up as he pondered his next move. Nobody but the convict had seen him. But he might remember seeing a stranger entering a church he had to know was empty. So it was time to leave.

But as he started to, he spotted a flash of white on the far side and hesitated, eyes narrowed. It was the guy in the white hat but he wasn't alone. There were six others with him, dressed in civilian clothes and hence neither cops nor convicts. He knew the French had detectives, but it was early for detectives and the half dozen men were headed his way while white hat stayed put, like a general.

Captain Gringo moved across the belfry to the other side

88

and looked out. Beyond the few rooftops of this semi-isolated hamlet, other open fields stretched farther than he really felt like running with six guys on his ass. His damned horse was tethered at the hotel and God only knew where old Gaston was. He moved back to his first vantage point. The six hadn't stopped the convict with the mule and the latter was rounding the corner. The six were moving abreast with a certain O.K. Corral flavor to their in-step strides, although none had drawn a weapon—yet.

He watched as they approached the bodies. The obvious leader stopped a moment, shrugged, and continued the advance. It now was definitely an advance, he could see. They didn't seem to feel a couple of dead guys were worth bothering about. That meant white hat was either local law or had made some arrangements with the local law giving him a free hand in whatever he had in mind. Captain Gringo swallowed the green taste in his mouth as he considered the odds on him not being what white hat had in mind. The odds were lousy. The last time he'd seen white hat in the neighborhood had been just before he and Gaston had been set up for a machine-gun ambush!

He drew his .38 and headed for the stairs. This belfry was a natural trap if they searched the church for him. He moved down to the main floor and looked around for a place to hide. The foundation stones of the altar didn't look high enough. He ran over there anyway, leaped up on the slab and grinned as he stared down the far side. There was a crypt behind where the altar had been. A flight of stone steps led down to a bronze door. He moved down and tried the door. It was locked. The son-of-a-bitch local Catholics had had too much respect for Protestant dead to strip the crypt of it's bronze, damn their hides!

The yard outside might be weedy enough to hunker down in. But as he gave up on the crypt he heard the sound of a boot heel crunching glass and knew he was no longer alone in here!

He crouched behind the altar foundation, tucking his .38 away and drawing the more serious six guns as he sincerely hoped they'd dismiss the slab as lousy cover, too. A voice with an American accent said, "There's nobody here, Smitty." Then some other bastard answered, "Where else could he be? The boss says he don't know nobody in these parts, so he can't be in any of them houses across the way. Murph, you check the belfry. What's that big slab or rock over there?"

89

Captain Gringo gauged the odds. They'd be even worse if he let them spread out. So he took a deep breath, popped up with a six gun in each hand, and said, "Peek-a-boo!" as he opened up at point blank range with both of them!

The results were almost as confusing to Captain Gringo as they were to the startled gun slicks. They naturally had their own guns out and were on the prod, but he had the advantage of surprise and a better aim as the old church reverberated to the roar of guns as the air grew hazy with blue gunsmoke. He dropped two in their tracks and then nailed another who made the mistake of staying in the same place after firing and missing. He drilled a man running in panic for the door through the spine as a slug spanged off the stone beside him and he shifted his aim to the two on the stairs. He dropped the one who'd fired and saw him rolling down the steps after his clattering gun like a wet rag doll while the other went up the stairs like a scalded cat. He drew a bead, pulled the trigger, and swore when his hammer clicked on an empty chamber. He swore and holstered the empty six guns to draw his .38 as the survivor vanished into the belfry and slammed the trap door shut to seal himself off up there.

Captain Gringo knew the sounds of gunplay carried and the bastard in the belfry could signal across to the main town, too. So he stepped over a corpse and started up the stairs. He heard the trapdoor creak. The guy up there was either sitting on or piling things on it to keep him from opening it. The tall American nodded grimly, raised the muzzle of his .38, and pumped four rounds up through the wood. He stopped when he heard a thud on the top of the trapdoor. He thumbed in more ammo and moved up a step. Then he saw the blood dripping through the bullet holes he'd put in the planks of the trap. He nodded, fired once more between two oozing bullet holes to make sure, and moved back to the main floor level. He didn't have time to go through pockets, but the one he'd spine shot was trying to rise, like a sea lion on it's flippers but moaning more like a gut-shot pig. Captain Gringo walked over to him, hunkered down to place the muzzle of his .38 against the side of his skull and asked in a pleasant tone, "Okay, Pal, who are you working for?"

"I'm hurt bad, Walker. I need a doc!"

"I already noticed that. Noticed you know my name, too. You want to chat about it or do you want me to blow your fucking brains out?"

"Look, Walker, it's nothing personal. We're just hired guns, like you."

"Tell me something I don't know, damn it! Who's the guy in the white hat?"

"He's called Klondike. I don't know his last name."

"Screw his last name. What's his game? Who's he working for?"

The wounded man coughed, gave a defeated little sigh, and fell forward on his face. He was still breathing, so Captain Gringo shook him and said, "Talk, Goddamn it!"

The spine-shot man didn't answer. He wasn't breathing, either, now. Maybe shaking him hadn't been such a swell idea. Captain Gringo heard voices outside and he moved closer to the doorway where he saw some peons on the roadway out front, staring his way as they talked over the gunshots and tried to get up nerve to come closer. He swore, ran across the church, and dove out a glassless window to do some serious crawling through the weeds he'd landed in.

He crawled a million miles, or so it seemed, keeping his ass down like he'd learned in Apache country; and when he came to a clump of gumbo limbo and risked a peek over the top of the weeds, he saw he was well clear of the old church and that nobody seemed to be following him.

He got his bearings and started crawling some more, back toward the main part of town. The weeds were dry and he didn't meet as many snakes as he was worried about; but if walking that open space had seemed a chore, crawling across it on his belly was a real bitch. He was sure it would take all day. But when he finally reached a fence line and gingerly rose to see nobody in sight, he checked his watch and saw he'd only spent a couple of hours out there playing lizard. It would be hours more before it got dark. He moved along the fence line, found a break that put him in an alley, and followed it to the main street. People were moving quietly, nobody seemed excited, so he stepped out innocently, got his bearings, and returned to where he'd left his horse tethered in front of the main hotel. Gaston was nowhere to be seen. But his mount was still there. Hoping he knew what he was doing, Captain Gringo found a wrought iron bench on the hotel veranda and sat down to light a smoke and read his papers. He unfolded the official news first, knowing he could get in trouble reading dirty stories by Zola in broad daylight. The paper was six weeks old and hardly seemed worth the effort

91

of struggling with the French it was printed in. Nothing important seemed to be going on in Paris these days except that, what the hell . . . ? Emile Zola had fled the country for England!

The paper hinted that the government was displeased with him for writing something called *J'Accuse!* It was small wonder the shopkeeper had been nervous about selling copies openly. It had to be filthy, indeed, if it shocked Paris. They regularly published magazines you could get arrested for reading in England or the States.

A woman was coming along the veranda from the beauty shop down the way. Captain Gringo pulled his boots in to let her pass to the front entrance. Then they both recognized each other at the same time.

She gasped, "Dick! What on earth are you doing in French Guiana?" as he stood up, leaving the paper on the bench, and touched the brim of his hat to say, "I was about to ask you the same question, Liza. Still working for British Intelligence?"

Liza Smathers *On Her Majesty's Service* took his arm, registered a worried glance, and whispered, "For God's sake, keep it down! Let's go somewhere private where we can talk!"

He thought that sounded reasonable, so he let Liza lead him inside and through the shady potted-palm jingle of the lobby. He noticed she was still skinny and flat chested since the last time he'd undressed her. But her cameo features under the piled black hair beneath her picture hat were still as beautiful as ever. She still looked like an innocent English schoolgirl, despite the many people he knew she'd killed in her day.

Liza led him up to her second story room and bolted the door behind them before she turned and said, breathlessly, "About that time I had to run out on you in Bogotá, Darling, I know you must be a teeny-weeny bit annoyed with itsy-bitsy me, but I had to do it. I see you got out after all."

"Yeah," he said, "it was a lot of laughs when the revolution started. I'm not sore, Kiddo. I knew you were ordered not to tip off the rest of us. I found the note you started to write me before you remembered your duty to the Queen and country and all that rot."

She smiled in relief and reached up to unpin her hat. The chest under the lace bodice stayed pretty flat, but what the hell. She said, "I knew you'd get away. Who are you working for here in French Guiana, Dear?"

He laughed, "I said I forgave you for running out on me in Bogotá. I didn't say I'd gone nuts. This time I know more than you do, Honey. You're working for Greystoke's section of British Intelligence and it would be silly for me to ask what you Lime Juicers are doing in a French colony, so let's just take our clothes off and skip the usual lies."

She turned away and snapped, "You seem to be taking a lot for granted, Dick," even as she threw her hat on a chair and let her hair cascade down the buttons over her spine. He stepped in close and began to nuzzle her neck from behind as he started unbuttoning her blouse. She said, "You bastard. You've always been able to read my mind. But we don't have much time. I have to be somewhere at sunset."

"Oh, is he good looking?"

"I'm on a mission, you idiot."

"So am I," he said, as he unpeeled her bodice and let her dolly varden skirts fall to the floor around her feet. He turned her around, naked save for her stockings and high button shoes. He didn't wear underwear in a hot country, either. So as he held her against his front, kissing her, she started unbuckling and undressing him and as his pants fell around his booted ankles she stood on tiptoe to mount his shaft like a witch on a broom. It wasn't in, yet, but she was lubricating it nicely with her parted genital lips as she came up for air and gasped, "Oh, my, I see you missed me! But let's do it right, for God's sake!"

So he stepped out of his pants, picked her up, and carried her to the bed. As she sprawled across it the sunlight through the jalousied blinds painted tiger stripes of light and shade across her cool-looking boyish body. But there was nothing cool about Liza as he got between her pale skinny thighs and parted the small apron of thatch with his shaft. She rose to meet him, shoe heels hooked in the edge of the mattress, and the nice thing about coming home to an old sex partner was that they didn't have to waste time in exploratory moves. She sighed, "Oh, better than I remembered it, and I've thought about you a lot, you mean thing!"

He could tell she hadn't been getting as much as him, lately. That was another nice thing about Liza. The sweet screwing British spy wasn't an easy lay. He'd had a hell of a time getting into her the last time they'd worked together. But

93

once the loaf was cut, Liza was generous as hell with extra slices! She came ahead of him, partly because he'd been well taken care of the night before and partly because he couldn't let himself go as completely as usual with a lady who could kill like a cobra at the damndest times. She gasped, "Don't stop!" so, knowing how she liked acrobatics, he rolled her over and finished in her rectum as she giggled and protested, "Oh, you're just awful! I'll bet you do that to Gaston, too! Is he still alive, by the way?"

He didn't answer. He was coming and it was none of her business whether Gaston was in Sinnamary or not. The sodomy served to stimulate her to new lows, as he'd hoped it would. So he lay on the bed as she went to the dresser to get a wash cloth. As she turned, she said, "For God's sake, you still have your boots on!" and he said, "Why not? I like the way you look in those long black stockings. Shall we take time out to strip all the way?"

"I haven't time," she said. "I have to go soon." And then she dropped to her knees between his open thighs and proceeded to make him come some more by wiping him clean and taking it between her lips. As he reclined on his elbows with his feet on the floor, gazing fondly at the bobbing part of her hair, he knew she was trying to wear him out faster than usual. The last time she'd preferred a long, all-night orgy. It made him feel a little used and abused, but she sure did that nice. He lay back and said, "Watch out, Old Faithful's getting set to shoot!" and Liza laughed as she removed her lips just in time to hop up on the bed and land like a sex-mad frog on a lily pad with it up inside her, gushing.

She said, "Oh, I felt that!" Then, as she started moving up and down with her legs spread wide on either side of his hips, she added, "Poor baby, I'll bet you haven't had another girl since I left you in Bogotá! Let Baby do all the work, but play with my titties like you used to, won't you?"

She was full of shit both ways. But her love box was pure heaven and her flat chest was a novelty. The first time he'd had her it had been a sort of rape occasioned by her feeling like a boy when he accidently brushed a hand over her chest and wondered if a fairy was playing a nasty trick on him. Her nipples were large and turgid as a woman in heat were supposed to be. But her upper torso looked like some fourteen-year-old boy had pasted them on his skinny chest. He'd never gotten around to asking if she had some glandular problem, since it seemed impolite in the first place and her

94

other glands worked swell in the second. Whatever quirk of nature had made her flat chested had given her little body hair as well; but the snatch inside that tomboy body was awesomely female. He chuckled as he remembered something and Liza asked, "What's wrong?"

He fondled one of her nipples, moving it around on the little pad of softness it rose from as he said, "Nothing's wrong. I was just thinking about the time you hid those emeralds up inside you. That was a hell of a big poke, even greased, wasn't it?"

She flushed and said, "I'm not too loose for you, you monster!" and proved it by clamping down hard, even as she started to giggle at her own memories of her duty to Queen and country. He rolled her over to finish right with her skinny legs hugging him and her nails digging gently into his buttocks. That reminded him of another lady. So when they stopped for a smoke and a bit of cooling off he asked, "Do you want to deal a bit before I do it some more? You know I've always leveled with you, Liza."

She took a puff on his cigar as she pulled his hand in her lap, saying, "I don't see how my current mission can have anything to do with you, thank God. We had no idea you were here in French Guiana. Who are you shooting for money these days, Darling?"

"Damn it, Liza. I told you I'm a soldier of fortune, not a hired killer."

"There's a difference? All right, I'll put my cards on the table. We heard a revolution is brewing down here. We want to know if it's true."

"Does Britain have designs on French Guiana?"

"Heavens, no. We've been cultivating France as an ally against the silly new Kaiser of Germany. Our only interest is that British Guiana and Trinidad are just up the coast, and these revolutions will spill over."

He thought and said, "I think I'll buy that. Britain's been buttering up Uncle Sam, too, and my old country would wave the Monroe Doctrine a lot if Her Majesty got greedy again. The U.S. and Britain just came within a gnat's wisker of war over the Venezuelan dispute and you folks are too cool to start up again with Grover Cleveland."

"You're right. He seems a rather surly chap. I'll tell you frankly that Whitehall's not worried about a home-grown revolt of these French colonists. France can swat them like a fly if that's all there is to it. We're trying to find out if anyone

95

else is stirring up trouble. You remember that nice-looking German military aide in Colombia?"

"Von Linderhoff? He wasn't such a bad egg. When the rebels in Bogotá started shooting at all foreigners on sight he worked with the rest of us to save our mutual tail. What about him?"

"Von Linderhoff's been spotted by our agents here in French Guiana. He's not working as an embassy aide this time. He's in mufti, meeting lots of people in dark places."

Captain Gringo whistled and said, "Yeah, I met a guy who says he's a Hollander and who can tell a Hollander from a German speaking English?"

"I can." She shrugged, adding, "You must mean Van Horn. We know he's with the rebel party, but he checks out as a real Dutchman, left over from the old days. We think he's mad, but I doubt he's a German agent."

"Does the name Claudette ring any bells?"

Liza shook her head and said, "Lot's of French girls are named Claudette, Dick."

"This one has a American accent and says she's with some Jewish organization that's out to free Captain Dreyfus. Are you saying Whitehall hasn't got a line on them?"

Liza frowned and said, "Not in connection with Dreyfus. I'd forgotten the poor sod was Jewish. The only important Jewish group London is worried about is a budding Zionist movement with connections between London and the Continent. If they ever get anyone to take them seriously their ideas about a Jewish home state in Turkish Palestine could stir up trouble near the Suez Canal. But, frankly, we think it's just talk."

"Well, this other Jewish outfit is talking big money. I turned down a fortune when they asked me if I thought I could get Dreyfus off Devil's Island. I needed the money, but M'selle Claudette sounded pretty wild and I didn't trust her."

Liza moved one of his fingers into her moist slit as she asked, "Oh? Was this Claudette built anything like this?"

He laughed and started fingering her clit as he considered. It was funny how the one you were with always seemed the best. He knew he could answer Claudette as truthfully when he said, "Baby, nobody is built like you and you know it."

"But you did lay her, didn't you, you brute?"

"Hell, what's with this jealousy, Liza? You've been around since the last time we played house and tonight, for all I know, you'll be doing it with some other guy."

"No I won't," she said, "If I meet Von Linderhoff at the meeting he's slated to attend, my mission is to kill him. Would you like to come along?"

"I'd like to come, but not along." He grimaced, snubbing out the smoke and rolling atop her again. She wanted it and she took it. Sobbing in mingled pleasure and . . . regret?

When they'd finished, she said, "You really have to go now, Dick. I never meant to spend so much time up here with you and it's getting late."

She was full of shit. It wasn't high noon yet. But he'd found out all she was going to tell him, too. So he sat up, lit up, and proceeded to get dressed as Liza studied him, reclining like a painted nude they'd forgotten to paint the tits for. She sighed, "God, you have a lovely body. Isn't it a shame we're both in such active professions? I wonder what it would be like to spend a month or more with you."

He said, "What can I tell you? We've made love twice in less than a year. We're ahead of the game for knockaround guys and gals. Before I leave, what's Britain's interest in the *Dreyfus Affair*, Liza?"

She shrugged one shoulder and said, "None, except we wish the perishing Frogs would settle it. The French are on the verge of Civil War over the poor twit, and we do so wish they'd find something else to talk about so that we can get them to arm against the damned Germans as we want them to."

"I noticed they're pretty worked up about it. Do you think Dreyfus is innocent or guilty, Liza?"

"Oh, there's little doubt he's innocent. He was what you Yanks call *the fall guy* for a cover up in high places. The French high command knows who was really selling secrets to the Germans, and they've taken care of him."

"They have? Then what the hell is poor Dreyfus doing in prison?"

"Taking the blame for his superior's blunders, of course. They got rid of the real French traitor, but they see no need for the whole perishing staff to resign. Poor Dreyfus wasn't popular in the officer's mess in any case. Anti-Semitism and all that rot. It's easier to leave him where he is and you're right that it's impossible to get him out. Where can I reach you if, uh, we want to compare notes some more, Dick?"

He started to tell her, but thought better of it. He said, "I'll be around, Liza. I like to put my head together with yours."

She called him a bastard again as he rose to let himself out.

He didn't know if it was because he'd neglected to kiss her goodbye, or because any kind of a goodbye upset her. That was the trouble with laying people you sort of liked.

He went downstairs, saw Gaston's mount was still next to his, and was wondering what to do about it when Gaston came down the walk to join him, saying, "I've been looking all over for you, Dick. Somebody just found two trustees dead on the edge of town and the police are asking *très* tiresome questions. Let's get out of here, hein?"

They mounted up and headed out before Captain Gringo told Gaston about his brush with the thugs. The little Frenchman said, "I might have known when they said they'd both been killed lumberjack style. Did anybody see you?"

"Of course not. What did you find out? Can we get a berth aboard that tramp moored at the docks?"

"*Mais non.* She is American Registry and you know every Yankee purser has your wanted poster pasted to his bulkhead. They are doubtless as dishonest as anyone else, but what could we offer that would top the rather alarming rewards out on you, hein?"

"Oh, well, at least we have a place to stay tonight."

"*Oui,* and the food's not bad, either. One assumes you will resume your droll discussion of African customs with M'selle Tonda?"

"I think she's mad at me, but the contrast should be interesting if she's not. Did you pick up anything else along the waterfront?"

Gaston shrugged and answered, "Too much. Everyone here is talking about a revolution, but no two stories are the same. They say they are expecting native trouble, too. Most of the whites here are more afraid of the Ashanti than they are the rebels or French garrison."

"I thought the coast settlers and the Blacks in the interior had some sort of agreement."

"So did everyone else, until recently. It seems some idiot has been selling modern arms to the Bush Negroes. A white mahogany cruiser came down the river with his dugout full of 30–30 rounds and the Ashanti have a new chief, or perhaps he would like to be called their king. They say he has a gilded stool and an admiral's hat and this would seem to make him feel important."

"Come on, somebody's always running guns and rum to natives. They might be able to fight pretty good on their own ground, but if they were to invade the coastal settlements the French military would make hash out of them."

"Oui, if they were not busy making hash of somebody else, hein?"

"Oboy, I see what you mean. What's the story on the new chief, aside from his fancy hat? Does he have a name?"

"Oui, it is M'Chuma. It seems to have the same effect on these settlers as Geronimo had back in your States."

"Holy shit!" Captain Gringo replied. "That's Tonda's husband, and Van Horn is holding her as a slave against her will!"

"Oui, one gathers M'sieur M'Chuma has grievances against the Whites in these parts. If I were you, Dick, I would not seek a personal meeting with King M'Chuma. You know, of course, that the *practique* thing would be to, ah, dispose of M'selle Tonda discreetly?"

"Jesus, are you suggesting I murder that poor girl?"

"I agree it does not sound gallant, but if both of you are to stay alive, make sure she never gets back to her husband to discuss you with him, hein?"

Paul Van Horn had gotten back to the plantation ahead of them. He was hopping around like a kid having to piss as they walked back from the corral to join him on the back veranda. He said, "Where in the devil have you been? I left no orders for you to leave the plantation."

Captain Gringo said, "You left no orders not to, either. We just rode in to pick up smokes and dirty books to read. What's up?"

"The damned Bush Negroes are up in arms, for one thing. How in the devil was I to know that damned Tonda would make up with her husband?"

"Tonda ran back to the Ashanti?"

"It would seem so. Her husband has become the chief and done some dreadful things to the witch doctor who banished her before M'Chuma inherited the golden stool. I don't know how she heard about it before we did this morning, but she must have, for she took off during the night. Regardless of the details, she seems to have made it. When we tried to catch up with her we ran into an ambush and were lucky to get out with our lives."

Captain Gringo nodded and said, "So that's where you've been. Your sister said you were trading with the Ashanti."

"A lot she knows! I *was* trading with them, and I hoped to enlist them on our side, until that damned girl messed things up. The *old* chief was a friend of mine. M'Chuma used to sit there glaring at me, and when I took Tonda from the village, simply to save her life, Goddamn it, M'Chuma swore he'd dance in my blood if ever he got the chance!"

Gaston sighed and said, "Ah, *oui,* that is why one should always be polite to the receptionist. For who knows when she may become the boss, hein?"

Captain Gringo asked Van Horn, "Has Tonda any reason to single you out for her husband's particular vengeance, Van Horn?"

Van Horn grimaced and said, "I've never had her personally, but a lot of White men have, including you if she followed my instructions last night. I don't know what could have gotten into the girl. I warned her M'Chuma would kill her if he ever got his hands on her again, but she kept saying she was in love with him or some such nonsense!"

Gaston sighed dramatically and said, "Ah, perhaps for her sake Love shall conquer all. But in any case this M'sieur M'Chuma will no doubt wish to settle the, how you say, hash of his poor wife's abusers. Don't look at me like that, Dick, they always say they have been abused."

Van Horn said, "Let's go inside. Watch what you say and let me do the talking. We have visitors. I've told them you two are buyers from the north. Don't let on you work for me."

They exchanged puzzled glances and followed the fat man into the parlor, where two men in fresh white uniforms sat by the cold fireplace. As they were introduced as one Captain Chambrun and a Lieutenant Granville, they both rose and clicked their heels. They were army, not gendarmes.

Van Horn waved everybody to a seat and yanked the pull cord for more booze. The two French colonial officers were well on their way to insobriety, which might help or mess things up, depending.

Neither officer seemed interested in him or Gaston, although Captain Gringo was ready to kill Van Horn for introducing them as Walker and Verrier instead of the names on their fake passports. Captain Chambrun was polite enough to speak English in front of a "Canadian spice importer" but the tall American took a seat and kept his mouth shut. For once Gaston seemed willing to do the same.

Lieutenant Grandville seemed a little left out and probably didn't understand as Chambrun and Van Horn picked up the threads of their conversation about the "jungle menace," as Chambrun put it. Van Horn said, "I am sure my workers can cope with any raids if M'sieur Le Captain will reconsider my suggestion about arms."

Chambrun sipped his drink and said, "Arming trustees is out of the question, M'sieur Van Horn. I am aware your somewhat Owenite policies have made you many doubtless loyal employees, but it is simply against government policy to allow the convicts arms. I don't make the rules. Although in this case I agree they make sense."

Van Horn said, "I assure you none of my workers would take advantage of it if they had more than their machetes to defend themselves with when the Ashanti strike."

Chambrun shrugged. "Perhaps M'sieur is right. Perhaps he is an idealist, hein? We are speaking of convicted murderers and rapists. The scum of France. Even if the particular scum assigned to this plantation should prove somehow improved by their association with you, the colonial governor would never allow it. There are thousands of other convicts and we know they are always planning escape, or, worse yet, revolt. If only a few weapons fell into their hands, the results would far outweigh anything a few savages from the jungle could hope to accomplish." He took another sip and added, "It's true this plantation is close to the tree line and obviously in more danger than the others. If you like, I can ask for a detail of soldiers to be quartered out here, hein?"

Van Horn looked like a fat baby who'd just been surprised with vinegar in the tit he was sucking, but his voice was cool as he said, "Oh, I don't think it's as serious as that, Captain! We don't have any place to quarter troops and . . . "

"They could pitch tents out back, *non?*" Chambrun cut in, curiously glancing around the spacious room. But Van Horn insisted, " I wouldn't want to impose further on the government. This season's crops are almost ready to harvest and I'll soon be returning most of the trustees in any case. This house, itself, is well clear of the bush and as you can see, it's built like a fortress. My free servants and me should be able to hold off any hit-and-run raids by the bush natives. My only reason for asking about a permit to arm the field hands was my natural concern for their personal safety."

Chambrun grimaced and said, "If the Ashanti know what's good for them they'll stay well clear of the thugs working for you. I have never understood your reasons for selecting such hard-core criminals from among the trustees labor force, M'sieur Van Horn. The army works closer with the police in this colony than in others, for obvious reasons. So I know for a fact that you seem to have gone out of your way to select the rotten apples from the barrel. One assumes M'sieur had a reason for choosing long-term Apache over petty thieves and swindlers?"

It was a good question, but Van Horn was good, too. He smiled and said, "I know it seems odd, but you forget I was raised here. I long ago discovered that petty thieves are lazy failures who fell into a life of crime simply because they were not fit workers."

"Ah? I take it men who chop up their wives in the bath tub swing a machete with more skill?"

"Exactly. I've found that the natural bully and street brawler has more natural energy. Most of my workers are not too bright, muscular types who got in touble with the law because they couldn't sit still. I agree they are worthless in a civilized community, but out here with nothing on their minds but their next meal and nothing to hit but men just as brutal as themselves . . . "

"Eh bien, I know your views on the reforming powers of hard work and firm but kindly discipline, M'sieur Van Horn. Now you know my views on letting one of those White savages anywhere near a serious weapon. You can't have an arms permit, and since you don't want me to provide a military guard detail, I see no point in further discussion of the matter. You will of course let us know if there are any distressing signs of an impending move by M'Chuma, hein?"

Van Horn nodded and Chambrun got to his feet. His junior officer blinked in surprise, gulped his drink, and followed suit. So Captain Gringo knew Grandville didn't speak a word of English.

As they all followed the two officers out to their horses tethered by the front veranda, Chambrun said, "One hopes there shall be no trouble. I am going into the jungle tomorrow morning in hopes of a meeting with the new tribal leadership. With a strong escort, of course. We know little of this M'Chuma, save that he is young and headstrong. Perhaps if we get to the bottom of what's disturbing him, we can calm him down with a few cases of trade goods. This is certainly no time for another bush war."

Captain Gringo saw the fat Van Horn just wanted to get rid of them. But he had a question. So he asked, "Are you expecting other trouble, Captain?"

Chambrun looked him over like he had some questions of his own to ask if he'd had more time. But his voice was polite as he replied, "I don't think anything will happen before you have your pepper aboard that American ship in the harbor, M'sieur Walker. But we are always expecting trouble. For some reason the, ah, colonists that France sends here seem unhappy with their new lives."

"Oh, I thought you were expecting something worse than the usual escape attempts."

"Ah, you've heard the local gossip about a grand uprising, too, hein? They plan revolts all the time. Unfortunately, this year it seems more serious. Some thrice accursed troublemaker has been running guns ashore, as if that stupid *Dreyfus Affair* didn't have people excited enough. Have you read Zola's *J'Accuse,* yet?"

Captain Gringo shook his head and replied, "No, but I heard about it. I thought it was a dirty book, like his *Nana.*"

Chambrun sighed as he untethered his horse, saying, *"Nana* loses it's point in the translations. Zola is another idealistic reformer. And if you think *Nana* was shocking, wait until you read *J'Accuse!* Zola promises to be another guest of Devil's Island if the government can find out where he's hiding these days. An exposé of Paris prostitution is one thing. This time he's attacked the French high command!"

The two officers mounted up, saluted, and rode off as Van Horn turned to Captain Gringo and said, "Damn it, I told you to be still! I'm trying to butter the bastards up, not irritate them!"

"I noticed," Captain Gringo said. "He turned you down on that gun permit before I said a word."

Van Horn pursed his lips and said, "He's only a captain and he's going into the bush tomorrow. I'm going over his head as soon as he's out of the way. His colonel is a rum soaked ass."

"Most high ranking officers who can't avoid a post like this have to be. But what do you need a permit for in the first place, Boss? You've already got more guns than your men can carry."

"I want you to start training them," added Van Horn. "We can't fire any weapons until we have a legal excuse for the sounds of distant gunfire, damn it!"

The tall American said, "Most of them probably already know how to pull a trigger. Want me to start them on some basic field tactics with dry fire?"

"Dry what?"

"Empty guns go click click click. You want them transformed from a rabble-in-arms to a field battalion, right? Okay, they have to know how to form ranks, move in lines of skirmish and so forth. Your guys are already natural fighters. But I can show them the basic shalls and shall nots. It's mostly shall nots. Green troops make the same basic mistakes with monotonous regularity. Once upon a time there was a company of colored troopers the real Apache had been making hash out of. In less than a week, the company left the base and was turned into soldiers, good soldiers."

"Really? I didn't know you could train a man to shoot and salute in only a week."

"Hell, the Tenth Cav had already taught them to shoot and salute. The other White officers tended to dismiss them as poor dumb coons and didn't think they could grasp basic tactics. I damned near shit the first time I led them on patrol. They bunched up when they should have spread out. They charged decoy Indians blind and brave. My Black non-coms yelled mother fucker instead of giving sensible commands and, well, it was a good thing the Indians weren't very good, either. I took them back, chewed them out, and started explaining the way it was done. Some of them couldn't read or write. But nobody likes to die in combat and the rules of soldiering aren't that complicated once somebody explains them to you."

"They sound complicated to me," Van Horn admitted, "but you're the expert. Tell Chef I said you were to train him and his men in this dry fire business. How long will it take you to train three machine-gun squads?"

"Too long, if you want good ones. I can probably teach them how to fire from fixed positions without having the breech block imbed itself in anybody on our side. If I can select good platoon sergeants and explain how machine guns are used defensively, they might come in handy. What kind of automatic weapons do the colonial troops have?"

"I don't know. But I can find out, if it's important."

"It's important. The machine gun's new and I notice the French army is cheap. You'll be badly outnumbered, at least until you can capture some arms and recruit more followers. If the government armories have some other Maxims, maybe. If they don't, your revolution promises to be long and bitter. Guys potting at one another with rifles takes forever to settle."

Van Horn told them to do their best and wandered off to do some paper work, jerk off, or something. As soon as they were alone, Captain Gringo told Gaston, "Let's wander out back and see what we can do with the slobs."

Gaston followed him from the house, but protested, "This is getting *très* serious, Dick. I deserted the legion, it's true, but I admit to a certain latent patriotism to La Belle. These worthless sons of France can't hope to win, but the blood they spill will be French and I don't like it."

"I don't like it either," Captain Gringo confessed, "but until we can get the hell out of here, we have to go along with the joke. There's going to be bloodshed anyway. I ran into Liza Smathers of British Intelligence in town and she says the Germans are stirring up trouble here, so . . ."

"Ah, I wondered where you'd been in town. Do you trust the British? Liza lied to us the last time, *non?*"

"That was in Colombia. Queen Vickie doesn't want a revolt in a French colony so close to her own. We know the young Kaiser is crazy, although I'll be damned if I can see his point, either. The Germans must know Uncle Sam would never stand for a German colony on this side of the pond and they seem to be busy enough carving up Africa, right?"

"Merde alors!" Gaston said, frowning "I think you just hit on something, Dick! I had forgotten the German colonies in West Africa! These orphaned Ashanti on this side of the sea ≥ak related dialects! What if German agents are inciting ↘ Bush Negroes over here to fight the French?"

"Hmm, the way I hear it, the Germans have been pretty brutal to the natives in Africa. But M'Chuma might not know that. Nobody can be as charming as a German when he doesn't have you by the throat. But what's the angle? How could Kaiser Willy gain by starting a jungle war in any part of the globe he isn't interested in?"

"I did not know there was a part of the globe the Germans were not interested in," Gaston spat. "I think it distresses them to see a map that is not all German green. You are probably right that seizing French Guiana for the Kaiser would draw some harsh words from your President Cleveland. But consider the advantages to Germany if the French army was tied up in a long tedious jungle war far from the

African continent! French West Africa joins the German Kameroon and who is to say just where the border is when one has business elsewhere, hein?"

Captain Gringo frowned. "Pretty crude, but they say Kaiser Willy has lousy table manners. You may be right. Between the *Dreyfus Affair* causing street riots in Paris and a three-way guerilla war between convict colonists, Bush Negroes, and the French military, France would be busy as hell."

"*Mais oui,* and we all know that sooner or later France and Germany mean to have another discussion on Alsace-Lorraine. France is not expecting another all-out war with Germany for at least twenty years. But Kaiser Willy may be feeling impatient."

By now they were near the workers' sheds and Chef came out to see what they wanted. "Le Grande Chef," Captain Gringo started, "wants me to teach you and your boys some basic infantry tactics."

"Most of the men are working in the fields, Captain Gringo."

"Okay, let's start with the ones goldbricking in the shade. They're usually the smart guys in an outfit."

Chef shrugged, turned, and bellowed for everyone to come outside. It took longer than it should have, but after a while Captain Gringo was facing a ragged, sullen line of about a dozen. None had brought their rifles or shotguns, but some had pistols and knives strapped to their bodies.

He said, in his high school French, "I'm sorry if you're having a hard time understanding me, but this is the best I can manage."

There were a couple of snickers. He stepped over to grinning lout and said, "I know my French is bad. Do y speak English?"

"No, my friend."

"Then wipe that stupid smile off your face, and I'm not your friend. I'm your commanding officer unless you think you can whip me."

The man he was chewing didn't answer. But a bigger one laughed and said, "Hey, *I* think I can whip you, big shot!"

Captain Gringo stepped over to him, smiled pleasantly, and knocked him on his ass with a vicious left hook before he said, "I think you're wrong" then stepped back to see what happened.

What happened was that the man he'd flattened came up

with blood in his eye and a knife in his fist, looking like he meant it!

Gaston drew his pistol and snapped, "Everybody back and give them room!" So the convicts scattered to form an interested circle at a safe distance.

Captain Gringo saw the guy wasn't thinking, so he didn't draw either of the guns strapped to his hips as the convict came in low with the blade held point first against his chest, the left hand out in a clenched fist. The American said, "Knife fighter, eh? It's not too late to kiss and make up."

"Kiss my ass," the convict said, "You hit me, you son-of-a-one-titted whore!" Then he charged.

Captain Gringo sidestepped and whipped off his gun belt as if to throw it aside. But as the enraged knife fighter slashed the hell out of the space and whirled on one heel to face him again, the big American swung the heavy gunbelt, guns and all, and slapped him to the dust once more. As he tried to rise, Captain Gringo kicked him in the face and flipped him on his back, like a flap jack. The convict landed spread eagle with a surprised expression but rolled over and tried to get up again, still gripping his knife. So Captain Gringo booted him in the ass and sent him skidding on his already battered face. Before he could recover, Captain Gringo sprang forward and licked the knife from his hand. But the guy just wasn't paying attention. He came up bare handed and waded in windmilling, screaming terrible things about Captain Gringo's mother. Captain Gringo landed a rabbit punch into an upcoming knee and the next time he went down he just lay there, muttering to himself.

Captain Gringo stood over him and said, "I've had enough. How about you?"

The convict sat up, spat out a tooth, and growled, "I give up." So Captain Gringo nodded and put his guns back on as he said, "All right, boys, the show's over. Line up and calm down. I don't like spit and polish any more than you do. But if you mean to go up against trained troops, you're going to have to know some basics. Forget salutes and standing at attention, but pay attention and speak when you're spoken to."

Gaston was facing them, too, so it was one of the trustees who called out, "Behind you, Captain!" and Captain Gringo turned to see the man he'd whipped coming at him again, with another knife he'd gotten somewhere in his pants!

"Oh, shit," he said, "enough is enough!" as he drew the

gun on his right hip and fired it point blank into the mad convict's red face. The face got even redder as the soft-nosed slug took him between the eyes and blew what brains he had out the back of his shattered skull. Captain Gringo stared down in distaste at the body at his feet, then turned and said, "You and you, drag this off somewhere and get rid of it." He nodded at the convict who'd sounded a warning and said, "I owe you. What's your name?"

The man shrugged and said, "Call me Pepe. I had to say something. The man had no honor. He was a Corsican and you know how they are."

Another grinned and said, "Pepe was right, Captain Gringo. We all heard him say he gave up. Corsicans have no honor."

Captain Gringo ignored him. There was always some brownnose trying to get in good with the brass. "All right," he said, "Pay attention. The basics of soldiering aren't too complicated or they wouldn't have such big armies. I'll try to keep it simple. But the battle is the place you pay for not having done your homework, and you all just saw what can happen to a fool who thinks all a fighting man needs is a nasty disposition and some hair on his chest!"

With Gaston translating the difficult words, Captain Gringo drilled the men until others started drifting in from the fields. Then he formed them up and drilled them too. Somebody that hadn't been paying attention bitched that it didn't seem fair to have to go through it all a second time, s Gaston pulled him out of ranks and kicked the shit out him while Captain Gringo continued his lesson. He cou see the real problem would be discipline. Few of these guy would have been to Devil's Island if they had any respect for authority. Those officers had been right about them being scum. But they were *tough* scum.

After a while it started getting dark and a servant came from the house to tell them dinner was about to be served. Captain Gringo dismissed the convicts and said they'd see if they could do better in the morning. As he and Gaston walked away, he heard one sigh, "*Merde,* that's what I was afraid of!"

They went inside and washed for dinner. As they reached the dining room the fat Van Horn and his pleasantly plump sister, Wilma, were already stuffing their faces.

108

The girl had piled her blond hair atop her head and wore a frilly white lace dress. She looked as if she were planning to go to the opera, if they had an opera in Sinnamary. The two were arguing with their mouthes full as Captain Gringo and Gaston sat down. Van Horn cleared his mouth for action with a healthy gulp of coffee and said, "No, no, and no! I told you it was not a social function at the colonel's home this evening, Wilma. You would be bored to tears if you came along."

Wilma swallowed her own food and snapped back, "I am bored to tears already, you oaf! I didn't get all dressed up to sit here listening to the damned mosquito songs! You have to let me come along. I refuse to stay here alone."

Van Horn nodded at Captain Gringo and said, "You won't be alone, you silly girl. These gentlemen will be here to keep you company."

Wilma looked at Captain Gringo as if she'd just spotted him slithering out from under a rock and sniffed, "I want to go to town with you. I never get to meet anybody but your shady friends and hired thugs."

Captain Gringo winked at Gaston and helped himself to some Spanish rice.

"I'll take you to the reception at the German consulate next week," Van Horn said, "if you behave yourself. My visit tonight is strictly business and no other ladies will be there."

Wilma picked up her dish, threw it at him, and when she saw she'd missed she jumped up and ran out of the room crying.

As a servant knelt to pick up the broken crockery behind him, Van Horn sighed and said, "You must forgive my sister, gentlemen. I fear life here bores her a bit."

Captain Gringo nodded sympathetically and said, "I noticed. I didn't know there was a German consulate here in Sinnamary."

Van Horn said, "Just a branch office, but they do give nice receptions. I don't think you should go with us, though. They say the new German attache is inclined to ask a lot of questions. He seems unusually interested in our affairs, considering the tension between his country and France at the moment."

Captain Gringo shrugged and said, "I don't speak German anyway. Do you?"

Van Horn frowned thoughtfully and asked, "What's that supposed to mean?"

109

"Nothing, Boss. I don't care where you get the ammo we need, as long as it's any good."

Van Horn shook his head and said, "You guessed wrong. I don't trust the Germans anymore than anyone else with a brain ought to. We don't need them to pull our chestnuts from the fire and I'm not about to exchange French colonial rule for German. As a Hollander, I don't like the Germans any more than the French do. My guns and ammunition are bought and paid for on the international black market. Are you satisfied?"

Captain Gringo said he was, although he privately wondered why Van Horn had to be so adamant. For a guy planning to overthrow the government he sure was busting a gut to sound like a French patriot.

Van Horn went back to serious eating and the two soldiers of fortune saw he was more interested in that than them. So they started eating to catch up in silent pursuit. But as the dessert was being served, Gaston cocked his head and murmured, "Listen!"

Captain Gringo nodded and said, "I hear it. Sounds like drums. A long way off."

Van Horn belched and said, "It's the Niggers. That's a talking drum."

"Do you know what it's talking about?"

"Of course not. Do I look like a Nigger? Its something they brought from Africa with them. Don't worry about it. The only time the Ashanti attack is when their drums are silent."

Gaston laughed and said, "Beat on, my jungle friends. But does it not concern you that your sister may be alone some night when and if those drums fall ominously silent?"

Van Horn said, "I'm not away that often. Besides, she h you and my convicts to guard her should M'Chuma start something."

The two soldiers of fortune exchanged glances. Gaston said, "I thank you for your confidence in Dick and me, M'sieur. But if I had a little sister I don't think I would want her guarded by inmates of Devil's Island."

Van Horn said, "They have women to service them. Those who still remember what a woman is for, at any rate. Most of the long-termers are homosexuals."

"Ah, *oui*, one must be *practique* in prison."

Captain Gringo didn't want Gaston to talk the fat man

out of leaving, so he said, "There's nothing to worry about with us here tonight, Gaston. I'm sure the boss knows what he's doing."

Van Horn nodded, downed his coffee, and said he'd be late for his meeting with the colonel. As he walked him out to his carriage, Captain Gringo said, "I thought you were going to wait until Captain Chambrun went into the bush before you went over his head, Boss."

Van Horn nodded and said, "I intend to. I'm on a buttering up and fact finding mission. I'll tell you at breakfast if I find out anything about the local garrison's heavy weapons."

"You want us to wait up for you?"

"Don't bother. I'll be spending the night in town. But for God's sake don't tell my sister. She's jealous about a certain French widow I've been ah, cultivating."

He got in his carriage and drove off as Captain Gringo went back inside, bemused. He knew some sisters could tend to be possessive of a big brother, but that was another angle to think about. Neither of them looked like they had much control of their appetites and he hadn't noticed any young men calling on Wilma with flowers, books, and candy.

He found Gaston chatting in Creole with the scar-faced lady from the night before. When he asked the little Frenchman how he felt about an after dinner smoke on the veranda Gaston yawned elaborately and said he was suddenly *très* fatigue for some reason. So Captain Gringo watched him goose the Black girl up the stairs and strolled out alone to enjoy a private smoke in the cool of evening. He found a rattan chair near a window and lit up. The light over his shoulder outlined him, so he moved the chair to one side. He could still see pretty well as he sat back to enjoy a quiet claro. He took out the forbidden pamphlet he'd brought from town to brush up on his French. The bastard version they spoke down here was already part Spanish and in the past few days he'd been picking it up pretty good. Most of the French words that weren't Latin based seemed related to English.

He opened Zola's *J'Accuse!* and started looking for the dirty parts. What Zola was accusing was the French Military, and he sure made them look shitty.

Most of it was stuff Captain Gringo had already heard, although Zola put it better. Aside from insisting Captain Dreyfus was an innocent Jewish officer framed by anti-Semitic superiors, he came right out and pointed the finger at both the spies in the French high command and the assholes trying to cover up their own mistakes with a whitewash.

Zola's main thrust was that the framing of an innocent man wasn't the greatest crime. He said it was against the interests of France. Half the decent officers in the French army were demoralized by the clumsy whitewash and more than one had resigned in protest, to their credit, as good Catholics and good officers. The pamphlet made a lot of sense to Captain Gringo and he wasn't even a Frenchman. He knew he'd hate to serve in battle under the jerkoff's who'd sent an innocent man to Devil's Island rather than admit they'd made what was really an unimportant error in judgment.

But the Dreyfus Affair wasn't his problem, so he folded the pamphlet and put it away. He'd been court martialed by assholes, too, and he'd had the sense to run. It was up to Dreyfus to escape from Devil's Island. Nobody else could get him off the rock. Not even Zola, since the muckraking journalist himself, was hiding out from the government these days.

Captain Gringo caught himself wondering where he could get a map of the main prison out there and warned himself to forget it. It was a very interesting challenge, but he had enough to worry about. He had no intention of fighting in another doomed revolution, but sooner or later they were going to expect him to if he didn't get himself and Gaston out of here before the egg hit the fan!

He sat back and took a long drag on his cigar as he weighed the odds on an early date for Van Horn's uprising. The fat man didn't look crazy and seemed to be planning ahead wit considerable patience. Yet the whole idea was doomed fro the beginning. There was just no way that an untrained rabbl was going to take a colony away from one of the bigges armies on earth; and now it seemed that even the Bush Negroes Van Horn had been cultivating were against him!

He cocked an ear to listen to the distant drums. He heard something else, closer. It sounded like someone was crying. He frowned and rose, looking about, and spotted a blur of white down at the far end of the veranda.

He wasn't sure he was making the right move as he drifted down that way, but Wilma Van Horn looked like she wanted company. She could have cried just as loudly in her own room if it were a private matter.

As he could see her better, she was sitting on the end rail of the veranda, crying real tears. He took the cigar from his mouth and said, "I couldn't help overhearing, Ma'am. Is there anything I can do?"

She sniffed and said, "You could take me to a nice party, if they ever *had* nice parties in this awful hole! Look at me! I'm all dressed up with no place to go!"

He nodded and said, "That outfit is very charming." It wasn't really a lie. The dress was expensive and Wilma wouldn't be bad if she could lose maybe twenty pounds. Make it thirty, as long as a guy was dreaming.

She stood and twirled in her high heels, holding the skirts out to the side and ending in a mock curtsy, as she sighed and said, "This came all the way from Paris. Paul's not stingy with money. I can have all the material things I want. But I'm bored, bored, *bored*. He never lets me go to town unescorted."

Captain Gringo nodded sympathetically and said, "The rules are sort of strict down here. Nice girls aren't allowed out without an escort in any South American country, and this is a prison colony, Miss Wilma. I'm sure your brother is only concerned with your safety and reputation."

She said, "Pooh, he's possessive, you mean. Don't you think a brother who treats his sister as a, well, wife, is a little strange?"

Van Horn had said his sister was the jealous one. Captain Gringo was aware he was skating on thin ice, so he took a silent drag on his cigar.

Wilma said, "It's true. Having a strict brother leaves a girl with all the restrictions of a wife with none of the advantages. [I] think he's afraid I'd get in trouble if I got out more. On the [rar]e occasions I meet a decent-looking man Paul always ac[cus]es me of flirting."

"Do you flirt, Wilma?"

"Of course. Don't all girls? What's the point of going to a ball in a Paris gown if one's not supposed to flirt? I've met several very dashing French officers in Sinnamary and I know they liked me. But when they asked Paul's permission to call on me, he refused them, saying I was spoken for. I ask you, was that just?"

"Maybe not just, but it could be practical. You, uh, know something about your brother's plans, don't you, Miss Wilma?"

"Call me Wilma—I'm flirting with you. I know Paul has some mad scheme to change things here in Guiana. All sorts of mysterous-looking people come and go at midnight around

113

here. But Paul won't even let me explore those possibilities. He says I talk too much."

Captain Gringo had to admit Van Horn had a point. Wilma was a spoiled and not too bright brat, it would seem. He took another drag on his cigar, wondering what he was supposed to do about it. She held out a hand and said, "Let me try that. I've never smoked. Paul won't let me. But while the cat's away, you'd be surprised what the mice can play with, eh?"

He handed her the Claro, but warned, "Don't inhale if you're not used to smoking, Wilma."

She ignored him and took a long deep drag. Then her eyes got big, she dropped the cigar and wheezed, trying to say something but only managing distressed gasps as she swayed off her perch. He grabbed her to steady her, saying, "I told you not to inhale" as she wrapped her plump arms around him to hang on, eyes watering and rosebud lips gulping air like a surfacing gold fish. She made quite a bundle in his arms. He could tell she owed the trim waistline to whalebone and Charles Goodyear, but the parts that bulged above and below the corset felt like nicely molded marshmallow. It was the part below that bothered him. In her high heels the big blond's soft tummy came right to the level of his groin and his damned fool shaft was rising to the occasion. He moved his hips back as Wilma got her breath again and wheezed, "Oh, Dear, I don't see how you men do it."

He said, "Yeah, smoking is an acquired taste and you're not supposed to start with Havana Claro cigars. They're a bit strong, even for a heavy smoker."

She said, "Oh, were we talking about smoking?" as she moved her pelvis closer, hooked a forearm around the nape of his neck, and kissed him hungrily.

He kissed back, as any man would have, since Wilma kissed great. But as he caught one hand cupping her big left breast he wondered what he was getting himself into. The last thing he needed right now was a big silly virgin, even if she wasn't related to the boss!

He decided he could forget the virgin part as Wilma tongued him expertly and drew him forward off balance with her considerable body weight. As her big rump perched again on the rail she parted her heroic thighs under the lace skirts and hauled him in until his erection was tucked between the lower rim of her corset and the soft bulge of her belly. She seemed to be trying to screw him with her naval, and as they come up for air, he said, "For God's sake, we're on the front porch!" "I know," she laughed. "The servants watch my room when Paul is away. But who's to dispute my right to a little fresh air before bedtime? Do you like flirting with me, Captain Gringo?"

"If you call this flirting, Wilma. You know what you're doing, don't you?"

She licked his lips with a teasing tongue and said, "I know exactly what I'm doing, unless you're holding a gun on me. I'll show that damned Paul. He wouldn't take me to town because he's afraid I'll flirt with his gentlemen friends in high places. He'd have a fit if he knew I was having even more fun with a gun-tramp like you, and you know where my low places are."

"Gee," he said, "thanks for the compliment, Doll" as Wilma began to raise her skirts with a free hand. He had one hand gripping the rail beside her hip as he bent his knees and moved his booted feet back to lower his center of gravity. As she got her skirt up around her own waist he unbuttoned his pants and hauled out balls and all. As he'd suspected, Wilma had no underpants on and as she tilted her pelvis to welcome him, it slid into her wide and enthusiastic love nest like it knew the way. She gasped in pleasure, locked her fingers behind his neck, and leaned back like a little girl in a swing as she raised her knees and gripped him by the waist with surprising strength. He kept one hand on the rail and grabbed the edge of her corset for purchase as she clamped down inside and he began to move. He laughed as he thought about that crazy afternoon with the sailors and the sea turtle.

Wilma asked, "What's so funny? I know I have a big be-, but . . ."

"Hey, I like your big behind. But this is kind of awkward, Wilma. I could do this a lot better if we could get out of these clothes in a horizontal position for God's sake!"

"I'm bashful. Move it faster. I think I'm coming, too!"

That made two of them, for despite her direct approach and awkward position, Wilma Van Horn was a sweet-smelling, pure female who's totally new feel excited him. He came with her, then had to grab wildly as she let go of his neck to fall back, sobbing in satisfaction, and she would have landed ass-over-teakettle in the flower bed below had not he pinned her to the rail with his imbedded shaft while he clutched at her corseted waist. That made for a hell of an interesting angle of attack, too, but he knew they couldn't keep it up. He hauled her upright and as she buried her head against his chest he

115

gasped and said, "Jesus, I'm not a circus acrobat, Wilma. Birds may do it in midair, but human beings are supposed to have something under them when they get laid."

She sighed and said, "I know. The birds probably land someplace. Damn, I wish it were safe to take you to my room . . . I know. Come with me."

He thought he just had, but as she was leading him by the cock he followed as she stepped off the veranda and dragged him out to the middle of the front lawn. They were apparently in full view of the house, but when he mentioned it, Wilma said, "You were just up there on the veranda. Didn't it look simply black to you, out here?"

He said, "I guess so" as he looked around. He could clearly see the rail they'd just torn off a piece against. But the nearby drive was lost in the gloom and everything away from the house was just a blur. Wilma was taking her dress off over her head, saying, "I wouldn't want to get this lace grass stained. You'd better strip, too."

"Wilma, right on the *front lawn?* I know it's dark, but Jesus Christ!"

Then, as she dropped her dress on the cool grass and stood there barely visible in nothing but her corset, stockings, and high button shoes, he grinned and said, "Well, when in Rome or other weird places" as he peeled out of his sweaty clothes and dropped them on the grass as well.

Wilma lay down, looking like a barroom Venus after closing hours. The guys who painted barroom nudes usually left the corsets off, but they gave them the same overblown curves and the impossible waistline added to the attractions above and below it. She possessed an hour glass figure beyond man evolution and he already knew she was a great lay, so he dropped into the saddle of her big pale thighs and this time they did it right. She was so soft it didn't feel like they were doing it on the ground. Her big, soft breasts felt like plump downy pillows to rest his chest on and he knew he didn't have to be as careful not to hurt such a big girl, so he let himself go. The contrast between Wilma's soft, white skin and Tonda's firmer, dusky curves inspired him. Liza had been less pallid than the big blond and her boyish flat-chested body, stark naked against him, had felt different, too. Whoever had said variety was the spice of life had obviously gotten around with women a lot, and he'd been right!

He wondered if women got as big a kick out of contrasting

116

partners. But he didn't ask. From the way she was moving, Wilma had done this before with somebody. But he wasn't one of those assholes who asked such questions. He knew he didn't like to think about another cock in his currently favorite place. Why some men asked a woman they were with about other partners eluded him. But as Wilma came, subsided, and purred, "Oh, don't take it out" she broke the spell by adding, "Am I as good at that Nigger wench, Tonda?"

He grimaced, but moved politely as he replied, "Who told you I'd be in a position to know, Doll?"

"I like it when you call me Doll. It makes me feel little and cuddly. I know you had Tonda last night. I told you the servants gossip. That's why we're not doing this in my room."

He didn't answer. Maybe if he just moved a little faster she'd lose interest in this dumb conversation. But, though she began to respond again, she insisted, "Come on, you can tell me. What's it like to rut with a Nigger? I've always been curious, but I've never had the nerve."

He said, "You're not missing anything in particular. Everybody feels the same in the dark and they do it just like we do. Some good, some not so good."

"Isn't anybody bad?"

He laughed and said, "To quote Gaston, 'Nine out of ten people are worth making love to and the tenth is worth trying as a novelty.' "

She laughed, said she'd have to remember that and added, "Then I'm just as good as Tonda? I thought that was why Paul preferred her to me."

He wrinkled his nose and said, "Your brother told me he ...ver messed with Tonda, and as for preferring her, you're *sister,* damn it."

She put her plams on his buttocks to take him deeper as she ...aughed and said, "My, aren't we ever Puritan all of a sudden? Does incest shock you? I was afraid nothing did."

He shrugged and said, "It's something I never got into. Not passing judgment, of course. My mother was a lady and I had no sisters. I can see how a thing like that could happen, you two being orphans and all."

"Paul says the Egyptian Pharoahs married their sisters, their daughters, and sometimes even their mothers."

"Well, it sounds like a complicated love life, but he did say he was planning to be king or something and it's none of my business."

"Will you take me away with you, Dick? I have some money set aside and we both know my brother's revolution isn't going to work."

He stopped in mid-stroke, saw she was crying again, and kissed her moist eyelids as he answered, "Let's not get carried away with this deal, Doll."

"Oh, I want to be your Doll. Not forever, if you don't want to marry me. Just until we get out of this awful country. Don't make me stay here with my cruel brother, Dick."

"Uh, you mean this sibling slap and tickle has been against your will?"

"Not exactly. You know by now that I love to do this and Paul and I started as children. I don't mind my brother sleeping with me. But I'm annoyed as hell that he won't let me sleep with anyone else! The real problem with incest is that it leads to such a dead end. We can't get married, even if he becomes the dictator or whatever. So what's to become of me? Who ever heard of an old maid who gets laid almost every night?"

He had to laugh, even though inside, he was kicking himself for having gotten into this fix, nice as it felt at the moment. But he wanted to keep her on his side, so he said, "I wasn't planning on going anywhere in the near future, Wilma. But maybe we can work out a trip to Paris or something for you. I agree that you're wasted here."

She started moving harder and he just had to post in the saddle as she did most of the work, purring, "Oh, I know you think I'm better than that Nigger wench. We're going to have to be careful, but now that *you're* here I don't mind plantation life as much!"

He laughed and then, since her corset was starting to ir ritate his belly, he withdrew, turned her over on her hands and knees, and went at her dog-style, gripping her cinched waist above the astounding spread of her star-lit rear. It kept her from babbling at him and she liked the novelty, too, judging from the way she tore at the grass with her fingers and teeth, panting with pleasure. But then, just as he was starting to come, he heard hoofbeats and the grate of metal wheel rims on gravel. He stiffened in place and Wilma moaned, "Why are you stopping? I was about to climax again!"

"Keep it down, for Chrissake!" he said. "I think your brother's carriage is coming back!"

She giggled and said, "I'm coming, too! He can't see us, Darling!"

118

Captain Gringo wasn't that optimistic. He withdrew and flattened in the grass beside her as he listened to the approaching carriage. They were maybe fifty feet from the drive and the carriage was a visible blur of moving blackness, now. He sincerely hoped to pass for a bush or something as he lay still, barely breathing.

Then the crazy big blond rolled him on his back and remounted, a heavy thigh gripping each of his hips as she eased onto his shaft, which surprised him by still being anywhere near an erection!

He gasped, "For Pete's sake, Wilma!" but she put a hand over his mouth and whispered, "Quiet, he'll hear you!" as she began to move up and down like the mean little kid she was. He was tense all over as the carriage rolled by, sounding as if it were about to run over his ear while the owner of this lawn was riding in it!

But then the carriage was past them and Wilma giggled, "He's gone and I came!" She sat straighter and began to bounce as she threw her head back and crooned, "I know something Paulie doesn't!"

Captain Gringo muttered, "They're both nuts!" as Wilma literally milked him to another orgasm. He tried to roll her over to finish right, but she said, "Don't be greedy, dear. I've got to get dressed and greet my dear brother like butter wouldn't melt in my mouth."

As she got off him she dropped her head to kiss his shaft, taking it between her lips for a moment before releasing it with a wet smack and adding, "Oh, nice. We'll do that the next time we have a chance."

Then she was crawling away to her dress on the lawn, her big pale rear waving teasingly as he sat up. She retrieved her dress and said, "I'll go in first as if I've been for a stroll. He'll ask where you are and I'll say I don't know. Then you come in, in five minutes or so, looking like butter wouldn't melt in *your* mouth, either, right?"

He resisted an impulse to ask her if she'd played this game before. He groped for his own things and watched, bemused, as Wilma slipped on her lace dress, smoothed her hair, and rose, saying, "Ta-ta for now. I'll tell you when I see another chance to meet like this."

And then she was gone before he could say he didn't like bedroom farce all that much. By the time he'd dressed she was entering the house. He knew she had a point about his own early entry. So he moved over to the drive, lit a smoke, and walked toward the road leading past the Van Horn plantation. But well inside the grounds he heard the snick of a gun being cocked and heard a voice call out, "Halt, who goes there?"

"Captain Gringo. Inspecting the perimeter. Who's on guard here?"

"It is I, Pepe, Captain Gringo. Le Grande Chef has posted guards on all approaches since we got the machine guns."

The tall American joined the shorter convict and turned to stare soberly toward the house. Fortunately the front lawn was a black, blank expanse. He asked Pepe, "Has anybody but Van Horn been by while you were on guard here, Pepe?"

The convict cocked an ear to the sound of distant drums and said, "No. I doubt anyone would be on the road tonight unless it was important business. Somebody was screwing on the lawn over there a while back, but that's not what I was sent to guard against, hein?"

Captain Gringo said, cautiously, "Oh? Did you see them at it, Pepe?"

"*Mais non*. It is too dark, as you can see, but I know the sounds of a screwing when I hear it. One of the boys must have been with a servant girl, hein?"

"That sounds reasonable. How do you trustees work that out? Do you draw straws or something?"

Pepe laughed and said, "M'sieur has noticed there are not enough women on this plantation to go around. Fortunately most of us are long-termers who have learned the joys of sodomy. Le Grande Chef seems to have chosen us with that in mind. He seems to think of everything, *non?*"

"Yeah, Alexander preferred troops who didn't need to fool with local village girls on the march. He must plan some serious marching. Uh, you say you're, uh, *practique,* too?"

Pepe said, "*Oui.* They made me a femme because of my size the first night I was in prison. By the time I'd finished my first sentence I'd learned to like it. Would M'sieur Captain enjoy a blow job?"

"Uh, thanks, but I'm not in the mood. Sorry."

Pepe shrugged and said, "*Eh bien.* I am on guard in any case. Perhaps on the trail you will remember my offer, *non?* Many of the boys will be most anxious to please you. But in all modesty, I suck and fuck better than most women. Chef usually requires my services. But rank has it's privileges and I find you *très* attractive, Captain Gringo."

"Uh, thanks, I guess," muttered the American, adding

120

something about getting on with his inspection and turning away, feeling awkward. He owed little Pepe for that shouted warning, but he didn't owe him *that* much!

As he strolled toward the house he wondered if Van Horn knew what the hell he was doing in recruiting so many homosexuals. He'd read his military history and the way the ancient Greeks had worked it, had been maybe as bizarre, but a lot more sensible. The Greek phalanxes had been divided up so that men of the same sexual natures served together. They'd have heterosexuals in one outfit and homosexuals in another. That way no grim mistakes could happen when strange soldiers found themselves sharing the same tent. Some of the Athenian outfits had played so much grab-ass on the march it was a wonder they ever got any fighting in, while the girl-liking Spartans had simply soldiered tough, ignoring their hard-ons. Putting both kinds together was asking for friction, and apparently some of Van Horn's private army still liked women. He knew that many a heterosexual would have clobbered poor little Pepe back there. It had been his own first instinct, and he was secure enough and had been around enough to know better. Most of his own kind tended to dismiss Pepe's kind as sissies to be swatted, not thinking how the average homosexual got into more fights than anyone else on his tragi-comic quests. It could only be hoped that the straight trustees had been in jail often enough to live and let live, and that the catamites among the convicts had learned not to push it when a guy said no. Taking on a trained army with a bunch of guys that hated one another sounded like a frantic notion!

He got to the house and walked into the parlor through the French doors. There was nobody there. He pulled the bell cord and when a male servant came in, he said he'd like a night cap and asked where Van Horn was.

The servant looked a little sly as he replied, "M'sieur and M'selle Van Horn have retired for the night, Captain."

That was something else to think about as he sat down by the cold fireplace alone. He knew it was dumb to feel annoyed about the rather piggy Wilma bouncing with another man right now. God knew she liked it and it wasn't as if Van Horn was stealing anything from anybody. He didn't think she'd play true confessions, despite Gaston's warning that all women did. On the other hand, a lady who confessed to incest on the first date wasn't exactly a clam, and she'd enjoyed flirting with getting caught out there on the lawn. He was sorely

121

tempted to haul Gaston off that colored girl and just run like hell!

They'd made it this far, hadn't they? How much more trouble could they get into between here and the Dutch border?

The servant returned with a tall, cool gin and tonic on a silver tray. Captain Gringo noticed he had faint tribal markings, too. He thanked the man for the drink and asked casually, "Are you Ashanti, too?"

The servant shrugged and said, "No, M'sieur. I am Ibo. Like the girl your friend is sleeping with. We were both captured long ago by the Ashanti. Our homeland is far to the north, in Dutch Guiana. Ashanti are very bad people. Not civilized, like us Ibo. They were going to sacrifice us, but M'sieur Van Horn bought us from them as slaves."

"Is slavery legal here in French Guiana?"

"No, M'sieur, but try telling that to the Ashanti! We are not really slaves of M'sieur Van Horn, of course, but the Ashanti must not ever hear this. They would come after us. They are cruel. You see, they were once slaves for a short while. Their tribal legends say that being a slave is the most terrible fate of all. They would rather make a slave out of an enemy than boil him alive over a slow fire. That is why it's so easy to fool them. We Ibo are smarter. We don't like slavery, but we know there are worse things that can happen."

Captain Gringo sipped his drink and said, "They say that girl, Tonda, ran back to the Ashanti after being a slave. Do you think they'll take her back?"

The servant shrugged and said, "I do not know. I said they were not civilized. I don't think an Ibo chief would want a woman like that. She was sold as an accused adulteress. If she can persuade M'Chuma she was not untrue to him, either here or there, she may have a chance. Otherwise she will wish she stayed here. I would tell you about Ashanti torture if it was not so close to bedtime."

Captain Gringo dismissed the servant and slowly sipped his drink as he ran that lovely bit of gossip in with the rest of this God awful mess. He looked at his watch. It was too late to make up any rational excuse to saddle two horses and ride off. Riding beat walking and they didn't seem to be confined to this plantation. Their best bet was to stay cool for now, make up some excuse to go to town in the morning, and play it by ear from there.

He finished his drink, put the glass down, and rose to head for his own room. It was a funny time to miss Tonda not being there. He'd had the skinny English brunette and the fat Dutch blond in the same day, for God's sake. He was just feeling horny because of the tense situation, he guessed. Maybe that was how bedroom farces worked. The excitement of dodging all over gave a guy a hard-on?

He opened his door and went in, switching on the light. He stared blankly down at the plump woman in his bed and said, "Wilma, what the fuck are you doing in here?"

"You took the words right out of my mouth, darling. I just had a bath and a douche and the corset was killing me!"

He said, "So I see." Without the corset she looked a lot fatter, albeit still nicely Junoesque. He said, "Isn't your brother's room just down the hall?" And she said, "Yes. He went out again. He said he'd be gone all night on some business. So we have this end of the hall to ourselves. Save for Gaston and that Nigger wench across the hall. I heard them through my wall and started getting kind of jealous."

"Your, ah, usual bed partner left you hanging, eh?"

"Pooh, Paul's too fat to do it right with the little he has to offer. I'm glad he didn't want me tonight. I want you some more! To tell you the truth, I was saving a little of myself to keep Paul from getting suspicious. But now it's all yours and I can really let myself go!"

He'd thought she had, out on the lawn. But as he shucked his clothes and rejoined her on a soft mattress, he saw she hadn't. The hell of it was, she felt completely different, inside as well as out, now that she'd unlaced that cinch around her internal organs. So he found to his surprise that *he'd* saved a little for an emergency, too!

Captain Gringo woke up feeling that something was missing. Then as he stared at the sunlight slanting through the shutters he knew it was Wilma. The sheets and pillow cases still reeked of her perfume and sweat mingled with the musky horse chestnut scent of human rutting. He grinned and ran a hand over the stubble of his jaw. That smelled like pussy, too.

He opened the blinds to air out the room as he washed

and shaved at the dry sink across the room. He ran the sponge all over himself and got most of Wilma off before going down to see if anybody was going to serve him breakfast. He found Gaston already consuming ham and eggs on the back veranda, alone. As he sat down, Gaston said, "'You certainly make noisy love, Dick. I know Le Grande Chef is out beating the bushes for some obscure reason, but do you think it was wise to make love to his sister so openly? S'Gawa, the lady I spent the evening with, tells me they are unusually close for brother and sister."

Captain Gringo grimaced and said, "The noise was her idea. I can screw as quiet as the next guy, but what do you do with a dame who's screaming at the top of her lungs for more?"

"Eh bien, give her more, most naturally. From the sounds one assumes you did. But when her big brother gets back . . ."

"We're not going to be here. This situation is too rich for my blood. Aside from the incest and sodomy going on all around, the whole scheme stinks. Those French officers yesterday didn't look stupid, even half drunk. Van Horn's running all over playing plot in the celler, so by now a lot of people have to know his plans, which wouldn't make sense if they were secret. I've been thinking some more about that ship in Sinnamary. We've been accepted here as legit gents. If we played our cards right . . ."

"Merde alors! I told you she's an American vessel!"

"So what? She's a long way from home. She'll be stopping at other ports of call before she goes anywhere near the States and right now any port of call would be an improvement. Shit, I'd rather go back to Venezuela, now that our last adventure there's had a little time to cool off. I know my way pretty good through an old-fashioned Hispanic revolution. What's going on here in French Guiana is just too fucking complicated. I can't think of anybody d⸻ ⸻e I'd trust a second!"

Gaston shrugged and said, "I'll ring for your breakfast." But the tall American said, "I'll eat in town and you're about finished. Let's get the hell out of here before Van Horn returns."

Gaston went on arguing as they walked out to the corral and selected two horses a little better than they'd had the day before. As they rode out, Chef was drilling a squad of men and shot them a new salute he'd been practicing. It made

Captain Gringo feel a little guilty, but what the hell, he'd given them some training and they were in better shape now to take on the French army.

They weren't in that much shape, though. And guilty or not, a guy had to look out for his own ass.

They rode into Sinnamary and tied up at the same place. He wondered if Liza was still at the hotel and if he could get it up on such short notice if she was. He told Gaston to come with him to the waterfront and let him do the talking. But they didn't make it.

Half way to the waterfront a full squad of gendarmes stopped them. The corporal in command smiled pleasantly and stated, "If you gentlemen will be kind enough to come with us." Since nobody seemed to be acting surly about his side arms, Captain Gringo smiled right back and said, "Sure, Corporal. Where are we going?"

"Just up the street, M'sieur. Our sergeant is talking to a witness and, forgive me, you were seen in this vicinity yesterday and you fit the description, although I am sure it is a mistake, *non?*"

The squad formed a polite box around them as they were frog marched past their horses and the hotel to a corner Captain Gringo remembered only too well. The corporal pointed at a stairway up the side of the building the tobacco shop was in. He didn't think they were after him for swiping a copy of *J'Accuse!*

He was right. Some other gendarmes and a petite redhead in a green dress were standing on the balcony of what seemed to be her room. He could see that anyone up here had a clear view of the weed-grown lots where he'd tangled with those muggers the day before!

They still hadn't disarmed him and Gaston, but somebody had either a pistol or a prick against his spine as the police sergeant smiled at them and asked the woman, "M'selle?"

The redhead laughed incredulously and said, "Heavens, no! I know these gentlemen. Just by sight, of course."

"M'selle described the man who killed those two convicts out there in broad daylight as a tall blond man in a straw planter's hat and a linen suit of European cut, with a two-gun harness around his hips, *non?* Forgive me, M'selle, but the tall one there fits your description exactly."

The redhead smiled exposing two pretty dimples and met Captain Gringo's eyes with a twinkle in her hellfire green ones

125

as she said, "I ought to know my own description, Sergeant. I didn't have to come forward as a witness if I had any reason to conceal the killer's identity, true?"

"Naturally, M'selle, but when you reported the killing, you said . . ."

"I said a tall blond man had some sort of a tussel with the men you found dead and I did say he wore a straw hat and a two-gun rig. But this is not the man I saw out there. I'm quite positive. I told you I've nodded to this particular gentleman before and I'd know the other if I saw him again, too."

The sergeant sighed, touched the beak of his cap to anybody who might feel the need of an apology, and said, *"Eh bien.* In that case we shall have to search further. I thank you gentlemen for being so co-operative."

The gun moved away from Captain Gringo's spine, so he smiled and said, "Hey, you were just doing your job, Sergeant."

The French non com still looked like he'd bitten into an apple with a worm in it, but he nodded and led his men down the steps as the redhead said, "Let's go inside where we can talk."

Captain Gringo knew how the fly must have felt when the spider invited him into her web. But he nodded at Gaston and they followed the mysterious redhead outside.

The hairs on the back of Captain Gringo's neck were tingling, for something fishy was going on here. The cops had seemed excited enough about finding a couple of dead bums out in the weeds. How could they have missed the half dozen bodies he'd left all over that abandoned church in the neighborhood?

Local peons had responded to the sounds of gunplay. What wrong with the local law? Those guys he'd shot it out with couldn't have got up and walked away before the cops arrived. There'd been a fix. The guy in the white hat had either cleaned up the mess damned suddenly or he had an in with the colonial government that allowed him to wash his own linen. The stiffs out in the weeds hadn't worked for white hat, so they'd been allowed on the police blotter and . . . yeah, the cops who'd picked him up just now probably didn't know about the more important fight across the way. That meant white hat was in with somebody higher up. So who the hell was he and what was his game?

The redhead's furnished room was shabby and non-descript, save for a new steamer trunk that was obviously the only

126

furniture she'd brought with her. It stood open and was almost as tall as she.

The redhead waved them to a couple of bentwood chairs, stepped over to the trunk, and pulled out a drawer as she introduced herself. "I'm Birdie Peepers. I work for James Gordon Bennet." Then she handed them each a large card and added, "These are press passes accredited to my newspaper chain. Fill them in with whatever names you're using at the moment. Most underpaid customs officials down here don't know the difference, as long as you show them *something*."

Captain Gringo stared at the documentation and asked, "You're a newspaper reporter?"

"Foreign correspondent, *s'il vous plait*. I mean to knock Nelly Bligh and the other girl reporters out of their socks with the scoop of the century and you boys are going to help me!"

As the two soldiers of fortune exchanged glances, Gaston asked Birdie, "Ah, M'selle speaks French?"

"*Oui, M'sieur,* but let's stick to Captain Gringo's English for now. I had to know French to get this assignment, but to tell the truth I'm not very comfortable as a Frog."

Captain Gringo asked, "Who's Captain Gringo?" in an innocent tone.

Birdie laughed and said, "Nice try, Lieutenant Walker of the 10th Cav."

He met her gaze unwinkingly as she perched on the edge of her bed across from him. She perched kind of nice. The green dress was wrapped around a trim little torso that didn't need foundation garments to hold it together. The dress was thin enough to tell.

She smiled and said, "My, you *are* as cool as they say. I suppose the two of you are wondering why I changed my story for the police just now?"

He raised an eyebrow, so she explained, "I described you so they'd pick you up. I told them they had the wrong man because you'd be no good to me in jail. I've been trying to figure out a way to approach you when I saw you in action from that window and I must say you move nicely for such a big man. Now that we've been properly introduced, I told you I was down here to get a story."

"I don't give interviews, Birdie."

"Pooh, they never sent me all the way down here to write about another soldier of fortune. These woods are full of your kind, thanks to the great depression in the States and a new

127

writer named O'Henry has a corner on telling your tale. I'm here to interview Captain Dreyfus. So far the damned Frogs won't let me talk to him."

Gaston looked pained and said, "M'selle, some of my best friends are Frogs. Would it be possible to call us Frenchmen?"

"Sorry, Shorty," Birdie laughed. "Even if I call them Frenchmen they're giving me a hard time. They say Dreyfus is being held incommunicado out on Devil's Island. You boys are going to help me slip into the prison out there for my papers."

Captain Gringo shook his head and said, "No we're not. Prisons make us nervous."

"I'm not finished," she said. "I'm not going to blackmail you by changing my mind to the police and those press passes may save your behinds some day. But there's more. My boss has chartered that tramp steamer down at the pier. So I can take you aboard and drop you off anywhere you like after I'm through here. How do you like it so far?"

"Keep talking."

"Okay, I know a little of your story, Dick, and you're in a situation a lot like Captain Dreyfus. A lot of people think both of you got a raw deal at your court martials. Suppose I got you to a safe hideout for a time and started a newspaper crusade to get you a new trial back home in the States?"

He brightened, heaved a sigh, and said, "It's a little late. Since you seem to be following my career, you know I killed the officer of the guard as I was making my departure the night before they planned to hang me."

"That could be considered self-defense, couldn't it?"

"That's the way I looked at it. But you know how picky the army can be."

She shook her head and insisted, "If Zola can get Dreyfus off, I can get you off. I'm a better writer than Zola."

"Last time I heard," he laughed, "Zola wasn't doing so hot. Dreyfus is still on Devil's Island and Zola is on the dodge."

"Pooh, he's in England where they can't touch him and he's still giving them hell. He has an opposition party man named Clemenceau asking questions in the chamber of deputies, now, and Anatole France has come out for poor Dreyfus, too. The movement's beginning to snowball and it's only a question of time. That's why it's important I interview him *now*. Before they let him out and somebody else gets the scoop!"

Gaston was trying to catch Captain Gringo's eye as he shook his head. But the tall American didn't have to be told her idea was dumb. He said, "Your talking about a maximum security prison fortress and a guy they're watching like a hawk. You're not the only one interested in getting to him, you know."

Birdie Peepers nodded and said, "I heard about that Jewish organization. The French have, too, and it's not helping Captain Dreyfus much. But I'm not navigating blind in a complete fog, even if you do think I'm a silly."

She rose gracefully and took a folded chart from her trunk, where all sorts of things seemed to be stashed. She spread it on her bed as both men rose to stand on either side of her. Captain Gringo noticed she wore sandalwood perfume as she pointed down and said, "This is a chart of the facilities on Devil's Island. As you can see, it's not a walled castle rising from the sea."

Gaston said, *"Mais non,* it seems to be a quite ordinary French prison camp. Those round circles would be the guard towers. I see the prisoners are kept in these barracks and ... *oui,* here would be the maximum security cells, sunk in the rock nearer the main headquarters."

"Dreyfus isn't in solitary," she said. "We know that much. More than one decent French officer feels sorry for him so he's being treated as well as the other lifers out there. Maybe a little better. You can see there's nothing much to keep anyone from coming ashore or leaving the same way."

Gaston nodded and said, *"Practique* and cheap, as usual. The main barrier to escape is the shark infested sea itself. It must be *très* frustrating to walk about out there, with nothing between you and freedom but an occasional dark fin cu, in, the placid water, hein?"

She nodded and said, "The guards find it easy enough to keep the prisoners from building a boat. At night they sweep the sea with searchlights to make sure nobody brings a boat in."

Captain Gringo grimaced and said, "That's what I just said. So how in hell could you expect us to put ashore without a burst of gunfire coming down a beam at us?"

She shrugged and said, "You're the professionals. All I need you for is to get me out there and bring Captain Dreyfus back with me. Once we're all aboard my hired tramp steamer it's high for the bounding main and an exclusive that will top Stanley and Livingston!"

"Holy bananas! You intend to rescue Dreyfus, too?"

"Of course. The fact that he's out there is hardly fresh

129

news. Stanley didn't just find Livingston, he saved him, remember?"

"Not exactly, but I see your point. It's too big a boo, Birdie. The odds are lousy going in and even worse on getting off the island alone, forgetting Dreyfus. Why not sit tight and let Zola do it the easy way?"

"Pooh, let Zola get his own story of the century! I thought if we could work out some sort of ruse, to distract the guards as we landed . . ."

"What kind of ruse, Birdie?"

"How should I know? I'm a reporter, not a soldier-of-fortune. If I were a knock-around guy in your shoes, Dick, I think I'd come up with something fast. I'm making you a hell of an offer, you know."

He knew. "I'll think about it," he sighed. "I have to know how many guys you have on that boat that we can rely on. I need to see what kind of gear we have to work with. Above all, I need an idea. Right now I'm drawing nothing but low cards from the deck and I have to find the joker."

She said, "Sleep on it if you like. I have to the end of the week to either get a story or give up. Dear James Gordon is acting bearish about the expenses I've run up so far. But all will be forgiven if I can come back with Captain Dreyfus and an exclusive. Meanwhile, as long as I'm here, have either of you heard of M'Chuma, the new king of the Bush Negroes?"

"Those are his drums you hear when the wind is right," Captain Gringo said. "What about M'Chuma?"

"What about him indeed. I interviewed Geronimo at Fort Sill just before coming down here. He was fun—not at all like I imagined."

Captain Gringo sighed and said, "He wasn't much fun when I was chasing him through Apacheria, Birdie. M'Chuma's not a defeated chief on a reservation. They say he hates Whites and he's sitting surrounded by a whole tribe of warriors who seem to feel the same way."

"You don't think you could get me up to his camp in the hills, Dick?"

"Good God, I'd rather try for Dreyfus on Devil's Island! At least if we're caught, we won't be tortured to death."

She looked uncertain, then shrugged and said, "Well, I'll worry about that another time. When do we go to Devil's Island, boys?"

"When I come up with a plan, if I do," Captain Gringo replied. "Meeting you and talking about that steamboat has changed things, Birdie. The first thing we have to do is mend some fences so that nobody's looking for us. Come on, Gaston. We'd better go back to the plantation and act innocent."

He told Birdie he'd be back around sundown, even if he had to fib about a date with her in town. He added, "The guy we're working for might ask questions, and he has a lot of informants among the convicts here in town. So it's going to have to look like you and I are . . . you know."

She smiled and said, "Oh, right, we'll put on an act about being lovers." Then she spoiled it all by adding, "You understand, of course, that this will just be for public consumption? I hope you won't think I'm old-fashioned, but I'm not that sort of girl."

He grinned wryly and added, "Hey, who said I was that kind of boy? The idea will be to have people thinking we're up here acting naughty-naughty while we're innocently plotting serious crimes against the state, see?"

She laughed her understanding and the two of them went down to the street. Gaston asked, "What do we tell Van Horn if he's back, Dick?"

Captain Gringo shrugged and replied, "We tell him we went to town, got mixed up with the police, and that I made a date with a redhead. Does that sound suspicious to you?"

"Mais non, but I don't think Wilma is going to like it."

"Screw Wilma. Come to think of it, Van Horn will probably want to since he didn't get to last night."

As they walked to their tethered horses, they heard a commotion coming their way and turned to see what the noise was about. Three weary-looking soldiers in gunsmoke-stained white uniforms were slogging grim-faced down the street, surrounded by convicts and civilians shouting back and forth. They recognized one in officer's kit as Lieutenant Granville, from the meeting at the plantation. Captain Gringo said, "Ask him what's up, Gaston. He doesn't speak English, remember?"

Gaston hesitated, nodded, and moved out to fall in step next to the dazed-looking junior officer as Captain Gringo followed along the walk, trying to follow the drift of their rapid-fire French. He didn't believe what he was hearing until Gaston peeled off, rejoined him, and said, "They are on their way to their headquarters, after a most distressing incident in the jungle. Chambrun is dead. Almost everyone is dead, save for those three who were near the end of the column when it marched into an ambush."

"I got that part. What was that shit about a machine gun?"

"Granville says they were raked by machine-gun fire in the jungle as they formed ranks to face the Ashanti."

"The fuckin' wild tribesmen hosed them down with machine-gun fire?"

"*Oui*, it sounds *très* mad to me, too, but Granville was there and he should know, hein? Life was so much simpler in the good old days when the natives knew their station in life. Now wild Indians have repeating Winchesters and they say the British have been meeting Afghan tribesmen with their own homemade copies of British repeating rifles. Is it not amazing how a man who sees no need to send his children to college seems to grasp the advantages of modern weaponry so easily?"

"Yeah. The White Man's Burden is likely to get heavier before it gets lighter. Let's ride out."

They saw other soldiers on the road as they headed for the Van Horn place. These guys looked clean and were jogging with rifles at port arms. So apparently somebody was already thinking of setting up defense lines.

As they neared Van Horn's gate they heard the distant woodpecker snarl of yet another machine gun. So Captain Gringo whipped his horse into a run and moved on the sound of the guns. There were two convicts, armed, on duty at the gate. He reined in and called down, "Get those weapons out of sight. We may have visitors and you guys are only allowed to hold hands."

They rode on, swinging wide of the house, and reined in again as they saw what all the noise was about. Van Horn and Chef had one of the Maxim guns set up and were apparently trying to mow down a row of distant bottles as other convicts watched with interest. Van Horn stopped firing as the two soldiers of fortune joined him, dismounting and tossing the reins to the nearest convicts. Van Horn said, "Oh, there you are. We were just trying out our new ammo. I met the smugglers and their new guide last night. We have enough now to train as well as fight."

Captain Gringo said, "Swell. The first thing we have to do is hide every fuckin' weapon on the place, and hide them good! This place figures to be crawling with security forces any minute. Didn't you hear what happened to Chambrun's column?"

"No. You two are the only ones who've been to town since I got back. What happened to Chambrun? Did he have his meeting with M'Chuma?"

"He sure did, and the Ashanti chopped the shit out of him.

Chambrun's dead. Along with most of his men. The survivors said they were mowed down with guns like these!"

Van Horn looked astonished and gasped, "Ashanti with automatic weapons? Where in God's name would they get them?"

"That's a good question. Have you checked since Tonda ran off to them?"

"You mean *our* guns? Impossible. The other two are . . . Chef, you'd better run and make sure, eh?"

As Chef trotted for the storage sheds, Captain Gringo said, "Even a stolen machine gun needs a gunner. Back in the good old days when they were still talking to you, did you notice many other Whites trading with the Bush Negroes?"

Van Horn frowned and said, "Not many. They don't trust the French as much as they do Dutchmen. And I'm the only Dutchman this far south."

"A German would look a lot like a Dutchman to M'Chuma, wouldn't he?"

Before Van Horn could answer, Chef called out from a doorway, "They are both here, Le Grande Chef! Nobody has trifled with our stored arms!"

Captain Gringo said, "Yeah, it fits even better now that we know it's not one of your boys going into business for himself. A very sharp German spy master named Von Linderhoff, added to an Ashanti chief who's heard Dutchmen are trustworthy, could sure account for a machine-gun crew backing a spear-tossing ambush!"

Van Horn wet a finger to test the wind. Then he said, "Listen, the Ashanti drums are still beating."

Captain Gringo listened to the distant murmur of jungle drums for a moment before he shrugged and said, "So much for anthropology. They used to tell us Indians never attacked after dark, too. Maybe M'chuma doesn't know he's supposed to warn us all by letting his drums fall silent, huh?"

"Well," Van Horn said, "Chambrun was on M'Chuma's home ground when they hit him. The Ashanti must have considered it a defensive move. Those drums right now are probably talking the ambush over. It's going to make M'Chuma look good and strengthen his hand."

"Yeah, and meanwhile it's put a crimp in your revolution. None of the other convicts will join you in the middle of a race war. When it comes time to choose sides in a race war everybody already has his uniform on and most of the French, convict or otherwise, are White. I wouldn't be surprised if the government doesn't bend the rules to arm some trustees, officially. The U.S. Army used Confederate P.O.W.s against the Sioux in a simular situation. Meanwhile, until you get that gun permit you've been after handed to you on a silver platter, we'd better hide everything but our personal side arms and get these guys out in the fields before some official drops by to warn us about the natives getting restless again."

Van Horn nodded and said, with a grin, "You're right. I hadn't considered how M'Chuma could be playing right into our hands. We may have lost him as an ally, but he makes a marvelous bogeyman!"

"Yeah, by the time they put a lid on him, half the convicts in the colony will have guns to play with. Are you going to call yourself emperor or just president, like the modest guy we always knew you were?"

It was just after sundown when Captain Gringo, Gaston, and Birdie Peepers shoved off from the rented steamboat in the ship's launch. The skipper of the bigger craft was the only one who had the least notion what they were up to and he'd told Birdie he didn't really want to know much about it. One got the impression he and his rag-tag crew were nervous about the French navy, even at the wages they were getting from her news syndicate.

The ship's launch lay low in the water, but was powered by it's own oil fired and silent steam engine. So they didn't have to row as they towed the raft he and Gaston had thrown together before shoving off. Captain Gringo rode in the bow with Birdie as Gaston manned the tiller on the far side of the upright boiler, so they didn't have to listen to him bitching. The redhead sat on Captain Gringo's left, with the breech of her bought-and-paid-for Lewis gun between them. The Lewis wasn't as good a machine gun as the Maxim, but Birdie hadn't known that when she'd armed herself to the teeth and the lighter Lewis had certain advantages in a hit-and-run situation. It fired it's 30–30 rounds from a drum mounted atop the action. So changing an exhausted magazine was quick and simple. The Lewis patent had a bad habit of jamming. But he'd checked the rounds and rejected those that looked the least bit bent. The gun sat on a post screwed to the forward thwart. If he had to, he could dismount it and use it as a weapon from the hip. He'd had no chance to zero in the

134

sights, so accuracy was up for grabs. He sincerely hoped he wasn't going to have to shoot anybody anyway.

It was too dark to see the horizon. But you could sort of tell up from down as the little boat bobbed over the ground swells. The sky was full of stars and the Atlantic Ocean wasn't. He craned out to one side for a look down their wake. He nodded in satisfaction and told Birdie, "We're in luck with phosphorescent wakes tonight. The little critters who make the water glow are seasonal and it's safe to splash this month."

She leaned over the side to splash her hand through the bow wave and he said, "Stop that. I didn't say the *sharks* were seasonal and the barricuda come big down here, too!"

"Sorry," she said. "I'm so jumpy I could scream."

"I wish you wouldn't. Hey, Gaston? Swing a point to starboard and let's see if I can make a star wink out."

The boat's bow swung as directed and he said, "Right. The island's where it's supposed to be. We're going to pass it a cable length to the south."

She stared hard and said, "Dick, I can't see a thing." And he said, "I sure hope so. If we can see them in the dark, they can see us."

They steamed on a few more minutes. Then, off to their left, a search light winked on and began to sweep the sea slowly with it's beam. Gaston swore and swung the tiller hard over, but Captain Gringo called back, softly, "Steady as she goes. We're not going close enough for that beam to pick us up. Stick to the course I gave you, damn it!"

Another light came on to sweep the white caps to the north. He told Birdie, "That's just routine. They don't want kiddies like us in their old swimming hole."

"It's so much scarier now that we're really out here, Dick."

"What did you expect? I told you it would be a boo. You can light the fuse now, Gaston. Make sure the bulk is between you and the island when you strike a light, right?"

Gaston muttered, *"Merde alors."* Neither of them saw any light from back there until he said, "It's lit. One trusts it's slow fuse as M'selle's supply voucher said. Otherwise we are all *très* dead."

They steamed on, bow pointed into the trade winds at a course that would pass the island to the south-east, just beyond searchlight range. On shore, they heard a door slam and someone was playing a mouth organ. Gaston whispered, "Dick, we are almost broadside to the island and I can't see what that fuse has to say about the matter, hein?"

135

"Steady as she goes," Captain Gringo replied. "I want the raft off to seaward. Can you get more speed out of this tub?"

Gaston answered, "Not dragging all that garbage through the water astern." So Captain Gringo shrugged and hung tight. Beside him, Birdie was shivering. He put an arm around her and she started to resist, then snuggled closer and said, "Oh, it sure is cold out here on the water. But don't get fresh."

" 'Fresh,' she says," he muttered, adding, "Lady hires wanted men to smuggle her into Devil's Island and she's afraid they'll get fresh!"

"Well, I know how men are."

"I'll bet you do. Honey, right now I'm too scared to get fresh with Lillian Russell."

"Oh? What's she got that I haven't got?"

"Nothing, Dollface. You all come with the same basic equipment, Allah be praised. Do you want my arm around you or don't you?"

"Well, it does feel comfy, but don't get ideas."

He swore softly under his breath and gauged the angle from the sweeping searchlight as he forced himself to slowly count to a hundred. Then he did it again and called back, "Okay, Gaston, cast off the decoy."

The boat leaped forward as the Frenchman in the stern released the painter towing the raft. Aside from that, nothing much happened. It wasn't supposed to, if they'd timed things correctly. He let Gaston steer them further out to sea before he called back, "Okay, let's swing hard port and get around to the far side."

So Gaston did and it only seemed like a million years until they were north of the island, still cruising beyond the searchlight beam. Captain Gringo muttered, "What time is it?" and then as he reached for his watch all hell broke loose.

Far to the south-east, where they'd left it, a powder charge aboard the raft went off with a roar. And then, having gained the doubtless undivided attention of everyone on the island, the raft started sending up distress rockets as a can of oil-soaked waste burned red, like a ship on fire. He saw both the previous beams groping for the "wreck" as two more winked on to join in, sweeping closer in for possible survivors in the water. He chuckled and said, "Now, Gaston."

Gaston said, "I wish I was home in bed." He then swung the bow toward the shore of Devil's Island and opened the silent throttle. As they approached the black mass, outlined

136

by the lights and red sky on the far side, they came in through the breakers and grounded the bow on a gritty little beach. Captain Gringo snapped, "Okay, Gaston, keep her in with the screw and be ready to back off on a moment's notice, right?"

"Mais non, I was planning to build a home here."

Captain Gringo grabbed the girl's arm and said, "Now. Move it fast and keep it down to a roar. Come *on,* Doll! This is one hell of a time to powder your nose!"

"Dick, I'm scared! I don't think I can do it!"

"Sure you can," he said, and hauled her after him over the gunwale. They splashed ashore and made the cover of some brush. "Wait here," he said, and moved inland up a steep slope, clinging to the shadows until he topped the rise and found himself on a flat open field of some sort. He saw men in both convict and guard uniforms standing about and craning their necks to see what the hell was happening at sea to the south-east. He walked casually over to a group of prisoners and one of them spotted him and asked, "What's going on?"

"Don't know. Just came from the office myself. Can you tell me where I can find Captain Dreyfus?"

The prisoner turned and shouted, "Hey, Dreyfus, somebody here wants to see you!"

A man in the near distance turned like a puppet on a stick and marched gravely over as Captain Gringo wondered who the hell they thought he was. Up close, Alfred Dreyfus was a stiff, slender man with a moustache and pince-nez glasses. He looked more like a Prussian officer in his shabby convict whites than a lot of Prussian officers could manage in full dress uniform. He saluted Captain Gringo gravely and said, "M'sieur?"

"Come with me," snapped Captain Gringo, knowing how to act chicken shit if it was required. Nobody said a word as he marched Dreyfus away from the others. It was easier than stealing chickens, for God's sake!

As they reached the drop off, Captain Gringo took Dreyfus by the arm to steady him. But the officer pulled away and asked, "What is going on? Why are we going down there? There is nothing there, M'sieur!"

"You're wrong, Captain Dreyfus. Have I got a girl for you."

He took Dreyfus down to the redhead and Birdie gushed, "Oh, Dick, you did it! Let's all get out of here!"

It sounded reasonable enough to Captain Gringo, but Captain Dreyfus said, "Out of here, M'selle? Are you suggesting I attempt to escape?"

"Don't you want to escape, Captain Dreyfus?"

"Are you mad? Why would I wish to do such a crazy thing?"

Birdie stared at him in astonishment. Captain Gringo said, "Speaking of crazy, correct me if I'm wrong, but this is Devil's Island and you are serving a life term here, right?"

"But of course. I understand this is in all the newspapers, M'sieur."

"Look, Dreyfus, this is interesting as hell, but let's talk about it in the boat, huh?"

A siren started wailing and Dreyfus said, "Ah, that is the signal for all prisoners to return to quarters. Someone seems to be having second thoughts about that ship in distress and a bed check seems in order. Forgive me, I must leave you now."

Birdie sobbed, "Hit him, Dick. Hit him and put him in the boat! They've driven the poor man out of his head!"

Captain Gringo shook his own head and said, "He might know what's he doing. Right, Captain Dreyfus?"

The downed but not defeated officer nodded gravely and said, "I am grateful for what you odd people seem to be trying to do, and I thank you for calling me by my rank. But they stripped me of my commission, M'sieur. They stood me at attention and ripped off my decorations. Then they broke my sword. Can you understand how a man feels at such a time?"

"Yeah, but let's stick to your court martial. A lot of people seem to feel you're innocent, Captain."

"I am innocent—that's why I can't go with you. Don't you see what the men who ruined me could make out of my escape? 'Ahah, we knew it! Now the dirty Jew has *proven* he's a traitor to France!' "

"That's what they'd say, alright. But, since you brought it up, what do you know about a Jewish organization who's also supposed to be working to free you, Captain Dreyfus?"

The French officer looked sincerely puzzled as he said, "A Jewish group? But why, M'sieur?"

Hey, you're the one who just said you were Jewish, remember?"

"*Mais non,* I did not call myself a dirty Jew. The people who falsely imprisoned me called me that. I do not consider myself a Jew. I am a Frenchman who's family happens to be

138

Jewish. I, myself, am an agnostic. I did not know how some of my fellow officers felt about my background until I was accused of treason."

"Doesn't that make you want to get in the boat, Captain? It sounds like your loyalty's a bit misplaced!"

"*Mais non,* M'sieur. My loyalty is to France and the French army. Despite my misfortune, I have never lost faith in the country I love or the many decent men in her army. I shall never betray my country or the army because of a few, how you say, bad apples?"

"Close enough. Let's go, Birdie. You got your story and the captain has to make bed check."

"Dick," she gasped, "we can't leave him here!" But Dreyfus had thrown them a salute and was moving away. Captain Gringo called, "Hey, Frenchy?" and when Dreyfus turned with a puzzled smile, he threw him the best West Point salute he could manage. It seemed to cheer Dreyfus up as he scrambled up the slope to rejoin his fellow prisoners.

Captain Gringo got Birdie back in the launch and called back, "Throw her in reverse and let's beat it!"

Gaston tried, but they were only out a hundred yards or so when a light suddenly went on and started sweeping it's beam to intercept them!

Captain Gringo shouted, "Down, Birdie!" as he dropped behind the Lewis gun and threw the arming lever. The beam was almost on them when he opened up and fired a full drum into the swinging light and anybody dumb enough to be anywhere near it!

The light went out with a satisfactory tinkle of glass and screams. And then as they got really moving, another switched on, groping blindly in the area they'd just left, so he shot that one out, too, and for some reason everyone on shore started making a lot of noise. Sirens and police whistles sounded off and somebody started firing blind out across the water. But since they didn't have the range, he didn't return the fire. He figured it was up to them to figure out where he was, right?

As the racket faded astern, Birdie was crying. He put a hand on her heaving shoulders and asked, "What's the matter, did you get hit?"

"No," she sobbed, "and I didn't get my story! All that work and risk for nothing! How was I to know he was some kind of Don Quixote?"

He pulled her up, sat her in his lap, and said, "You dumb little dame, you just got your story and it's a good one! Dreyfus was right. He would be just another guy on the dodge if he came with us. He's better news as a Don Quixote. There aren't as many of them around. Jesus, I'm not a writer and I know what I could do with that scene on the beach back there!"

She brightened and said, "Oh, you may be right! He's still loyal to his colors, after all France did to him! I guess that does make him a real hero, and he was sort of nice-looking, too!"

Then she kissed him, soundly, and sighed, "Thank you, Dick. I think I have my scoop after all!"

He was about to return the kiss when Gaston called out, "Excuse me, my love birds, but we seem to have another launch pursing us!"

"Jesus, are they gaining?"

"No. We seem to have the swifter craft. But I thought you ought to know."

Devil's Island must have a cable running to the mainland. The shoreline of Sinnamary was lit up like a Mexican street carnival and white clad troops were running up and down it like chickens with their head cut off as the launch approached. But the chartered steamship was blacked out and for a girl who didn't think ahead, Birdie couldn't have planned it better. Gaston simply steered them up the shadow lane of the ship and they tied up to the ladder on the offshore dark side while the police and troops guarded the waterfront with their lives and considerable shouting.

The skipper and mate were waiting for them at the top of the ladder. The skipper gasped, "Jesus, Miss Birdie, we've got to cast off and get out of here. The Frogs are acting crazy."

But she said, "Pooh, how can you tell? My, uh, criminal associates here tell me we're home free. Isn't that right, Dick?"

"I think so," Captain Gringo said. "They didn't spot us, so they have no description out on us or the launch. Nobody escaped from Devil's Island after all. So after they figure that out, they ought to simmer down and just wonder what the hell we were about."

The skipper sighed and said, "I hope so. From all the yelling on the quay it seems they think wild Niggers just raided the place. The Frogs have soldiers watching the bush inland and now they have to worry about sea raiders, so they're pretty frantic. They should welcome a break."

"Look," Captain Gringo warned, "we're not dealing with a bunch of banana banditos. Right now they're rattled and have every right to be because not a thing that's happened makes military sense as they learned it at Saint Cyr. But they're forming defense lines and once they finish they'll make the usual moves to police up their interior. They'll be boarding this vessel to ask questions in a little while, so we'd better have our stories straight."

Birdie said, "Pooh, I got what I came for, sort of, and there's nothing to keep you and Gaston here. Why don't we just weigh anchor and steam out of here right now?"

Captain Gringo shot the skipper a disgusted look. The old tramp steamer mate nodded and told Birdie, "We'd wind up in bigger trouble with the French navy, Miss Birdie. A vessel's not supposed to leave a port without clearance from the harbor master. If we were to light out in the middle of all this excitement a lot of Frogs would wonder why!"

He turned to Captain Gringo and said, "My crew has no idea what's been going on and Mr. Slade and I can hide the machine gun if you still need it."

"Don't hide it," Captain Gringo said. "Clean it and put it back in it's case. It's reasonable for a vessel in these waters to pack emergency gear. Nobody on the island got a good look at us, but they might get it out of Dreyfus that there was a woman with us. Gaston, here, can blend into the French crowd with no trouble. I'll take Miss Birdie to her room ashore and when and if they board, you don't have any idea what's happened and they can look around all they want, right?"

"Dick," Birdie added, "I think I'd feel safer and certainly more comfortable in my stateroom aboard this ship. We've plenty of room for you two and . . ."

"Don't you ever pay attention?" he cut in, adding, "Carry on, skipper. Gaston, get on the other side of her and let's mosey down the gangplank like innocent tourists."

Birdie was still bitching as they took her ashore and headed for her rented room. They passed soldiers and some trustees with arm bands and rifles, but nobody challenged them. There were bonfires at intersections and the people of the town who weren't milling about in the streets seemed to be leaning out their windows shouting questions back and forth. He cocked his head and couldn't tell if the Ashanti drums were still throbbing in the hills. He grinned over at Gaston and said, "Well, we sure have a good excuse if we ever see Van Horn again. Nobody's going to be moving on the roads tonight except the military. They'll probably call on Cayenne for help and dig in until troops from the main colonial garrison can get here."

He'd no sooner spoken when the air above them was ripped like a big canvas sheet and Gaston gasped, *"Mon Dieu!* That's a 155 if ever I hear done passing over!"

The big shell crumpled down somewhere to the west and Captain Gringo said, "Yeah, there's at least one gun boat out there lobbing harassing fire. I told you they'd go by the book."

Birdie asked what he meant and he explained, "They don't know where or who they're shooting at, but an occasional shell coming down in the vicinity makes people duck and slow down. The idea is to keep the enemy off base 'til you can get your own people into position."

They came to a cross street and Gaston said, "I know a rather disreputable back-alley bistro down that way, Dick. I think I'll join the crowd at the bar and, as you say, blend in, hein?"

"Right. We'll meet in front of the usual hotel in the morning, if the coast seems clear. If you run into Van Horn or any of his men, we were caught by surprise here, too. Tell him the last time you saw me I was with a lady. You don't know who she is and we don't know anybody else in town."

"Merde, don't coach me, coach M'selle Birdie," snorted Gaston, peeling off to fade into invisibility.

Captain Gringo led Birdie up on the walk that passed Liza's hotel and to her corner room, hoping to attract less attention in the shade of the arcade. But as they reached the entrance of the hotel a tall bullet-headed man wearing a white civilian suit and a Prussian monacle almost bumped into them. He stopped, clicked his heels to let them pass, then gasped, "Herr Walker! What are you doing in French Guiana?"

Captain Gringo sighed and answered, "Hi, Von Linderhoff. Heard you were in town."

"Zo? You have then the advantage on me. But I might have known you were here. It's rather noisy tonight, *nicht wahr?* Are not you going to introduce me to your charming companion?"

Birdie started to say something, but Captain Gringo nudged her and said, "Get your own girl, Von Linderhoff. I don't know what all the excitement's about. I thought you might."

The German smiled crookedly and replied, "I am here on an open diplomatic mission. I trust your papers are in order, Herr Walker?"

Captain Gringo didn't know if that was a veiled threat or not. You could never tell with guys like Von Linderhoff. He answered, "Look, we once made a deal when it was to both our advantages, remember?"

"I do indeed. Civilized gentlemen must play 'the great game' by some rules and those Colombian rebels were behaving like maniacs."

"Okay, I have a hot tip for you and you don't know who I am or what I might be doing here, right?"

Von Linderhoff hesitated, then nodded. "My word as an officer and gentleman, since I see no way anything you could be up to would work against the cause of my Kaiser."

"Yeah, I know he wants the French to enjoy a lot of peace and happiness. I know you're another professional and I found you trustworthy the last time we fenced. So here's the tip: British Intelligence knows you're here and they're out to terminate your date with destiny, ol' Buddy."

Von Linderhoff smiled sardonically and said, "Is that all? I have my own agents watching the attractive lady that Greystoke of Whitehall sent to kill me in bed. Naturally, she won't get me in bed or anywhere else. But I thank you for your concern, and I believe you are dealing from the top of the deck. Tell me one thing, Walker. Are you here in connection with the *Dreyfus Affair?*"

Birdie flinched but kept quiet and fortunately Von Linderhoff was watching Captain Gringo with his one good eye. "I give you my word" Captain Gringo answered "that I have no intention of doing a thing to hurt or harm Captain Dreyfus. I'm mulling over an option to do some shooting for local interests who couldn't care one way or the other about the *Dreyfus Affair.*"

The tall German officer stared hard for a long unwinking minute. Then he nodded and seemed satisfied. "In that case we part friends, or, in case anyone should ask, as strangers, *nicht wahr?*"

"Right. I don't know you and you don't know me. I'd tell you to watch out for stray rounds when the real fun and games start, but, knowing you, it would be as silly as telling my granny how to pluck a chicken."

Von Linderhoff laughed, clicked his heels again, and marched off. As Captain Gringo hurried Birdie on she asked, "Who was that man and what happened to his poor eye?"

"Don't worry about it," he said. "It's a long story and I just told him I didn't know who he was or what he's doing here."

"But you *do* know, don't you, Dick?"

"Yeah, it's getting more obvious by the minute. Here's your stairway. Let's get inside fast."

They took the stairs two at a time and as he followed her inside, Birdie flicked on the lights. He flicked them off and said, "You're not thinking. This is a corner house and we're on the second floor with a clear field of fire from those vacant lots to the north."

"But it's so dark in here, Dick!"

He stepped to the jalousied window and adjusted the blinds, letting in a zebra pattern of streetlight as he said, "This'll be enough to get around and it's a dumb time to curl up with a good book."

Then he grabbed her, spun her around, and threw her head first across the bed.

She screamed, "Have you gone crazy?" as he pinned her face down and began to run his free hand over her body, feeling for weapons and only finding some interesting bumps and depressions in her well, put together torso. He said, "Well, you're not packing a derringer in your garters and I'd have noticed one higher, I think." He rolled her over and ran his hands over the front of her bodice as she sobbed, "Please, I'm not that kind of a girl!" while he frisked and found nothing but a pair of very sweet little tits. She wasn't even wearing a corset. The waistline was all Birdie. He sat beside her on the mattress and removed his hands from her, but said, "Just stay put. I'll smack you if I have to."

"Don't hurt me," she whipered. "If you want me that much I'll let you, but please don't hurt me."

"Cut the old-fashioned girl bullshit, Birdie," he said, "I bought it for a while, but a guy in my business learns to think on his feet and your story just won't hold water."

She tried to rise but he shoved her down as she sobbed, "Let me take off my dress. Don't tear it."

"Later, maybe. It's questions and answers time. You hired a whole tramp steamer. You have a stateroom aboard her."

"Of course, but . . ."

"But, shit, Birdie. Tell me how come a lady with a private

stateroom on her own boat saw fit to rent this dingy little room over a tobacco shop. A tobacco shop that sells forbidden political literature in addition to cigars."

"Dick, I don't know anything about the shop downstairs. Do I look like a girl who smokes cigars?"

"You look like butter wouldn't melt in your mouth. There's a lot of that going around down here. You want me to tell you why you rented this room with such an interesting view? You didn't need a place to sleep. You had a place to sleep. You weren't up here when I had that fight with the two convicts. You never saw it."

"Dick, that's crazy. How could I have described you to the police if I hadn't been here at the time?"

"Easy. You made it up. You knew I was in town. You'd seen me on the street and were trying to figure out a way to meet me and get me to help you. When you heard there'd been a fight and that the police were looking for witnesses, you rented this room with a view and *back dated!* You described me so the police would pick me up and you could be a swell kid. It worked pretty good and you must have had a turn when you found out I really was the guy who'd fought and killed those two thugs, right?"

She started to cry when he said, "Knock it off. I'm not sore about the way we met. I just want some answers about why."

"You *know* why, damn it! I wanted to get out to Devil's Island and I knew you could do it. We just came back from there, Dick! What on earth can you suspect me of?"

"I'm trying to think of something. You claim to be a reporter, and you've been reading up on the *Dreyfus Affair* more than I have. So how come I knew more about it than you? I could see Captain Dreyfus is sure to be freed the easy way. I suspected he'd know that even before he told me. You know what I think all you do-gooders are trying to do? I think you're trying to get him killed!"

"Dick, that's crazy. I was only trying to help the poor man."

"Bullshit. He's got Zola and Anatole France helping him already. He's got the leader of the opposition party. Clemenceau, demanding a new trial, and if Clemenceau wins the next election there will surely be one. There will also be a stink-to-high heaven when an impartial board of new officers starts sifting the evidence. They'll find all the wet rocks German agents and French traitors have been hiding under. Der Kaiser will be as embarrassed as hell. He's not ready for his next big war with France, yet, and a lot of plans will have to suffer some hasty changes once the French High Command knows where all the bodies are buried!"

She sniffled and said, "Well, maybe you're right. You just met a German spy master on the street and . . ."

"*I* never said he was a German spy master, Birdie. You asked me who he was, remember?"

"Damn it, Dick, you're trying to trick me."

"Trying, hell, I'm succeeding. Who are you really working for, Birdie?"

"I told you, James Gordon Bennet. Do you want to see my press pass?"

"I already have one of my own and I wouldn't know James Gordon Bennet if he walked in the door right now. Are you with that Claudette and her Jewish whatever?"

"For God's sake, do I look Jewish?"

"Not particularly. Neither did Claudette, and I don't think either of you are working to free Dreyfus for any Jewish organization. Dreyfus isn't interested in the new Zionist movement and few orthodox Jews would give a damn about an apostate who considers himself a Frenchman. On the other hand, a Central European is a Central European. Hebrew isn't anything like High German, but Yiddish is really a form of Old High German, spoken in the ghetto neighborhoods as a *lingua Franca.* A German agent would have little trouble speaking Yiddish. It would be like an Englishman putting on a thick brogue, and most of us wouldn't know the difference."

"Oh, then you think those Jews who tried to hire you were really German spies?"

"Think it? Hell, I'm sure of it. I turned them down because I could see it was a dumb move for any real friends of Captain Dreyfus. But it wouldn't be a dumb move for Germany. If I'd gone in slam-bang, Dreyfus would have been killed in the escape attempt. If not by the guards, by some other convict on the German payroll. But you were smoother and got me to actually go out there and . . ."

"And Dreyfus wasn't hurt!" she cut in, grabbing his hand and pressing it to her breast as she added, desperately, "You forget I went with you, Dick! Does that strike you as a smart move for a German agent who wanted a bloody riot out there?"

He moved his palm over her erect nipple, thoughtfully, as he frowned and said, "Okay, score one point for Birdie. But it was still pretty dumb and I'm feeling used and abused."

She sighed, "I may have been used, too. I admit playing a teeny-weeny trick on you to meet you, but . . ."

"You mean you blackmailed me into take one hell of a chance on getting all of us including Dreyfus killed!"

"I'm sorry. But it turned out all right in the end, didn't it? I really am a reporter and I really have a swell scoop and I really mean to try and get you a fair shake when I get back to the States, Dick. Can't we still be friends?"

She had his hand by the wrist and was helping him massage her breast now, so he leaned down to kiss her and when he started unbuttoning her bodice she kissed back enthusiastically. He decided he'd asked enough questions for now and noticed her chest felt a lot nicer bare. But as he started hauling up her skirt, she rolled her mouth away from his and gasped, "Oh, what ever are you doing? I don't want to go all the way. I just wanted to make sure there were no hard feelings."

"Baby," he said, "you'd be surprised at the hard feelings I have for you right now, but relax a bit and let me show you."

He rolled atop her as she got the skirt up around her waist and though she didn't resist, he parted her thighs with his hips and ran his free hand down to unbutton his fly. She protested, "Please, Dick, I'm not that kind of a girl!"

And then her eyes widened as he entered her and she gasped, "Oh, I mean I *wasn't* that kind of a girl!" and proceeded to move her hips to meet his thrusts with a skill that belied her maidenly modesty. He'd figured she had to have laid somebody to get the job, if she was really a girl reporter. He was willing to concede that newspaper women like Nelly Bligh held their positions on ability. Birdie may not have been a very clever secret agent and she was one God awful reporter but she was a terrific lay.

She climaxed fast, or said she had, and asked if they couldn't take their clothes off and do it right. That was the most sensible thing she'd said since he'd met her. So he stopped to peel her to the buff as she undressed him, kissing his flesh as she unbuttoned, and protesting all the while that she never did this sort of thing as a rule.

But apparently rules were made to be broken as they went at each other stark naked across the covers, she forgetting her Victorian upbringing and getting on top to tease her nipples across his lips as she moved up and down with a rotary wiggle to her rollicking little rump. She felt marvelous as he explored her with his hands. It aroused him to think of her and big Wilma at the same time, for the little redhead was another delightful contrast. The cynic who'd said all cats were gray in the dark hadn't gotten around much. No two women were alike, Allah be praised, and Birdie was a cut above average. He came as she contracted in a sobbing orgasm and fell limp with her firm little torso glued to his chest and a well turned knee in each of his arm pits while he ran his hand up and down her back, letting her milk him with her post orgasmic spasms. He decided he really wouldn't mind a hell of a lot if God pulled the plug on the universe right now. It was funny how detached and sane a man felt at a time like this. Someone had once said that nobody should make an important decision until he'd had a good meal and a good lay to settle his mind. Someone had been right.

Birdie kissed his collar bone and asked, "Are we friends, now, Dick?"

"Better than friends. I think we're lovers and I'm looking back to a long ocean voyage with you, Kid."

"Oh, we'll have to be careful aboard the steamer. I have my reputation to consider."

He didn't answer as she moved experimentally and added, "Of course, if we do it discreetly, nobody has to know."

"That's what I just said. We'll let the excitement die down and leave quietly in a day or so. Meanwhile, let's keep this room ashore so we don't have to be discreet."

"You don't want to leave in the morning, Darling?"

"...nt to? Can't! Until they think they have the situation under control the authorities here will be touchy as hell about people coming and going."

"Oh, speaking of coming, could we roll over? My legs are getting cramped."

He laughed, rolled atop without withdrawing, and cupped a firm buttock in each of his own palms as he began to move in and out with long slow strokes. Birdie moaned in pleasure and started pounding on his rear with her little bare heels as she pleaded, "Faster, don't tease me, Darling!"

So he did as she asked and, for a girl who didn't ordinarily do this sort of thing, she sure came fast and often. They'd wound up near the edge of the bed, so as he got one foot on the floor he doubled the other leg and got her in a sideways position with one leg around his waist and the other up like a can-can dancer so that he could kiss her toes while he rammed her at the new angle and caught up with her, feeling it from his insteps up as he exploded in her petite pelvis. She

148

said, "Don't stop!" but his one leg was cramping, so he got that off the mattress, too, and pounded her to glory with his feet on the floor and her tail bone on the edge as she flattened the bare soles of her feet against his chest and wriggled madly, gasping, "Oh, my God, I feel like a chicken on a spit and I love it!"

He did, too, but all good things must come, so after they did he withdrew to sit up, fumbled for a smoke and looked for his wits again.

He thumbed a match to light up, admiring the way the match flame played on the curves and dimples of his little bedmate. He lit up and offered a drag, but she said nice girls didn't smoke and added, "If we have to stay here a while I might be able to get a story on . . . what *is* going on, Dick?"

He hesitated, decided he wasn't giving anything away a lot of other people didn't already know about, and just in case she was as innocent as she claimed, he said, "I think the *Dreyfus Affair* is over. But that was a side show. If they can't knock him off to shut him up before he's released, the best move for his enemies would be to drop it and hope nobody takes it seriously. By now everyone's mind is made up one way or the other on the *Dreyfus Affair*. Those on his side will go on saying he's innocent no matter what, and the anti-Semites in France will insist he was guilty to the day they die."

"I hope you're right, Dear. But what's the main show?"

"Not sure. The original plan, as it was sold to me, was a convict uprising backed by some planters who don't like to pay taxes to Paris, with the wild tribes out in the bush keeping the French troops off base. But now the Ashanti have a new chief and it seems to be a whole new ball game. Damned few Frenchmen, even convicts, are going to want to shoot at the only army standing between them and a general massacre of Whites."

He took a thoughtful drag on his Claro and added, "If the guy's planning the coup have any sense, they'll follow our example and just lay low while the military shows M'Chuma the advantages of civilized behavior."

Birdie said, "I had a briefing on young Chief M'Chuma, Dick. He's said to be progressive. A French missionary I spoke to said he was counting on M'Chuma to settle the hash of some witch doctors who'd been getting out of hand. The old chief had some kind of lingering illness and the witch doctors had him in the palms of their hands. M'Chuma's not a Christian and doesn't seem to want to be one, but the missionary said he wasn't a bad sort, for a heathen."

Captain Gringo shrugged and said, "Whatever he is, he doesn't seem to want to join the rebels against the French army. He doesn't like the French on either side, judging from the way he's been shooting up both sides. He smoked up some guys I know are rebels, and then wiped out an army column. Your missionary must have met him before he came to power. You never know a man until you've played cards with him, gone after the same girl, or given him a little rank. I've seen more than one swell private turn into a raving bastard after making Lance Corporal. M'Chuma seems to be the same type."

"He may just be misunderstood, Dick."

"Lots of guys who kill people are just misunderstood, Kitten. It's not our problem. The French military can handle him now that they know he has modern weapons and doesn't like them. They have a handle on the rebel plot, too. So if those nuts rise in the near future they'll find out what a 155 shell can do. The little brushing up I've had on the local French powers that be have impressed me. The guys are pretty good for this neck of the woods. The easy wins against the rotting Spanish empire down here have made everybody think he's another Simón Bolívar. But Bolívar never took on a major colonial power."

Birdie wasn't listening. She said, "If you and Gaston could get me out to the bush to interview Chief M'Chuma . . ." So he cut in, "Have you been smoking opium, Dollface? The Goddamn French army is forming a defense line between here and the jungle hills, so in the first place there's no way to get to M'Chuma if you wanted to. And you wouldn't want to if you paid attention. The guy's a certified savage who hates Whites and the last time I looked you were white all over!"

"They say he speaks English, Dutch, and French," she insisted. The Missionary who told me about him said M'Chuma enjoys a good religious argument and had a twinkle in his eye while they discussed the advantages of Mumbo Jumbo over the Trinity. I'm sure he wouldn't hurt us if we approached him right, Dick."

"Honey, you don't approach armed tribesmen right. You don't approach them at all! I know you interviewed Geronimo. You should have known him when he was sniping at the

Tenth Cav from the rimrock. Atilla the Hun must have been a good host, when he wasn't mad at you. But M'Chuma is mad as hell and I know one of the reasons. One of his favorite wives was taken from him to serve as a love toy for White riff-raff and I shudder to think how he'd pay us back if he got his hands on a White woman about now!"

"Then you won't take me?"

He snubbed out his cigar and said, "Sure I'll take you. How do you want it this time, dog-style, old-fashion style, or shall we think up something new?"

She sighed and said, "Damn it, I wish you wouldn't treat me like a silly girl." But then as he rolled her over, pulled her up on her hands and knees to enter her again from the rear she started acting silly as hell and he assumed he'd convinced her it was wild enough here behind the French lines. He still had a lot to learn about Miss Birdie Peepers, girl reporter.

By morning he'd had Birdie in every position that didn't hurt and the street outside lay quiet under a soft rain. Off in the misty distance the talking drums of the Ashanti muttered hollowly and every once in a while the French gunboat offshore sent a round rumbling across the gray sky to remind anyone listening that La Belle France could be one tough lady if she was needlessly annoyed. He figured the French military had the same ideas as he about that machine-gun ambush of the jungle patrol and no doubt Herr Von Linderhoff was explaining a lot at the German consulate. Getting another round of ammo into the bush was going to be a problem, now that the authorities were on full alert. Any agents with the Ashanti would be leaving soon, if M'Chuma let them.

He dressed, woke up Birdie, and told her to have her trunk taken openly to the steamboat, explaining, "We've established that you were here all last night. By now they'll have snooped around the tramp steamer and satisfied themselves. Stay on board until Gaston and I join you."

"Where are you going, Darling?"

"Recon patrol. Have to make sure nobody went crazy and got picked up by the gendarmes last night in all the excitement. I'd hate to have you drop me off in Costa Rica with a warrant for my arrest wired ahead. I have to make a graceful exit by returning some front money, too. It's bad for a soldier of fortune's rep to double cross a client who looks like he might survive to gossip about it."

"Take me with you? I don't really have much of a story yet."

"Hey, I told you what to do, damn it. Nice girls don't associate with the kind of people I do business with. I'll give you an exclusive as soon as I know what the hell is going on."

He kissed her goodbye running a fond hand over her nude curves as he considered how great it would be to make love to her in broad daylight when he returned. The kiss turned out longer than planned and he almost gave in to her entreaty for another quick one. But he was firm and departed to look for Gaston. The bistro the little Frenchman had mentioned was closed and shuttered. Gaston had doubtless found someone to spend the night with, too. He grinned and went to the livery where they'd left the horses. He tipped the convict hostler to saddle the one he'd ridden in from Van Horn's and headed back to the plantation.

On the edge of town he was stopped by a roadblock manned by gendarmes and some convicts with arm bands and guns. It was obvious Frenchmen stuck together in a real emergency. They didn't arrest him, but the sergeant-in-charge said he was travelling at his own risk if he left town. He said he had to, so they told him he was crazy and let him through.

The security lines had been drawn around the real estate that mattered to the government, so there were a few scattered farmsteads and shanties along the road this close to town. But he saw they'd been deserted by their worried owners and stood open mouthed and empty. Or, at least, they *looked* that way until he spotted movement in the open doorway of a pasteboard and palm thatch shack to his right.

He rode on to a clump of gumbo limbo, cut suddenly off the road, and slid out of the saddle to tether his mount and circle back on foot through some growing corn, guns drawn.

He eased up to the rear of the suspicious shack, spotted an open back door, and moved in fast, guns cocked and ready for anything. Then he had a good laugh at his own expense when the stray cat he'd flushed darted out the front way, hissing and scared.

He holstered his six guns as he watched the cat cross the road, shaking his own head as he muttered, "Jesus, you're sure getting edgey in your old age." Then he stiffened as he saw three riders coming up the road, one of the riders wearing a white hat! Nobody was supposed to be on the damned road unless they had serious business to attend to.

Captain Gringo nodded as he drew his guns again and stepped closer to the doorway, albeit still in the shade of the overhanging thatch. He and the guys trailing him had the whole open countryside to their lonesomes, with no nosey French officials likely to butt in, and he was getting tired as hell of that white hat.

They were riding abreast, guns drawn, and trotting their mounts as they tried to catch up with a rider who'd vanished down the trail ahead of them. Captain Gringo dropped to one knee, bracing the gun in his right hand on his left knee to take dead aim as he let them line up in his gun sights, and then, when he had the three of them set up like domino pieces he emptied the six gun into them, rapid fire, dropped the first gun, and shifted the other to his right hand to continue the process as they rolled about in the dust with their horses running every which way!

He saw he was being redundant by the time he'd emptied the second six gun into them, so he holstered both empty weapons, drew his .38, and stepped out cautiously. He looked up and down the empty road, saw nobody seemed interested, and moved in on the men he'd ambushed, .38 ready for sudden moves.

There weren't any. The only one still breathing was the guy he'd blown out from under his white hat, and he was breathing sort of raspy. Captain Gringo walked over, kicked him in the ribs, and said, "Howdy, Klondike. I understand you've been looking for me."

Up close, the shot up mystery man was a middle-aged guy with a drinker's nose and yellow teeth bared in pain. He stared up at Captain Gringo and groaned, "Jesus, Kid, you're really as good as they said you were. I'm embarrassed as hell about this. I s'pect I'm kilt, too!"

"I think you're right. But you can still hurt, so let's talk about the way you've been tailing me. Are you working for any government in particular or are you just a bounty hunter?"

Klondike grimaced and said, "Bounty hunter is a harsh

153

way of putting it, son. I'm a licensed private detective, recognized as such by the French Colonial Government."

Captain Gringo nodded and said, "Right. That accounts for the way they let you sweep that gunfight in the old church under the rug. I don't suppose you saw fit to tell them there was a nice reward on my head, huh?"

"That wouldn't have been professional, son. Let the damned Frogs do their own work if they want to share in rewards, right? That head of yours sure is worth a lot of money, these days. But if you'll just get me to a doc we'll say no more about it."

Captain Gringo didn't answer.

Klondike licked his lips and said, "No shit, son, the rounds you put in me are starting to smart. You got me fair and square and it won't hurt you to get me some medical attention. Nobody but me and my boys knew about the papers on you, so the Frogs won't arrest you if you help me, see?"

"Oh, sure, that would be smart as hell of me, wouldn't it? If they don't have a telephone at the hospital you'll just have to send a note to the police."

"Now why in thunder would I want to do that, son? If the damned old Frogs arrested you they'd get the reward, not me!"

Captain Gringo glanced down at a nearby body and said, "You wouldn't want revenge for your men, huh?"

Klondike shook his head and answered, "Revenge ain't professional. I told the boys you were good and they knew the chances they were taking. I'll tell you true, as soon as I'm up and about I may try for that reward on you again. But I doubt like hell I'll be in shape to pester you for a good six or eight weeks, so what do you say, as one Yank to another?"

Captain Gringo smiled thinly and said, "I say you're a pretty dedicated son-of-a-bitch, but I admire your gall. I won't risk a hair getting help for you, but I'll fetch that horse of yours that's grazing up the road and I'll help you aboard. Then I'll take you with me to a place I know where you can't make trouble until I'm ready to move on."

Klondike tried to sit up, failed, and said, "I ain't sure I can ride, Walker."

Captain Gringo told him that was his problem and moved slowly up the road so as not to spook the bay gelding

154

cropping weeds a hundred yards up the road. The gunfire and the still-throbbing distant drums had the bay on the prod and he showed the whites of his eyes as Captain Gringo approached with soothing words. But the horse didn't resist when the tall American gathered the reins and headed back to the men he'd put on the ground. He saw Klondike had now managed to prop himself up on one elbow. As Captain Gringo led the bay toward him, the bounty hunter raised the derringer in his other hand. Captain Gringo let go of the reins, crabbed to one side as Klondike fired, and blew the side of the treacherous bastard's skull away with his own .38.

This time the spooked bay just kept running. Captain Gringo muttered, "Some guys just never learn!" as he stood there reloading all his guns. Then he walked to where he'd left his own mount and rode off, satisfied he'd cleaned up at least one small detail, but all too aware that he and Gaston still had a mess of chores cut out for them in the near future.

The open countryside was deserted and a man got lonesome fast riding by banana and coffee groves with jungle drums throbbing like some angry giant's pulse. He knew some of what he heard had to be just echo, but that didn't help much.

He made it to the Van Horn plantation and swung in, noting no guards at the gate. He rode past the house and dismounted out back by the convict compound. There wasn't a soul in sight. He left the horse saddled, tied to a corral post, and stepped into the nearest shed. The convict called Pepe was on a bunk with another guy. Pepe was on the bottom, playing the woman's part, and neither seemed aware of Captain Gringo as he grimaced and said, "Excuse me."

The convict on top looked up and flushed beet red, but Pepe smiled sensuously and said, "Oh, good morning, M'sieur. Would you like to be next?"

"No thanks. Where the hell is everyone, Pepe?"

"Out chasing Niggers. Claude and I were left here to guard the plantation."

"Carry on, then. Maybe someone in the house can tell me what the fuck is going on."

Pepe laughed, "Ooh, la, la! Fucking is my favorite subject!"

155

Captain Gringo left them to it and looked in the shed where the weapons were supposed to be stored. They were gone. Van Horn had taken three machine guns as well as the bigger boys in his outfit. The question now was where and why.

He walked up to the house and big blond Wilma met him on the porch, wearing nothing but an open kimono a size too small for her. She had one big cantalope peeking out at him as she sighed, "Oh, Dick, I thought you were with my brother and the others! This is marvelous! We have the whole house and the whole day to ourselves!"

As she flattened herself against him, he took her in his arms to be polite, but said, "Hey, we're on the back porch. What about the servants?"

"Screw the servants. Better yet, screw me. We can go into the solarium if you're bashful. Nobody comes in there unless I ring for them." Then, as she took him by the hand she added, with a low lewd laugh, "Nobody come in there but *us*, I mean."

As she led him down the veranda to the glassed in wing, he said, "Listen, Wilma, I have to know where your brother and the others went. This could be serious. The French authorities are on the alert and this is a lousy time to be leaving the plantation at the head of an armed mob of convicts!"

The solarium was furnished with potted tree ferns, hanging flower pots, some bamboo chairs and a big rope hammock with a nest of throw pillows. Wilma dropped her kimono on the tile floor and climbed into the hammock stark naked, like a big pink pig in heat, albeit a reasonably attractive one. She rolled on her back, hooked a knee over either side of the hammock and said, "This is serious, too. I'm so hot for you I could die. Where on earth were you last night? You'll never believe what I had to use to put myself to sleep!"

"A banana?" He grinned, feeling a tingle despite himself. The contrast was even better than he'd imagined, thinking of her while laying the little readhead. He wondered if thinking about Birdie while he pawed Wilma's big melons would be as interesting, but, damn it, he was in a hurry.

He said, "No fooling, Wilma, where did they go? I tried to ask that Goddamn Pepe but he was in the middle of a Greek orgy and didn't make much sense."

She laughed and said, "Oh, we haven't tried that. I'll let

156

you put it in like that if you'll play with my clit while you're doing it."

He saw she wasn't in the mood to talk but she laughed and said, "you must know, they went after the bush Niggers. They raided us last night. They've gone crazy."

"So I heard in town. But what about the authorities?"

"Oh, didn't you know? It's all right to arm convicts now. Paul has permission from the military. Just during this emergency, anyway. He saw the colonel last night and they say if he'll be responsible it's all right to issue arms to his plantation workers."

"Oboy! Your brother was right. The colonel is a moron. But even if he has permission to arm his workers, that wouldn't include the right to lead them anywhere, would it?"

"How should I know, dear? I guess nobody much cares who shoots M'Chuma now, as long as somebody does. Paul said we have to make sure the Niggers are subdued before he carries out any other plans. But never mind all that, what about us?"

"I have to get back to town," he said. "I'll never catch up with your brother's expedition, even if I was dumb enough to try alone in the bush. Will you be all right here?"

"I'll be all right after you make me come. The servants and me have plenty of guns and Paul said M'Chuma wouldn't dare advance this far into the coastal settlements."

Wilma got on her hands and knees on the tile floor and said, "Do it to me dirty. I like it Greek once I'm really hot!"

He tried to think of a graceful exit line. But what do you say to a naked lady who's pointing her derrière at you and fingering herself? He knew he'd had all he really needed and was just showing off, but what the hell, he knew he'd never see her again and they may as well part friends. In her own wild way, Wilma Van Horn had been a gracious hostess to him.

She welcomed him perversely as he rose on his knees, took a big hip in each hand, and let her guide him into her rose-bud anal opening. Even as she leaned back into him, she hissed, "Oh, I think's it's too big that way." It would have been too big if it had been all the way up, for despite the spread of her big smooth rump, she was tight as hell back there.

He asked, "Am I hurting you, Wilma?" and she said, "Yes, I love it. It makes me feel like a tiny virgin." So he did his best to thoroughly deflower her, if that was what they

157

were doing. He was pretty sure she'd done this before, too. So he let himself go and she gasped, "Harder, faster, I'm coming!"

She did, too, although he was damned if he could see why she should. But if Pepe and others like him enjoyed it there, there had to be something to it. He didn't have to worry about how he was getting there. It felt like he was in some little girl who'd somehow wound up inside a big bawdy blond. He exploded and she popped off to roll on her back, panting, "Put it in the front way, now!" So he fell forward to subside in her arms as she milked it to the last drop with her vaginal contractions. She was almost purring, sex drugged half asleep on the hard tiles. He was tempted to join her, but he withdrew, wiped himself off on her silk kimono train, and sat on a chair to dress as she murmured, "Oh, don't go. Let's take a little nap and do it some more."

"Later," he said, knowing it was a white lie, but she didn't argue as he rose, strapping on his gun rig. He looked down at her, wistful because he knew he'd probably never see her again and there sure was a lot of her to see. Then he blew her a kiss and ducked out to remount and ride back to town. He'd leave the horse in the livery for them to recover. He'd pay the livery, but keep the rest of his front money. Was it his fault Paul Van Horn had started without him? It was definitely time to haul ass out of this crazy country!

Captain Gringo met Gaston as he was retethering his mount in front of the hotel. The Frenchman said, "I've been looking all over for you. Where have you been?"

"Later. Is your horse still in the livery?"

"*Oui*, why?"

"We'd better put this one with it and board ship. Van Horn's gone nuts, too. If nobody's arrested Birdie and her crew we might be safe in weighing anchor."

"Ah, that is why I have been searching for you, Dick. M'selle Birdie is not there. The skipper says she took the first mate and a couple of other crewmen with her."

"With her? With her where?"

"Apparently into the jungle. I would not have let her go, but the skipper could not talk her out of it. She seems to think she can get an interview with M'Chuma, the Ashanti leader and . . ."

"Oh . . . shit!" sighed the tired American.

Gaston said, *"Oui,* she is obviously mad, if she's still alive. But there is nothing we can do about it, now. She left hours ago and by now will have reached the treeline. I think her skipper would leave without her and his crazy crew members, if we approached him right."

Captain Gringo cocked his head to the sound of a distant ship's siren and said, "Oh, oh! It looks as if he's already figured things out for himself!"

Gaston stepped away from the curb to stare down the street at the moving plume of smoke as the tramp backed off the pier at the far end. He spat, "Species of insects! What do they think they are doing, hein?"

Captain Gringo shrugged and answered, "Same thing we'd do, if we had the chance. You could have been more diplomatic, but I see you scared him shitless. So he's leaving while the leaving's good."

"Oui, and leaving us stranded, the cowardly son-of-a-raddled whore! What do we do now, Dick?"

"We get your horse and ride."

"Ah, *oui,* now you are making sense. The Dutch border is *très* far, but with two good mounts and a full day ahead of us . . ."

"We're not heading for Dutch Guiana. We have to overtake Birdie and those idiots with her."

"Merde alors, Dick! I just said you made sense! Do you mean to make a liar out of me? The girl and the three men with her are as good as dead. I see no reason to join them."

"Come on, I'll walk this mount with you to the livery. Let's see, we have three guns apiece and . . ."

"And M'Chuma has at least one machine gun and God knows how many spears! This is madness, even for you. I have a good mind to kick some reason into you."

"You aim a foot at me and you'll draw back a stump! We've got to try and save them, Gaston. Heroics aside, Birdie can still get us out of here and she's promised to publicize my case in the press."

"Ah, for a moment I thought it was love."

Captain Gringo shrugged and said, "Love's a strong word, but let's say we're a little close for me to want her dead. Come on, move your ass and let's see if we can save hers!"

159

The Ashanti drums sounded a lot louder as they reined in at the treeline, miles from anyone who could possibly be on their side. Captain Gringo stared morosely at the thick undergrowth between the soaring trees and said, "We'd better leave the horses here and leg it in the rest of the way."

Gaston sighed, "I agree the jungle is not the place for a horse. It's not the place for anybody with a bit of sense! Leaving aside the doubtless truculent personages beating those damned drums, we'll never find them, now. This jungle is not an orange grove, Dick. It spreads for hundreds of kilometers in every direction, *non?*"

As he dismounted, Captain Gringo said, "We're not navigating by sheer guesswork, damn it. We followed the direct trail from town and I see it leads into the Goddamn trees over there. Birdie and those crewmen are green horns, so they'd naturally follow the trail leading toward the drums, right?"

"*Oui,* but I hardly think it's right. This would seem to be the same trail Chambrun walked to his ambush the other day! Permit me to observe that the Ashanti know this trail and have no intention of letting anyone use it!"

Captain Gringo tethered both horses to a gumbo limbo as he pointed west with his chin and said, "Follow me. I'm not dumb enough to walk up a trail like a big ass bird. We'll scout parallel to it."

"Fine. How shall we be able to follow the trail if we are not on it?"

"The way Chambrun should have, if he'd been an old Indian fighter. Once we're under the top story trees, the going won't be too rough. But the sunlight on the trail allows all sorts of crud to sprout, so we just have to stay on the safe side of the natural hedgerow. Any ambushers should be on our side of the trailside bush, looking the other way for a sucker, see?"

"*Oui,* I see. Let us hope *they* do not see, hein?"

But Gaston followed as Captain Gringo bulled through the vertical wall of greenery, wishing he had a machete. Most of it was gumbo limbo and sea grape, but the jungle had evolved some son-of-a-bitching stuff that grew like oversized thorny celery and a sneaky little vine that thought it was chicken wire and bed springs, lacing the whole mess together.

Aside from a well swung machete, the only thing that stunted the rampant growth of tropic greenery was shade. So once they'd forced their way in a ways the underbrush faded into a sickly vine here and a monster toadstool there between the giant trees. The surface between the elephant gray buttress roots was like the floor of a henhouse that hadn't been cleaned in a very long time. Here and there a fallen branch lay mouldering but aside from being slippery and disgusting underfoot, the going wasn't difficult. To their right they could see the thick green wall of vegetable excess along the sunlit trail. In every other direction the view simply faded out in the cathedral gloom of the rain forest. High overhead the canopy of spinach green was pinpointed by twinkling stars of sky. But it seemed to be raining gently. There was a constant drip of condensed moisture, sap, and monkey shit. A band of howler monks kept pace with them, shouting insults down from the canopy and occasionally breaking off a twig to drop in their general direction. Between the howls of the simians they could hear the Ashanti drums throbbing through the gloom. Gaston spat and observed, *"Merde alors,* this is not a friendly forest, Dick."

Captain Gringo told him to shut up and swung closer to the trail. With their right flank guarded by the impenetrable hedgerow they were still open to attack from almost any other direction, and someone on the trail might hear them, if they didn't hear talking on the trail first.

The ground began to rise gently and the trail they were scouting started swinging in *S* curves, making for dots and dashes of cover as they proceeded up the slope more directly. They left the howler troop behind, no doubt bragging to one another about repelling an invasion of their territory, so it got gloomier and quieter, save for the distant drum beats and an occasional wet plop. They were about an hour in when Captain Gringo stopped and held a hand up for silence as he stared thoughtfully at the next big bend in the trail. Gaston stepped beside him and murmured, "I hear them. Hornets, *non?"*

"Flies, I think. Lots of 'em. Cover me."

Gaston drew one of his pistols as he stepped into a buttressed niche and Captain Gringo eased forward, drawing one of his own pistols. He came to the bend, moved around it, and saw the fresh stump of a huge mahogany. As he eased further he saw where the big tree had crashed down across the trail, flattening gaps in the trailside brush. He moved to the

161

log, looked along it and whistled under his breath. Then he signaled Gaston to join him as he followed the log through the break. The narrow trail the felled tree had blocked was a scene of carnage. Bloated bodies in the tropic whites of France lay sprawled in every position, covered with ants and the buzzing of flies he'd heard. Gaston joined him and gasped, "Ah, *quelle horreur!* This was Chambrun's column and one can see they had no chance!"

Captain Gringo stepped out on the red earth of the trail, picked up a spent cartridge and said, "This is a Lebel, French issue. So they got off a round or two going under. The ambushers took their guns, but, yeah, here's another couple of Lebel brasses. Chambrun had a lot to learn about this kind of fighting, but he and his boys tried. That must be him over there. I see they took his head, but they left his shoulder straps."

Gaston shook his head and said, "Now you see why I deserted the legion. Our damned officers always showed more courage than sense. I don't know what they put in their food at Saint Cyr, but when in doubt a French officer always orders a charge."

Captain Gringo shrugged as he moved down the line of soggy shot up and beheaded corpses. He stopped and looked back. Then he nodded and said, "I see how it went. They came to what they thought was a windfall log across the trail. If they had flank scouts out, the ambushers picked them off in silence. As they bunched up behind the log to figure the next move some son-of-a-bitch opened up with a machine gun and that's all she wrote. Most of these guys never knew what hit them. Look at that rag on the thorn bush there. There was no way to get off the trail and they were butchered like hogs in a bowling alley."

He stepped over the legs of a corpse on the trail, glanced down, and said, "Oh, no!"

Gaston joined him and nodded, *"Oui,* that is the heel mark of a woman's shoe. M'selle Birdie got this far and did not like what she saw, since the one footprint in the soft spot there is moving the other way, *non?"*

Captain Gringo heaved a sigh of relief and said, "Yeah, there's a man's heel mark and he was headed back to Sinnamary in a hurry, too. Birdie and the three dopes got this far, saw how serious things could get out here in the bush and had second thoughts."

"Let us follow them, hein?"

Captain Gringo hesitated, then nodded and said, "Yeah, there's a time to save the world and a time to look out for your own ass. I don't know how the hell we're going to leave Sinnamary without that ship, now. But Birdie will be waiting for us at her place and we'll work it out."

They headed down the trail, spotting an occasional small sharp heel mark as they made better time on the firmer footing. They'd traveled maybe a quarter mile when they came around another bend and stopped, thunderstruck. Gaston made the sign of the cross and murmured, *"Mon Dieu,* is there no mercy in heaven?"

Four human heads were impaled on stakes across the trail. Mercifully the faces were turned to the east, facing civilization, but there was no mistaking the long redhair hanging down from Birdie Peeper's severed head. The stakes were crawling with ants. The message was obvious.

Captain Gringo retched, growled deep in his chest, and turned around with a look of cold fury. As he started back up the trail Gaston tugged at his sleeve, pleading, "Let it go Dick. I agree with your feelings, but the odds are simply impossible!"

Then, as he saw he'd have had as much luck stopping a moving switch engine, Gaston followed, muttering, *"Merde alors,* this disgusting loyalty is going to get me killed yet!"

Captain Gringo bulled past the bloated corpses at the ambush and returned to the log blocking the trail. As he started to move sideways into safer ground he glanced over the big bole and said, "Oh, Chambrun's guy did better than I thought!"

A French soldier lay face down on the far side of the log, still wearing his head. Half under him lay a naked black corpse with a Lebel rifle pinning it to the trail with it's long trifoil bayonette. Gaston said, *"Oui,* this soldier advanced well, despite all those bullet holes in him, and at least one Ashanti paid for the ambush with his wretched life. This little scene seems to have been overlooked amid the no doubt confusing aftermath of the attack."

Captain Gringo moved thoughtfully up the trail. Gaston said, *"Mais non,* Dick. We should not be in this natural trap."

Captain Gringo said, "Shut up, I see something else." He stepped to the thick wall of the undergrowth and hauled a tripod leg he'd spotted from the greenery. A Maxim machine gun and it's trailing ammo belt was attached to the tripod. As he sat it upright on the trail and dropped to one knee he nodded, yanked the arming lever, and ejected a bent round

163

as he nodded again and said, "Give a greenhorn a gun like this and he'll jam her every time."

Gaston grinned and said, "Incredible! They abandoned a machine gun in working order?"

"They didn't know it was in working order. They thought it was busted and who's going to haul a useless load of scrap metal through a jungle?"

He looked at the coils of ammo belt and added, "This is a fresh belt. They used one on the French column and screwed up trying to reload. Things are looking up for *us*, though!"

He gathered the ammo belt in a coil, shoved his left forearm through it, and unlocked the tripod pin to lift the machine gun bodily from it's mount. He hefted it and said, "The water jacket's empty. Remind me to only fire short bursts."

"I'd rather get you to accompany me to Sinnamary. Even with a machine gun the odds are *très* disgusting, Dick!"

"Yeah, but you've got to admit they're a lot better than they were a few minutes ago. Let's go!"

He moved back to the break with the heavy Maxim over his shoulder and followed the downed tree into the open gloom beyond. Then he started walking uphill, toward the drums. Gaston could hear as well as anybody, so he swore and said, "How many warriors do you think M'Chuma has with him at the moment, my old and reckless?"

"Don't know. From what I've heard of the Bush Negroes it could be about a thousand all told. I doubt if we'll find more than five hundred or so at his main camp. Those drums wouldn't still be beating if they were all assembled in one place. Since they're talking drums, some sub-chief's might be arguing back and forth about their next move."

Gaston groaned and said, "Not more than five hundred, *merde alors!* You don't have five hundred rounds in that gunbelt, you idiot!"

"Quit your bitching. We have our six guns, too."

"Ah, *oui,* I forgot our side arms. No doubt we can gun the entire Ashanti nation with a couple of braces of pistol fire."

M'Chuma, Lord of the jungle and king of the Ashanti sat on his gilded hardwood stool wrapped in jaguar skins and wearing a feathered crown as he listened with a frown to the distant talking drum of M'Fisi's band. The young chief was

164

surrounded by a bodyguard of warriors stripped for action and leaning on the hardwood shafts of their long spears while his own drummer waited nearby for M'Chuma's next dictated command. No women or children were at this end of the village, for war was a man's business. M'Chuma scratched at his balls under the smelly jaguar robes his position made him wear despite the heat. He wanted a woman. But that would have to wait, too. Ashanti warriors fought better with hardons, according to tribal tradition, so nobody had any sex for days.

His drummer turned and said, "M'Fisi says the French are many and that the shelling from the sea has made it unsafe to travel, O King."

M'Chuma growled, "I understand drum talk, you fool. M'Fisi is well named. I don't know what a hyena is, but the elders say that in the old country they were cowardly beasts, too."

M'Chuma, The Iron One in his own dialect, turned to one of his captains and said, "If we march alone, many of our women will be widows."

The captain, a graceful man of thirty, shrugged and said, "All women will be widows sooner or later if they belong to real men. My king has been insulted. I am ready to die anywhere he sends me."

There was a bubble pipe burble of agreement and M'Chuma rose, holding out a hand to his spear carrier. But as he took his spear by it's gilded shaft a runner staggered into view, dropped on all fours before M'Chuma, and panted, "Two White men are coming, alone, O Kind and Merciful King. Don't order my death until you see I do not lie!"

M'Chuma frowned and growled, "Alone? Coming this way?"

"I swear it, Lord of the universe under the trees! They are on the trader's trail, walking as if they owned it. One is short and the other is as tall as you, meaning no insult to your majestic carriage! They are armed, but their actions do not seem threatening. Our scouts are watching from all sides, of course. But we thought you'd like to know before we killed them."

M'Chuma's guard captain said, "Let me kill them, my King. It's good to go into battle with blood on one's blade, even if they are only lost travelers."

"No," M'Chuma said. "I must study this strange happening.

My children know that some Whites are not evil and there is wisdom in the words of this runner. I shall hear what they have to say before I dance to their blood."

And so, as Captain Gringo had gambled, M'Chuma and his bodyguard advanced down the trail to meet them. As they spotted the crowd of Ashanti blocking the trail ahead, Gaston sighed and said, "Well, your ears have led us to the black bastards. Now let us pray your mouth can get us out of this alive, hein?"

Captain Gringo grounded the heavy machine gun and un-buckled his gunbelt to let it fall at his feet as Gaston swore softly and did the same. The gesture was not lost on M'Chuma, who handed his spear to a servant and strode forward to speak to them. He said, "I am M'Chuma, King of the Ashanti and Lord of tributary tribes. What are you doing in my forest?"

Captain Gringo said, "You speak good English. I'm called Captain Gringo and this is my friend, M'sieur Verrier."

"He is French? I am sorry, but he must die. I don't think I wish to kill any English or Dutchmen but the French have abused us and we mean to pay them back."

Captain Gringo shook his head and said, "You're wrong. It's not the French you're after. It's Van Horn, the planter. He's tricked both you and the French. As we speak he's on his way here with an armed band and he means to wipe you out."

M'Chuma frowned and said, "Impossible. Van Horn has traded with us for years. He says he is our friend."

"He says a lot of things. He's lied to the French government and gotten a hunting permit to kill Ashanti and seize their lands. He lied to us. We thought he was arming to rebel against France, but he's not that dumb. He wants to expand his plantation lands and the treaty you have with the colony forbids this as long as your people live in this forest at peace with France."

M'Chuma looked dubious and asked, "How do you know so much about me and my people? You are strangers here."

Captain Gringo nodded and said, "That was why it took me a while to figure out Van Horn's game. I know more about you than you think. Your wife, Tonda, told me you were wise and good. I hope she was right."

M'Chuma's face softened and then went hard as he asked, "You spoke to my woman before the French took her away to sell in another colony?"

Captain Gringo muttered, "Oboy." Then he said, "If Van

Horn told you that, it was another lie. He told me she'd run off to rejoin you when she learned you were the new chief. The French government had nothing to do with her disappearance."

"Then where *is* my Tonda, damn it?"

"I'm sorry, your Majesty, I think they killed her and buried her somewhere. They didn't expect you to become chief and they were afraid she'd tell you how she'd been treated on the Van Horn plantation."

M'Chuma swayed as if struck, recovered, and gasped, "That Dutchman defiled my woman? He swore the last time we spoke that she was only a guest at his plantation, to save her from the witch doctors who are no longer with us. He said he was my friend! I believed this!"

"Yeah, he still thinks he has you fooled. That's why he left his sister and plantation guarded only by a couple of fairies as he went looking for you. He's got over a hundred armed convicts and two machine guns like this one. He used to have three, but he used this one to ambush some French soldiers who wanted to parley with you. The French think you did it. That's why they keep lobbing those shells into this bush."

"You are confusing me with all this news! I know nothing of an ambush!"

"I didn't think you did. They set it up so you and your people would get the blame. They even left a dead Black man posed with a dead Frenchman that simply never could have moved that far with so many bullet holes in him. Fortunately, I found them first and couldn't figure out why a war party that had time to take heads hadn't recovered their own dead and a perfectly good rifle."

"Heads? We are not headhunters. Some Indian tribes take heads, but it is not an Ashanti custom."

"I know. I read that in a book. It made me wonder when we found all those decapitated bodies. I couldn't see you manning machine guns, either, no offense. That's why I came to warn you. By bulling through without wasting time on scouting we've beaten Van Horn's column, but he knows where your village is and he can't be far behind. Do you want to help me or do I have to take them on with just my friend, here?"

M'Chuma frowned thoughtfully before he said, "You say you have dared my wrath to help us. I find this strange. Who asked you to take part in this business?"

Captain Gringo's eyes were cold as he said, "Van Horn killed a woman of mine, too. He left her head on a stake to make it look like you and your people did it. If you need another reason, I just don't *like* the fat bastard! I don't want him to get even richer by trickery and slaughter."

"But I don't know you. How do I know this is not another White man's trick?"

"Easy. Help me set up a defense of your village. If I'm not telling the truth, it won't be needed. If Van Horn's men get here before we're set up it will be too late!"

M'Chuma nodded and said, "That makes sense. Come with us. We shall do as you say, for now. But if you are a liar, you will never leave my village alive. It is true we don't take heads and the story about us eating people is another lie. But there are many ways 'to make a man die slowly, and both of you will know them well if this is some kind of a trick!"

Chef turned to Van Horn in another part of the jungle and said, "Hey, listen, the drums have stopped!" as he held up a hand to halt the rag-tag column of white clad convicts. Van Horn peered ahead through the dripping gloom and said, "Push on, I know where M'Chuma's village is and those drums were a bore in any case."

"Yes, but doesn't it mean they've all assembled, Le Grand Chef?"

"I hope so. Our two machine guns set to fire crossfire into the grass shacks should clear the vermin well. I wish to God you hadn't abandoned that other one, Chef."

"Look, I told you it was busted. That American you hired to show us the ropes warned that they got out of order easily. Where the hell did he and that little guy vanish to, anyway? I wish I had them with us right now."

Van Horn shrugged and said, "Captain Gringo was too smart to be useful. He doubtless left on that American tramp steamer that we spotted from the ridge back behind my place. It's just as well. We'd have had to get rid of him later and he might have been a disposal problem. Once we wipe out the Ashanti the colonel will be easy to deal with and, oh, look, another mahogany and there's a nice quinine tree just beyond."

Chef grinned and said, "Yeah, there's a fortune in here,

even before we clear it for crops. Somebody should have run the spear-chuckers off this prime land a long time ago, Le Grande Chef."

Van Horn smiled smugly and said, "I know. They weren't as smart as me."

They came to a narrow game trail. Van Horn nodded and said, "I know where we are, now. As I planned, it took longer coming this way, around the back of M'Chuma's village, but they'll never be expecting an attack from this direction." He held up a hand and called back, "All right, boys, listen to me. We'll be coming to the cleared millet fields around the main Ashanti village in a few moments. I want you to form a skirmish line like that American taught you. We'll come out of the treeline abreast and it's only a short advance across open ground to their stockade. Move shooting from the hip in a crouch as you cross the cleared ground and the millet will give you some cover, but move fast and don't stop until you reach the stockade. The machine guns will hose ahead of you and the stockade was never intended to stop anything more serious than a goat. Our bullets will go right through it and the first men to reach it should be able to hammer it flat with their body weight. Smash the stockade and flatten out to pick your targets. The machine-gun fire will sweep over you and blow the straw huts down like the big bad wolf in that story. The idea is to lick them good and make sure no survivors go whimpering to the government with a tale that might jibe with mine. Are there any questions?"

A convict held his hand up and yelled out, "Yeah, Le Grande Chef. What if the black bastards are expecting us?"

Van Horn shrugged and said, "I don't expect that, but if they are, so what? They don't have a dozen old trade muskets between them and if you're dumb enough to let a Nigger get near you with a spear or machete then you don't deserve to live. Naturally, any casualties we take will add to the veracity of this punitive expedition."

There was a worried mutter, but no further questions. Van Horn grinned and said, "Right. Let's move it out in line of skirmish."

The long ragged line of convicts started moving abreast through the trees, guns at port with the machine-gun crews on either flank, and Van Horn and Chef in the middle. They saw light ahead as the forest floor tilted down to a murky jungle streamlet. As they reached the bottom of the draw they paused, for beyond the stream lay a clear slope up to

169

the Ashanti stockade on higher ground. Chef said, "They've just harvested the millet, the bastards! The stubble is only ankle deep!"

Van Horn hesitated, said, "Well, apparently it was riper than I thought. But, hell, there's nothing moving up there. We've caught them napping. So let's go!"

He pointed his six gun at the stockade and charged forward, firing, as the machine guns on either side opened up to blow splinters from the flimsy stockade and the whole line surged forward, shooting from the hip!

There was no return fire, not even a spear, and as the skirmish line moved up the gentle slope the gun crews ceased fire to lug the heavy weapons forward. That's when Captain Gringo and M'Chuma sprung their trap.

The big American rose from an apparently harmless clump of weeds on Van Horn's right flank, firing his own machine gun from the hip along the line of advancing convicts while Gaston and a squad of M'Chuma's warriors jumped one gun crew crossing the stream and filled them with six gun rounds and spears. At the far end, M'Chuma in person stepped from behind a tree buttress to blast his trade musket, charged with a handful of nails, into the other machine gun squad and then stood, looking dignified, as his grinning warriors mopped up, shouting "S'kee! S'kee!" as they plunged their blades into the screaming Whites!

The main party, caught in the open on the stubble Captain Gringo had ordered cleared, went down like duck pins as he hosed them with hot led, aiming low so that a man with his legs shot out from under him could fall into the fire. The gun on his hip got hot but he ignored the blisters and gambled on the head spacing as he emptied the belt into anything and everything that moved. But of course one or more made it back down to the stream since he couldn't be everywhere at once with his lead spitter.

Chef, wounded badly but too scared to let it slow him down, splashed through the mud, screaming in terror, as he met a grimly smiling Ashanti and his spear. He gasped, "Oh, no!" as the Ashanti drove the tip in just above the belt buckle and ripped up, spilling Chef's guts, and Chef, in the mud.

Van Horn staggered for the trees like a dignified drunk, three bullets throbbing hot in his fat as he wondered what had gone wrong. Gaston stepped over a dead convict machine gunner and raised his pistol. Van Horn looked owlishly at him and said, "Please don't!" as Gaston fired, pumped another round into him to make sure, and muttered, "I didn't do it for you, my friend."

A few others lay still alive, moaning on the stubble, as M'Chuma joined Gaston and said, "I wish you hadn't done that. I wanted to talk to him about my woman as he died over a slow fire."

Gaston said, "Oh, I am *très* mortified at my own inability to think ahead!"

Captain Gringo dropped the Maxim before it could blister his hands further and walked down to join them. M'Chuma grinned boyishly and clapped him on the shoulder, saying "You are a good fighter as well as a newfound friend, Captain Gringo. I'm so sorry you are not black. You would have made a good Ashanti."

Another warrior came over to burble at M'Chuma. The king nodded and bubbled back, explaining as he left, "I said it was safe for the women, children, and old ones to return to the village. He says they did little damage firing into the empty huts. I still don't know how you could foresee an attack from this direction."

Captain Gringo said, "It was the best way for them to hit you and I gave them some basic infantry tactics before I caught on to what they were up to."

M'Chuma laughed, "I'd like you to teach my men some, too, before you leave. You shall stay while we have a victory feast. I will give you trade rum and women and we will make a night of it as the survivors scream over slow fires, eh?"

Captain Gringo grimaced and said, "It sounds like fun. But I have a better idea. You said you liked my advice, right?"

"Yes, I never would have thought to clear the millet. If only you weren't such an ugly color I'd make you a general. What is this idea of yours?"

"I want you to deliver the few prisoners alive to the French government under a parley flag. Wait, don't cloud up and rain all over me until I've finished! The French still think you and your people ambushed Chambrun's column. These convicts know you didn't. The French will get the whole story of Van Horn's plot out of them and you won't have those 155s dropping in on you anymore, see?"

M'Chuma scowled and said, "I'm not afraid of the damned French."

"No, your Majesty, but they're sure afraid of you and I think you'd better make peace before somebody gets hurt."

M'Chuma turned and gazed up the corpse-covered slope.

Then he laughed and said, "Ha, somebody on my side, you mean. Wait until I tell that cowardly sub-chief, M'Fisi, about the fun he missed here. You are an awful spoilsport, but I see the wisdom in your words. We shall turn the survivors over to their government. They are convicts already and the French will keep them even longer as slaves. That will serve them right!"

He turned back to the fat corpse of Van Horn, spat on it, and added, "I never would have let this one go. There were many questions I wanted to ask him about my woman, Tonda."

Captain Gringo's voice was gentle as he said, "She loved you to the end, M'Chuma. That's all you have to remember about the lady."

M'Chuma stared soberly at him, a dangerous question in his eyes. Then he nodded and said, "If you say this is true, it must be so. You are right. Nothing else that happened matters, now. Come, my warriors can deal with this carrion. You and my little friend Gaston have never received a proper Ashanti welcome and we have much to celebrate, thanks to you."

The next morning Gaston limped over to Captain Gringo's hut and called out, "Dick, are you still alive?"

Captain Gringo looked up from where he lay on piled skins with a sleeping black beauty nestled on either side of him and said, "I think so, but what the hell was in that rum we drank?"

Gaston came in, hunkered down, and sighed, "It tasted like gunpowder. I vaguly remember servicing eight women before I passed out. Do you think this could be possible?"

"We were both too drunk to count. What's going on out there? It seems pretty quiet."

"Everybody left is sleeping off the party," Gaston said. "M'Chuma just left with the prisoners under a flag of truce. I thought you'd like to know."

"Yeah, good, I told him I wasn't in the mood to talk to any French cops and he seemed to understand. I used to have some clothes around here. Let's give them a few hours lead and see about getting our own tails out of here."

As he sat up, one of the girls sleeping with him moved drowsily to fondle his shaft and Gaston cackled, "Well, now, who says we have to hurry, hein?"

172

He started to unbuckle his pants but Captain Gringo said, "Knock it off. You can jerk off on the trail if you're still horny, you old goat. I want to get somewhere sensible before dark and it's already broad daylight."

He gently removed the girl's hand and slid out from between them as Gaston sighed, "Oh, I like the little one. Was she good?"

"They're all good, and let's not wake them up for Petes sake!"

"Let Pete get his own ass," chuckled Gaston as he handed Captain Gringo his pants. The tall American started dressing as the one who'd been playing with him groped absently, found the other girl's lap, and began to finger her. The girl being stimulated fluttered her eye lashes, smiled sweetly, and murmured something that sounded like dirty words through a bubble pipe. Gaston said, "I like the sounds they make. It saves so much tedious dialogue when a woman has no proper way of saying no. Let me just tear off a quick one, Dick? She's very pretty."

"No, Goddamn it. We've still got to get out of French Guiana and the army may send somebody up here to look things over after they talk to M'Chuma."

"Ah, you do have a convincing way with words. Sleep on, my pet. We must march."

As they left, the Ashanti girls weren't exactly sleeping, but they probably had no idea who they were going sixty-nine with, so what the hell.

Outside, a couple of little kids were screwing in the dust. No doubt inspired by the example of their elders. Gaston chuckled and said, "I've never had one quite that young, but why can't we take them along for pets?"

"You want the little boy, right? Let's see, there's a trail leading north, but we don't know chief M'Fisi and he might want to prove he's a he-man on white strangers. We can't go back to the plantation. Ol' Wilma will probably get to keep it, but it's likely to be crawling with gendarmes for a while."

"*Oui*, no doubt M'selle Van Horn will screw her way out of her late brother's mistakes. We can't go west. There's nothing but jungle all the way to Brazil and the Brazilians have *très fatigue* questions for us, too. That leaves the horses we left, *non?*"

"If they're still there. Let's find out."

They didn't. They took the main trade trail toward Sinnamary and made good time downhill for a few hours. But then, about noon, they heard voices in the jungle ahead and stopped. Gaston listened and said, "Ah, a burial detail from town. No doubt *très* curious as to certain details, *non?*"

"Yeah, we'd better swing wide and try to come out just above Sinnamary."

"We are going into town again? Is that wise, Dick?"

"Wiser than being caught out in the open country by excited patrols. Traffic up and down the coast is going to come to a halt for the next few days. They'll have road blocks all over until they get a handle on just what the hell's been going on. But our faces are known in Sinnamary and nobody ought to be looking for us in particular."

"Ah, *oui,* we can hole up in the room you shared with the unfortunate redhead, *non?*"

"Don't be a dope. By now they've brought her head back to town and some cop will be sitting on her steamer trunk. Where did you hole up the other night in town?"

"Oh, we can't go there. I had a rather dramatic discussion with the lady's pimp."

"Jesus, you got in trouble?"

"Mais non, he did. I ask you, is it just for a woman to pick a man up in a bistro and take her to her room *before* she tells him she is a business woman? I told her her suggestion that I pay later was too droll to consider, so she called for her pimp and I was forced to show them both I am not a tourist to be taken advantage of, hein?"

"Oh, shit, that means you have a waterfront thug looking for you as well as the cops!"

Gaston shook his head and said, *"Mais non.* I doubt if the bodies have been discovered yet. I locked the door as I made my departure."

"Jesus H. Christ! You killed them both?"

"Oui, it was the *practique* thing to do, since only a fool leaves a witness who keeps threatening him with tiresome words about the police. Apparently she was fond of her rather apelike pimp. So I left them quiet in each other's arms. When someone notices the smell, let us hope they will assume it was a lover's quarrel. I left the knife in her hand."

Captain Gringo groaned aloud and said, "Jesus, you keep saying it makes you nervous to travel with *me!* Okay, we can't go to Birdie's and we can't go to your late lady friend's so that leaves . . . I know, the hotel. We have some money and business will be slow there now, in any case."

174

"I love a good joke. But didn't you say both a British and a German spy were staying at the hotel, Dick?"

"Yeah, but I doubt either Liza or Von Linderhoff would turn us in."

"I admire your trusting soul, but what if you're wrong?"

"We'll be in a hell of a mess. Do you have any better suggestions?"

"*Non*, let us press on to Sinnamary and hope for the best, hein?"

The hotel's room clerk looked down his nose at them until he saw the color of their money. Then he sh ved the register at them and placed two keys beside it, saying, "You will both need a room with a bath, of course."

Captain Gringo smiled as he signed and said, "We've been out in the bush." And the clerk sniffed again and said, "So it would seem, M'sieur."

Gaston signed and followed Captain Gringo up the stairs, muttering, "That was a bit fresh if you ask me. Do I smell that bad to you, Dick?"

"I can't tell. I'm all covered with the same jungle mold and sweat, too."

They came to their adjoining doors and he said, "So far so good. We'd better get cleaned up and a fresh change of clothes wouldn't hurt. You know my size and ought to attract less attention on the street right now. I'm going to stay holed up until I'm in shape for questions from a curious cop."

Gaston agreed and they split up. Captain Gringo found that the suite he'd taken was layed out like Liza's. Hers was just down the hall, as he remembered. He wondered if she was still here and why he cared. Since the last time he'd been with the skinny tomboy from British Intelligence he'd been screwed skinny and his poor old love tool needed a rest.

He locked the door, undressed, and moved naked into the adjoining bath to run a tub. The water was warm and clear and he got in before it filled, luxuriating as it rose around his grimy flesh. He'd had no idea he'd gotten so dirty.

A voice from the other room called, "Dick?" and he cursed himself for not having thought to bathe with a gun strapped on. That voice was far too high to be Gaston and even the Frenchman couldn't have a key to this place!

175

Liza Smathers appeared in the doorway to say, "Oh, there you are. What are you doing here?"

"What does it look like I'm doing? I'm taking a bath. How the hell did you get in here?"

"I meant what are you doing in Sinnamary; I thought you'd left. I saw you in the lobby and followed to ask why you hadn't left with that tramp steamer as everyone thought. As to how I got in, that's a silly question to ask a trained spy who wears hair pins, isn't it?"

She came in and sat on the commode, unbuttoning her dress as she added, "I'm glad you're still here. I need you." Then she sniffed and said, "God, you smell like you've been fucking."

"I just came in from the jungle. Most of it's monkey shit. Why are you taking your clothes off, Liza?"

"I thought I'd join you. But that's not what I really need you for. You've no idea what a break this is. Everybody thinks you're gone. It gives us the advantage we need on the Germans."

He stared down wistfully at the murky water around his flaccid shaft and said, "Slow down and let me get used to one thing at a time, Liza."

She dropped her dress on the tiles, unbuckled her shoes, and said, "I intend to, Darling."

As she rose to move her slender boyish body over to the tub he said, "Wait a minute, this water's dirty." But she said, "You know I like you dirty, you lovely animal." And then, as he opened the tap wider and pulled the plug she climbed in, putting a bare foot on the bottom of the tub on either side of his hips. As she lowered herself she mused, "You sure fill a tub, don't you? I don't think there's room."

He said, "Hell, let me up and we'll do it right on the bed out there."

Liza laughed and said, "We've done it in bed already. Let me see, now . . . oh, I know."

She raised a wet foot to hook one knee over the rim of the tub as he admired the view up between her thin athletic thighs. She braced her weight on her hands to either side, raised the other leg to hook it the same way, and lowered herself, wide spread and gingerly as she added, "I think you'll have to aim it, Dear."

He didn't think he could, as it was still half soft despite the exciting approach. But as he soaped it, it rose to the occasion and he held it at attention while Liza dropped into his

176

lap, legs spread at an astounding angle as she threw her head back, thrusting her tiny tits at him, and sighed, "Oh, delicious!"

He couldn't do much, pinned to the hard bottom on his butt, but the saucy English girl began to move up and down, splashing soapy water up between them with each thrust. For a girl who likes sex dirty, she sure was scrubbing his belly nice with her soapy little brush and it looked wild as hell.

Liza came fast and subsided as he still throbbed within her. He said, "Hey, don't stop now!" And she said, "I ought to. I'm a little cross with you. Who was that redhead I saw you with the other night?"

"Just a friend. For God's sake, Liza, move!"

"Phoo, if I know you, you did this to her, too."

"Never in a bathtub. If you're not going to move, let's get out and do it right."

The thin English beauty began to oblige him with teasing movements as she said, "I ought to make you suffer, but I know she chartered that tramp steamer, so now I have you all to myself again. How come you didn't leave with her? Wasn't she any good in bed?"

He didn't like to speak ill of the dead, but if Liza didn't know anything he wasn't going to tell her. She was a fantastic lay, but about as trustworthy as a basket of cobras, and he knew she wanted more than this.

Meanwhile, nothing felt better than Liza's soapy snatch, so he got his own hands on the edges and lifted them both from the tub as she giggled and clung to him wetly, marvelling, "My God, you're strong as a bull, too."

He moved over to the commode and sat her on it, still inside. She gasped, "I don't have to go to the toilet, damn it!" Then as he began to move in his new kneeling position, she leaned back against the flush tank and said, "Oh, how terribly ingenious!"

He didn't answer. He came, amazed that he still could. She said, "I felt that." And he said, "Yeah," and picked her up and carried her out to the bed. They were both soapy and wet as he placed her on the coverlet. He slithered on top between her slippery thighs, and then, as he tried to get it in again, he couldn't. Liza panted, "Hurry, I want more!" as he fumbled his limp slippery traitor against her pink wet opening. He said, "Funny, this has never happened before!"

Liza slid a hand down between them to help, felt what was there, and sighed, "Oh, dear, that redhead must have been too greedy to believe!" She started to laugh when he said, "Damn it, she had nothing to do with it. I was at a party last night and they must have put something in my rum."

"I smelled what they put in your rum, you poor dear. But, oh well, God knows it's nice and clean. Let Mamma raise her little bashful boy."

She rolled him on his back and kissed her way down to his disaster, taking it limp in her mouth as she cocked a leg over to expose her open groin to his bemused stare. He stiffened as she swallowed the whole smaller-than-usual offering and he didn't know whether he liked it or not. There were times when common sense told a guy to quit. But then as he began to tingle in her teasing mouth he decided he might survive after all. Liza moved her hips from side-to side as she lowered her excited gates of heaven to be kissed in turn and, what the hell, it sure looked nice and clean, so he put two fingers in her vagina, shoved a pinky in her winking rectum, and began to tongue her clit. She moaned and tried to swallow him alive at the other end as it started rising again. She gagged but gamely kept at it. Fully erect now, he could tell what she wanted from the way her internal muscles were milking his questing fingers. He licked her turgid clit until she came and fell weakly off him. Then he swapped ends and mounted her right to finish as she pleaded, "Wait, I'm too excited and ... oh, heavenly!"

This time he knew he was finished for a while, so he said so. She said, "We'll worry about your impotency later. If that's what you want to call it. My God, you know how to satisfy a woman. It makes seducing you on Her Majesty's Service a pleasure."

He sat up on one elbow to study her as he said, "Now we get to the really dirty stuff, right?"

She put a hand in his lap to fondle him as she smiled and said, "I did have another proposition for you, Dick."

"I was afraid of that. I thought you and the guys you work for didn't need me this time. I guess it would be a waste of time to remind you I've never been British, don't want to be British, and haven't a thing against the French if only they'll leave me the hell alone?"

She said, "I assure you what I have in mind is in the interest of both France and your own country as well as mine."

"Yeah, you and that agent Graystoke are always telling me that, but every time I do a job for you some son-of-a-bitch wants to shoot me."

"This time it's simple. Dick. First hear my offer. I don't know what you're doing here in French Guiana, but if you have any sense you'll get out, fast. The French are sending in their own counterintelligence teams and they're good."

"I know. I've been trying to get out. It ain't easy."

"You're wrong. I have a private yacht moored in the harbor. I know you feel safest in Costa Rica, so I'm willing to drop you and Gaston off there as we cruise north. How do you like it so far?"

"A safe sea cruise with you? That's hardly twisting a guy's arm, Doll. Get to the part I won't like."

She jerked his shaft playfully and said, "I'm looking forward to a sea voyage with you, too. All right, I was sent here to make sure the Germans didn't get away with their planned assassination of Captain Dreyfus. You must know something about the case?"

"Sure. If Dreyfus finds himself free and talking, it's going to fuck up a lot of German spies in the French army."

"Exactly. And after the last fist fight in the chamber of deputies it seems certain that they'll have to give Dreyfus a new trial in Paris, with a lot of reporters taking notes. Von Linderhoff's section is here to see if Dreyfus couldn't die in an escape attempt or something. Somebody tried the other night but fortunately it didn't work. They were driven off by the Devil's Island garrison before they could land."

"That sounds reasonable. Did I guess right about the so-called Jewish organization out to rescue him?"

"Of course. They're German agents. Most of them have been rounded up in Cayenne, thanks to us. British Intelligence tipped the French off and I told you they were good, given a bit of guidance. Naturally, we don't tell France everything. For one thing we don't know how many French officers are on the German payroll and for another thing, they'd shoot you before I could take that cruise with you."

"Are you blackmailing me, Liza?"

"No, I just want to screw you silly all the way to Costa Rica."

"I noticed. But you want a little favor, right?"

"Well, it would be awfully decent of you if you saw fit to get at a German agent I haven't been able to get near."

"Jesus, Von Linderhoff?"

"Yes, he's been very tiresome. He knows me and knows I'm a Brit, so he keeps avoiding me, and last night he took a shot at me, the beastly thing. If I were to announce in advance I'd be at the reception for the new American consul, and his agents saw me there, his guard would be down when you went after him, don't you see?"

"No, I don't see. Von Linderhoff knows me, too. We worked together one time. He knows my rep, too. I'd have a hell of a time getting anywhere near him. He knows I'm in town and he must have guys watching for me, too."

Liza shook her head and said, "You're wrong. The sleeper agents we have watching the waterfront reported you gone aboard that tramp steamer. So the Germans watching should have reported the notorious Captain Gringo's departure, too! *I'm* the only one he's watching out for. I know where he'll be tonight and I have a pass key to his room on the next floor. If you just wait there for him . . ."

"Gee, I don't know, Liza. Von Linderhoff's not a bad guy for one of them, and while *you* may not see the distinction between a soldier of fortune and a hired assassin, *I* sure can! What happens if I say no?"

She lowered her head to kiss his virile member again and sighed, "Nothing much. We'll get somebody else to do it and you won't be sailing to Costa Rica with me after all. I'd feel beastly turning you in, after all the fun we've had, but I certainly could never justify any further help to my superiors at Whitehall."

She began to suck in earnest as he lay back and said, "We get new passports and a few bucks as well as safe passage out of here?"

With her mouth filled, she said, "Mmm humm." It felt funny as hell.

He lay staring at the ceiling as he considered his options and knew one of them was Liza all the way to the only banana republic that wasn't out to kill him on sight. There were some nice little things waiting for him there that he hadn't seen in a while, too. As Liza worked it up for him again he took her head between his hands to draw her face up and kiss it. But as he rolled atop her, she said, "You haven't given me your answer, Dear."

He said, "You know what my answer has to be, damn it. Von Linderhoff's not a bad egg, but I've never been this friendly with any man and, what the hell, since it's me or him, it'll just have to be him."

Captain Gringo sat in the dark hotel room with the bowie knife in his hand, dying for a smoke and wondering what time it was. He'd let himself into Von Linderhoff's room a million years ago and he still felt sort of shitty about what had to be done. Gaston had volunteered to murder the German and Captain Gringo knew Gaston was good. But Von Linderhoff was good, too, and there were things a man didn't ask another to do for him.

The cynic who'd said love and hate were opposite sides of the same coin had been full of shit. Captain Gringo's heart was pounding and he felt tense as a coiled spring, but he wasn't looking forward to the thrill of shoving eight inches of cold steel into a man with anything like the enthusiasm he'd have had for shoving less deadly inches into a woman.

He didn't like the idea of using a knife, even though gunshots in a crowded hotel in the center of town was out of the question. Gaston had brought him fresh clothing. It still lay neatly folded on his bed downstairs. His trail soiled duds were likely to be even messier by the time he was finished here. He had a tub filled with water waiting, too. He'd leave the blade in Von Linderhoff to keep the bloodshed to a minimum. Then he'd dash down the nearby stairwell, whip into his own suite to wash, change, and make it to Liza's yacht by midnight. Gaston had volunteered to stay and cover his withdrawal, but he'd told the little Frenchman to go down to the waterfront and keep an eye on Liza's crew. He had her word she'd be waiting when he'd finished here, but Liza was in a dirty business at best and she'd double crossed him once before.

Von Linderhoff hadn't. The last time they'd had dealings, the sardonic Prussian had kept his word as an officer and gentleman. Captain Gringo knew the German would crush him like a beetle if it were in Germany's interest, but to give the devil his due, the Kaiser's man in South America didn't seem to be a bastard just for practice.

"I can't do it," Captain Gringo muttered to himself, rising from the chair he'd placed near the closed door. He didn't know how he was going to explain this to British Intelligence but enough was enough. This wasn't soldiering, it was premeditated murder, and the guy they wanted killed had never done anything to him.

He reached for the doorknob with his free hand, but just at that moment the door opened and Von Linderhoff came in, groping for the light switch. Captain Gringo grabbed his wrist and pulled him inside, kicking the door shut with his foot as he ripped the blade up through the space the German's guts should have been. But the wirey Prussian had dropped and twisted away, rolling across the rug as he groped for his shoulder holster. Captain Gringo dove on him head first, pinned him to the floor by the throat, and stabbed down hard. The blade knifed through the leather of the holster over Von Linderhoff's heart, broke on the Mauser steel inside, as the Prussian grabbed Captain's wrists with his own strong hands and gasped, "Wait, let's talk!"

Captain Gringo twisted his knife hand free, and raised the blade high, trying to figure out a soft spot the blunted blade would work on as he sat on the German's chest. Von Linderhoff said, "Stop it, Walker. We're both being set up, you fool!"

Captain Gringo put the blade against the German officer's throat but held off from slicing as he snapped, "Move a muscle and you're dead. How did you know it was me? It's black as a bitch in here."

Von Linderhoff relaxed and said, "Ach, that's easy. I'm stronger than anyone else that Englishwoman has working for her. You have me, you big dumb Yankee. But before you cut my throat I have some news for you."

"Keep talking."

"The fight is over. You'll be killing me for no reason and the French police will be after you, too."

"A lot of people are after me. What do you mean the fight is over?"

"The *Dreyfus Affair*. I didn't come here to get the man killed. I came to check on the team another department sent. Most of them have been rounded up by the French, thanks to your friends from Whitehall, and I didn't like their plan to begin with. I just sent a coded cable to Berlin, advising them to let nature take it's course. Dreyfus is already a martyr and I see no reason to make a Holy Ghost out of him. All our dirty linen has been aired in the newspapers already, thanks to that damned Zola. Our best move now would be to simply laugh the case off as a political problem for the French to decide. After all, we *Germans* never had any interest in Captain Dreyfus. The sooner the affair dies down the sooner we can start rebuilding our bridges to the French High Command, *nicht wahr?*"

Captain Gringo nodded and said, "That makes sense, even for you guys. But how do I know you're telling me the truth?"

"My word as an officer and gentleman? I dealt from the top of the deck the time we worked together to get innocent bystanders out of that blow-up in Colombia, remember?"

"Yeah, and it surprised the shit out of me. I know you're not a bad guy, Von Linderhoff. How come you work for such a nasty government?"

"That's British propaganda. Der Kaiser is no better nor worse than his beloved grandmother, Victoria. Look at the map of the world and tell me if Germany has taken half of it in this century!"

"Yeah, you guys are planning to grab everything in the *next* century, right?"

Von Linderhoff sighed, "That's the way the Great Game has always been played, my young friend. Germany was divided and weak when the British and you Americans robbed both kinds of Indians. Now we just want our share."

"Screw power politics, get to the part about my being used. There's been a lot of that going around lately."

"Will you let me up?"

'No, you're doing fine flat on your back. It's a good position for guys like you. Assuming British Intelligence has you wrong, how are they screwing me?"

"Zum Gott! Isn't it obvious? You're being used as a tool. I'm here on a diplomatic visa with the full knowledge of the French government. So if you kill me it will be murder pure and simple, and do you really think the British will admit they even know you when you're caught?"

Captain Gringo thought and then he sighed, "Fair is fair and when you're right you're right. I don't want to kill you, Von Linderhoff, but they made me a pretty good deal."

"Maybe I can top it. I assume they offered you safe passage out of this prison colony? Very well, I have my own sea-going yacht tied up just a little way from here. We have twin diesels and I was about to leave in any case, so . . ."

"Oh, great, you'd love to get us out on the open sea where we could continue this discussion in private under the guns of a German crew, right? You must think I'm pretty country, Von Linderhoff. Thanks a lot, but I'd feel safer with the English lady and, no offense, she's a lot better looking, too!"

The Prussian chuckled and said, "Ach, that Liza is flat chested and much nastier than me, even though I admit you're

183

just not my type. But seriously, Dick, you'd better reconsider killing me for her!"

Captain Gringo kept the blade where it was but said, "I already have, or we wouldn't be chatting like this. Do you want to make another deal, man-to-man?"

"I don't have much choice, do I?"

"Damned A. But if I let you live you have to give me your word again on a couple of things."

"Name them. You have my undivided attention as well as my word."

"Okay, I'll have to tell them I killed you. You'll stay here, with the lights out and the door locked until we've left aboard Liza's yacht. If she finds out you're alive she'll be sore as hell and I'll be stranded here. If that happens you'd better pray the French cops catch me before I can get back to you again. Do we have a deal?"

"Of course. Now will you get off my damned chest?"

Captain Gringo tossed the knife aside and removed the pistol from the Prussian's shoulder holster before he rose and helped Von Linderhoff to his feet. They shook on the deal and Captain Gringo stepped out into the deserted hall. He went downstairs, changed his clothes, and dropped the Mauser in a waste basket. Then he locked the door behind him and went down to the lobby trying to look innocent.

As he turned in his key a couple of men in plainclothes stepped up on either side and one of them said, "You will come with us, M'sieur."

He didn't think the thing poking him in the floating ribs was a candy cane, so he kept his hands on the desk as he smiled and said, "Of course. Where are we going?"

"Upstairs to room 307."

That was Von Linderhoff's room!

Captain Gringo started for the stairs with the two cops on either side as he played dumb, his mind in a whirl. He said, "I don't know anyone on the third floor. My room's on the second."

The cop covering him said politely, "We'll see. Don't take this personally, M'sieur. We're just doing our job, and, hopefully, there's nothing to the tip we just received, hein?"

They didn't talk much as the three of them puffed up the stairs. Captain Gringo wasn't bothered as much by the climb, but he was looking for an opening and the bastards were too good to give him one.

As one kept him covered the other knocked on Von Linderhoff's door. There was a long silence. Then the German answered it in his shirt sleeves and asked, "Yes?"

"May we come in, M'sieur? We have received an unsigned note that a murder had occured in this room. We have to check it out, if you'd be good enough."

The German laughed and switched on the overhead light as he opened the door wide, saying, "Why Dick, I didn't know you were staying at this hotel."

Captain Gringo said, "Yeah, small world, isn't it?"

One of the cops stepped in, swept his eyes over everything, muttered a curse and looked in the adjoining bath. Then he dropped to his hands and knees, looked under the bed, and rose with a very annoyed expression. He asked, "Do you gentlemen know each other?" Von Linderhoff nodded and said, "Our paths have crossed from time to time. What's this all about, M'sieur L'Agent?"

"I don't know," the French detective replied. "The note was in a woman's handwriting. It said that M'sieur Smith, here, had plans to murder someone in this room. You are Herr Von Linderhoff, from the German consulate?"

"Of course. And M'sieur Smith, here, is an American businessman who's never murdered anyone to my knowledge."

The candy cane was no longer pressed against Captain Gringo's ribs, but the one who'd been covering him said, "How curious. You say he's an American, yet he's registered as a Canadian."

Von Linderhoff shrugged and said, "Ach, how should *I* know the difference? I'm a German and all Englishers seem alike to me. Isn't is obvious we've been the target of some obscure attempt at a practical joke, officers?"

The cop in charge put one finger alongside his nose and said, *"Cher-chez la femme,* hein? Obviously one of you has annoyed some lady and she tried to make trouble."

Von Linderhoff smiled crookedly at Captain Gringo and said, "I told you she was naughty, Herr Smith. But all's well that ends well, *nicht wahr?"*

The two cops excused themselves and walked off muttering. Captain Gringo said, "That was pretty decent of you, considering."

Von Linderhoff nodded and said, "I know. I'm still bruised. But I get so few chances to put one over on British Intelligence. She's going to wet her pants when she finds out we both survived her nasty ploy, *nicht wahr?"*

"Yeah. Meanwhile, you're supposed to be dead, so stay that

way until I find out what the fuck she thinks she's pulling!"

He went downstairs again and this time made it out to the street without getting arrested. He steamed down to the waterfront and found Gaston seated at a tin table with a rum and lemon. He said, "Come on, that fuckin' Liza's pulling another fast one!"

Gaston rose, leaving some coins on the table, but as he fell in with the angry American he said, "She's gone. I was wondering where you were so long. Did you kill the *Boche?*"

"No. What do you mean she's gone, Goddamn it."

"As I regarded the tranquil harbor lights I observed her yacht departing. There seemed to be nothing I could do about it, so I waited, and here you are. Where are we going in such a hurry, Dick. I just said your skinny Englishwoman has left us high and dry!"

Captain Gringo snapped, "I know. But I said we were leaving tonight for Costa Rica and we're getting hot as hell as well as high and dry. So we'll just have to hitch another ride!"

Gaston caught on as they approached a schooner tied to the quay. It was rigged fore and aft and a white German ensign hung from it's jack staff. As Captain Gringo marched up the gangplank a man in neat sailing kit appeared at the top and asked, "May I help you, Mein Herr?"

Captain Gringo snapped, *"Achtung!"* And when the crewman stiffened to attention automatically he decked him with a vicious left hook, stepped aboard, and drew his pistol.

There were seven more on board. Five men and two women. As Captain Gringo lined them up to frisk them down the girl in the loose kimono said, "Please don't hurt us. We are only servant girls. I am the, how you say, chambermaid?"

He looked her over and liked what he saw. He nodded at the darker mestizo next to her and asked, "What does she do, when she's fully dressed?"

"Maria is the cook, I suppose."

He grinned and said, "'All right. All you men forward to the sail locker. We'll put you ashore just up the coast if you behave yourselves. If I have any trouble with you I'll feed you to the sharks. Gaston, lock 'em up and see if you remember how to start those diesels."

As Gaston started herding the German crewmen forward, one of them protested, "This is piracy, Mein Herr!"

Captain Gringo nodded and said, "You are so right. You girls can't be carrying concealed weapons. So both of you sit

186

down and stay put while I cast off. We pirates can get mean as hell, so don't make any trouble."

They didn't want to make any trouble. So in less than three minutes the pirated yacht was under way, with the crewmen locked up and the creole girl sitting in Captain Gringo's lap as he steered for the high seas. For some reason Gaston seemed to need the little dark one with him as he ran the engines down below. The moon was rising and a gentle sea was running as the girl in his lap ran her fingers through his hair and begged him not to make her walk the plank.

He said, "Reach in my shirt pocket and put one of those cigars in my mouth, will you? What's your name, Honey?"

"If you please, M'sieur, I am called Fifi. Where are you taking us now that we are in your power?"

He said, "You please me very much, Fifi. We're on our way to Costa Rica. Do you want to come along or do you want to go ashore with the others?"

Fifi struck a light for him and said, "I have heard it is most pretty in Costa Rica, and you are pretty too. Maria and I signed on for adventure and this is all terribly exciting. I have never been captured by pirates before. One assumes you will wish to abuse us all the way to Costa Rica?"

"You're damned right. I don't know what the guy who owns this boat offered you, but we've got plenty of booze and a pleasant voyage to offer."

Fifi laughed, "That's good enough. I did not think that cold old German would be much fun, but anything is better than staying in a French colony. There is simply too much free competition for girls in our line."

"Okay, be good," he said, "and we'll take you along." So Fifi got off his lap, got out of her kimono, and knelt naked on the duck boards between him and the wheel as she started to unbutton his fly. He said, "Hey, wait 'til we get rid of the crew. We'll anchor during daylight hours in the coves along the coast. It's a long trip and I'm in no hurry."

But then, as she started to work on him with her lips he braced his legs out to either side of the wheel and leaned back to enjoy the watch on the tiller. Once she had it up, Fifi said she wanted to steer, so he let her. Sitting naked on his shaft she gripped the spokes and said, "Oh, this in fun."

He liked the hourglass of her pale back in the moonlight. But if he remembered correctly her smaller, darker companion had been prettier. Damn that Gaston. He'd grabbed the cute mestizo first. He was probably doing this very thing, right now, in the engine room. But as Fifi began to bounce, Captain Gringo decided to be philosophical. After all, they had plenty of time to swap, more than once, between here and Costa Rica.

The forward hatch opened just as he was coming. Gaston came back to the cockpit, blinked, and said, *"Eh bien* the engines are running themselves and I see you have the situation under *firm* control back here. I wish I could say the same, but the dark one is a little young for me and now she's crying on her bunk for some reason."

Captain Gringo laughed, "In that case, take the wheel with Fifi. I'll uh, go forward and have a talk with her."

"THE KING OF THE WESTERN NOVEL" IS MAX BRAND

6 EXCITING ADVENTURE SERIES
MEN OF ACTION BOOKS

MEN OF ACTION BOOKS

DIRTY HARRY
By Dane Hartman

He's "Dirty Harry" Callahan—tough, un-orthodox, no-nonsense plainclothesman extraordinaire of the San Francisco Police Department... Inspector #71 assigned to the bruising, thankless homicide detail ...A consummate crimebuster nothing can stop—not even the law! Explosive mysteries involving racketeers, mur-derers, extortioners, pushers, and sky-jackers; savage, bizarre murders, accom-plished with such cunning and expertise that the frustrated S.F.P.D. finds itself without a single clue; hair-raising action and violence as Dirty Harry arrives on the scene, armed with nothing but a Smith & Wesson .44 and a bag of dirty tricks; un-bearable suspense and hairy chase se-quences as Dirty Harry sleuths to unmask the villain and solve the mystery. Dirty Harry—when the chips are down, he's the most low-down cop on the case.